PERFECT STORM 3

BOBBY AKART

WELCOME

Welcome to PERFECT STORM 3, the third installment in the
Perfect Storm survival thriller series by Author Bobby Akart.
Join Bobby Akart's mailing list to learn about upcoming releases,
deals, contests, and appearances. Follow this link to:
BobbyAkart.com

PRAISE FOR BOBBY AKART AND PERFECT STORM

"Bobby Akart has written yet another engaging, believable and suspenseful thriller that keeps you on the edge of your seat!"

"This series has been a wild ride! It opens with a literal bang and keeps going from there.
I'll never look at the Northern Lights the same way again (Eek!)."

"... sucks you in and takes you for the ride of your life. Holy Cow! Who knew something as beautiful as the Northern Lights could portend such chaos."

"Bobby Akart continues to deliver the top thrillers of the year. Year after year after year!"

"A gripping story and compelling characters."

"I grade books by whether I want to stay up all night reading or not. This was a stay up kind of book."

"Author Bobby Akart has put together another scorcher of a story in Perfect Storm."

PERFECT STORM 3

by
Bobby Akart

OTHER WORKS BY AMAZON CHARTS TOP 25 AUTHOR BOBBY AKART

The Perfect Storm Series
Perfect Storm 1
Perfect Storm 2
Perfect Storm 3
Perfect Storm 4

Black Gold (a standalone terrorism thriller)

Nuclear Winter
First Strike
Armageddon
Whiteout
Devil Storm
Desolation

New Madrid (a standalone, disaster thriller)

Odessa (a Gunner Fox trilogy)

Odessa Reborn
Odessa Rising
Odessa Strikes

The Virus Hunters
Virus Hunters I
Virus Hunters II
Virus Hunters III

The Geostorm Series
The Shift
The Pulse
The Collapse
The Flood
The Tempest
The Pioneers

The Asteroid Series (A Gunner Fox trilogy)
Discovery
Diversion
Destruction

The Doomsday Series
Apocalypse
Haven
Anarchy
Minutemen
Civil War

The Yellowstone Series
Hellfire
Inferno
Fallout
Survival

The Lone Star Series
Axis of Evil
Beyond Borders
Lines in the Sand
Texas Strong
Fifth Column
Suicide Six

The Pandemic Series
Beginnings
The Innocents
Level 6
Quietus

The Blackout Series
36 Hours
Zero Hour
Turning Point
Shiloh Ranch
Hornet's Nest
Devil's Homecoming

The Boston Brahmin Series
The Loyal Nine
Cyber Attack
Martial Law
False Flag
The Mechanics
Choose Freedom
Patriot's Farewell (standalone novel)
Black Friday (standalone novel)
Seeds of Liberty (Companion Guide)

The Prepping for Tomorrow Series

Cyber Warfare
EMP: Electromagnetic Pulse
Economic Collapse

Copyright Information

ACKNOWLEDGMENTS

Creating a novel that is both informative and entertaining requires a tremendous team effort. Writing is the easy part.

For their efforts in making the Perfect Storm series a reality, I would like to thank Hristo Argirov Kovatliev for his incredible artistic talents in creating my cover art. He and Dani collaborate (and conspire) to create the most incredible cover art in the publishing business. A huge hug of appreciation goes out to Pauline Nolet, the *Professor*, for her editorial prowess and patience in correcting this writer's brain farts that happen more frequently with age. Thank you, Drew Avera, a United States Navy veteran, who has brought his talented formatting skills from a writer's perspective to create multiple formats for reading my novels. A round of applause for Kevin Pierce, the beloved voice of the apocalypse, who brought my words to life in audio format.

Now, for the serious stuff. While the Perfect Storm series is based on scientifically plausible events, certain parts of the story have been fictionalized for dramatic purposes, and they're not intended to reflect on any actual person or entity.

Accurately portraying the aftermath of a devastating perfect solar storm required countless hours of never-ending research and interviews with some of the brightest minds in the world of planetary science.

Once again, as I immersed myself in the science and history, source material and research flooded my inbox from around the globe. Without the assistance of many individuals and organizations, this story could not be told. Please allow me a moment to acknowledge a few of those institutions that without their tireless efforts and patience, the Perfect Storm series could not have been written.

Many thanks to the preeminent researchers and engineers who provided me assistance, tutelage, and scientific background at the following:

The Space Weather Prediction Center in Boulder, Colorado
The Aerospace Corporation in El Segundo, California
The Haleakala Observatory, home to the Daniel K. Inouye Solar Telescope, in Maui
NASA's Jet Propulsion Laboratory in Pasadena, California
The Geophysical Institute at the University of Alaska, Fairbanks

A special note of thanks to Joel Smith, a certified personal trainer and good friend who, in the course of casual conversation one day, provided me the inspiration for Fred Stewart. Fred was a man who'd been observed sleeping in his car by Joel and some of his friends. They often wondered about his life.

Well, within seconds, I created a character bio for Fred, including a full name, his career, and how he would fit into the Perfect Storm series. You see, every character has a story to tell, both real and imaginary.

Of course, a special thank you to the Team, my loyal friends who've always supported my work and provided me valuable insight from a reader's perspective—Denise Keef, Joe Carey, Shirley Nicholson, Bennita Barnett, and Colt Payne.

Thanks, y'all, and Choose Freedom!

ABOUT THE AUTHOR, BOBBY AKART

Author Bobby Akart delivers up-all-night thrillers to readers in 245 countries and territories worldwide. He has been ranked by Amazon as #25 on the Amazon Charts list of most popular, bestselling authors. He has achieved recognition as the #1 bestselling Horror Author, #1 bestselling Science Fiction Author, #5 bestselling Action & Adventure Author, #7 bestselling Historical Fiction Author and #10 on Amazon's bestselling Thriller Author list.

His novel *Yellowstone: Hellfire* reached the Top 25 on the Amazon bestsellers list and earned him multiple Kindle All-Star awards for most pages read in a month and most pages read as an author. The Yellowstone series vaulted him to the #25 bestselling author on Amazon Charts, and the #1 bestselling science fiction author.

Since its release in November 2020, his standalone novel *New Madrid Earthquake* has been ranked #1 on Amazon Charts in multiple countries as a natural disaster thriller.

Mr. Akart is a graduate of the University of Tennessee after pursuing a dual major in economics and political science. He went on to obtain his master's degree in business administration and his doctorate degree in law at Tennessee.

With over a million copies of his novels sold in all formats, Bobby Akart has provided his readers a diverse range of topics that are both informative and entertaining. His attention to detail and impeccable research has allowed him to capture the imagination of his readers through his fictional works and bring them valuable knowledge through his nonfiction books.

SIGN UP for Bobby Akart's mailing list to learn of special offers, view bonus content, and be the first to receive news about new releases.

Visit www.BobbyAkart.com for details.

DEDICATIONS

With the love and support of my wife, Dani, together with the unconditional love of Bullie and Boom, the princesses of the palace, I'm able to tell you these stories. It would be impossible for me to write without them in my heart.

This story was written during a difficult time in our lives. For my long-time readers, you know that our English Bulldogs, Bullie and Boom, affectionately known in my stories as the princesses of the palace, are the center of our universe. At Christmas in 2021, Boom Chukka suffered a significant tear in her gastrointestinal tract caused by chewing a pressed rawhide bone.

Because of Dani's watchful eye, she noticed Boom-Boom's gums turn more and more pale. I also noticed that her poop became black and tarry. Both of these were symptoms of internal bleeding. I relay this to you because, one day, you might experience this with your beloved pups.

Internal bleeding is nothing to be trifled with. Without urgent care, your fur babies can die within days, if not sooner.

We rushed Boom Chukka to our vets in Georgia. The entire team, led by Drs. Rambo and McNair, came to her rescue. By the early evening of New Year's Eve, her packed cell volume (PCV) and hematocrit (HCT) fell below twenty percent where thirty-five percent is normal. Thanks to a dog-to-dog blood transfusion from Dr. McNair's dog, Liza, Boom-Boom was able to survive long enough to transport her to the University of Georgia Veterinary Hospital in Athens.

Just before publication of Perfect Storm 3, Boom Chukka required surgery. An epulis, a stalk of pinkish tissue, had formed on her jaw and the mass had begun to grow over her back teeth. Five years ago, Woolie Bullie was required to undergo surgery that removed half of her lower jaw to prevent the spread of an epulis to prevent her from undergoing radiation treatment. Placing an English Bulldog under anesthesia at this late stage in their lives was a risky proposition. However, we trusted Dr. Rambo to perform the surgery and closely monitor our beloved Chubby. (Doomsday series readers might recall the introduction of Chubby and the Roo in book two, Haven.) Boom Chukka pulled through like a champ and the tissue was declared benign.

With the help of God watching over our entire family during this difficult time, Boom Chukka fought to live another day, and then another. As of this writing, Bullie and Boom are the ripe age of thirteen. However, they firmly believe they're one-year-old pups.

I urge you to love those who are closest to you, including your four-legged, bestest pals.

AUTHOR'S NOTE

March, 2022

For years, I've tackled the disaster thriller genre. As an author, the hardest part might be choosing how to destroy the Earth, therefore imperiling all of mankind. Look at all the options I've written about: asteroids, nuclear electromagnetic pulse attacks, pandemics, earthquakes, volcanoes, bioterrorism, cyber warfare, pole shifts, etc.

However, in a class by itself, is severe space weather. If its ominous name didn't clue you in, severe space weather can cause some serious complications to life on our planet. Much like earth-based weather, it's uncontrollable. It also has the potential for massive destruction and disruption of modern technology. Imagine the collapse of power grids; radio blackouts; satellite interference or even destruction; and airline operations ceasing, all in less than a minute. Without electricity, how would you communicate with your family, call 9-1-1, get clean water or keep food from spoiling? With a radio blackout, how would airplanes land safely? Massive solar flares have the potential to change life as we know it.

Now, if I haven't gotten your attention, let's take a look at the science and a little history, shall we?

Severe space weather is the result of large-scale eruptions of plasma and magnetic fields from the Sun's corona. Known as coronal mass ejections (CMEs), these eruptions can create magnetic storms in the magnetosphere and Earth's upper atmosphere, which can damage power lines, cause blackouts, and even dislocate Earth's radiation belts, damaging satellites.

Thankfully, such magnetic storms are classified as low frequency, but high impact. To be an impactful magnetic storm, CMEs from the solar disk must be fast and massive, launched from near the center of the Sun and directed toward Earth's magnetic field. CMEs also need to have a strong magnetic field with the opposite orientation of Earth's own magnetic field. Although classified as low frequency, when these conditions are met, CMEs are high-consequence occurrences. Here are some examples.

In recent history, the collapse of the Hydro-Quebec grid occurred in March 1989 leaving the province of Quebec without electricity for 9 hours. The outage closed schools, businesses, public transportation and grounded flights at Dorval Airport. Citizens found themselves stuck in traffic on darkened roads without street signals and many workers were stranded in office buildings, elevators and stairwells. The storm was felt in other parts of North America as well, with approximately two-hundred solar storm-related events reported including the failure of a transformer at a New Jersey nuclear power plant.

Amazingly, the 1989 magnetic storm that struck Quebec pales in comparison to other magnetic storms in our history.

The strongest storm in recorded history to directly impact our planet came in September of 1859. The CME behind the Carrington Event, as it became known, was first seen by Richard Carrington, a British amateur astronomer. Nearly eighteen hours after it was observed, the powerful CME impacted the Earth's magnetosphere, triggering a severe geomagnetic storm that disrupted telegraph networks around the world. The rare, fast-moving (CMEs normally impact Earth around 36 hours after being observed) CME hit the planet with highly charged particles enveloped the Northern Hemisphere. Telegraph operators were electrocuted, and fires were ignited as flames traveled along the telegraph lines.

The 1921 Geomagnetic Storm, also known as the New York Railway Storm, included geomagnetically induced currents that would have been 10 times more intense than those responsible for the 1989 Quebec solar storm. Taking place over several days in May 1921, the New York Railway Storm is widely considered the largest recorded in the twentieth century. It is this perfect solar storm event that forms the scientific basis for my book series.

SUNSPOT CREDITED WITH RAIL TIE-UP

New York Central Signal System Put Out of Service by Play of Northern Lights.

The sunspot which caused the brilliant aurora borealis on Saturday night and the worst electrical disturbance in memory on the telegraph systems was credited with an unprecedented thing at 7:04 o'clock yesterday morning, when the entire signal and switching system of the New York Central Railroad below 125th Street was put out of operation, followed by a fire in the control tower at Fifty-seventh Street and Park Avenue.

This is the first time that a sunspot has been blamed for such a piece of mischief. From other accounts it appeared

The New York Times
Published: May 16, 1921
Copyright © The New York Times

Park Site

ghts Given
)onor.

0,000 EACH

nd Surgeons to
College and
taffs.

SUNSPOT AURORA PARALYZES WIRES

Unprecedented Disturbance Is Attributed to Solar Manifestations.

BROADWAY LIGHTS DIMMED

Theatre Crowds Returning Home Amazed at the Brilliancy of the Skies.

WASHINGTON, May 14.—The un-

REJECTS 'FOO

Brooklyn Grand
121 of 129 P

After He Arres
for Rum La

ELECTRIC DISTURBANCES AFFECT FRENCH WIRES

Aurora Not Visible, Its Absence Being Attributed to Atmospheric Conditions.

Copyright, 19** by The New York Times Company

By Wireless to THE NEW YORK TIMES.

PARIS, May 17.—The disturbance which interrupted telegraphic transmission in the United States last week has been making itself felt also in

WHAT IF FICTION BECOMES REALITY?

A word of caution when thinking about history and the timeline of events. It's easy to dismiss any discussion of past catastrophes when one considers events like super volcano eruptions taking place every seven-hundred-thousand-years as in the case of Yellowstone. Massive solar storms occur far more frequently. Let's look at a recent event from just ten years ago.

On July 23, 2012, two CMEs erupted from an active patch of sunspots on the far side of the sun which is monitored by the Parker Solar Probe that circles the sun ahead of Earth in the same orbit. Emerging about fifteen minutes apart, the CMEs quickly merged into one massive shock wave of charged particles that washed over the probe's sensors.

Behind the shock wave, this energy raced along at about 2250 kilometers per second—five times their normal speed at Earth's distance from the sun—and the magnetic field strength there was more than ten times that normally seen at Earth's orbit.

If pointed in our direction, such a combination would have produced the strongest geomagnetic storm to have struck Earth in history. It could have knocked out satellites and earthbound power grids, researchers say. Fortunately, the event, a prime example of a *Perfect Storm*, was directed into a region of space where the solar wind and the magnetic field had been weakened by a solar flare 4 days earlier.

While the flare occurred in Earth's orbital plane, the solar matter missed us by the equivalent of nine days. Similar to the Carrington event, the particles traveled from the sun to the Earth in just seventeen hours. Had Earth been in the way at the time, the global damage toll would have crested the $10 trillion mark: the first fourteen-figure natural disaster in history. It was only luck that caused this perfect storm to miss us.

I add this example as a word of caution to us all. These severe solar storms happen with regular frequency. We dodged a powerful catastrophic solar flare in 2012. Next time, we might not be so lucky.

REAL-WORLD NEWS EXCERPTS

CANNIBAL SOLAR BURSTS MAY BRING AURORAS AS FAR SOUTH AS NEW YORK

~ SPACE.com, August 17, 2022

Cannibalization can occur when the sun launches two eruptions within a short period of time.
The sun has spat out two clouds of plasma in the past two days, which might trigger beautiful aurora displays observable much farther south than usual, including New York City.

The two coronal mass ejections (CMEs), eruptions of charged particles from the sun's upper atmosphere known as the corona, burst from the sun on Aug. 14 and 15 respectively, according to the U.K. forecaster Met Office. As the CMEs cross the 93,000,000-mile distance between the star and our planet, they might cannibalize each other creating a single super powerful CME.

CME cannibalization occurs when the sun launches two eruptions within a short period of time, with the second of the two being more energetic, and therefore faster than the first.

A GIANT SUNSPOT THE SIZE OF THREE EARTHS IS DIRECTED TOWARD OUR PLANET

~ *The Space Weather Journal, June 22, 2022*
The fast-growing sunspot suddenly doubled in size in a span of 24 hours.

A sunspot nearly triple the size of Earth is within firing range of our planet, and may send out medium-class flares in the near future.

"Yesterday, sunspot AR3038 was big. Today, it's enormous," the Space Weather Prediction Center in Boulder, Colorado reported.

"The fast-growing sunspot has doubled in size in only 24 hours," the SPWC added, noting that the magnetic field surrounding it has the potential to blast X-class solar flares toward our planet.

SURPRISE SOLAR STORM WITH DISRUPTIVE POTENTIAL SLAMS INTO EARTH

~ *Live Science, June 28, 2022*
Experts were initially unsure what caused the freak geomagnetic event.

Scientists were recently left scratching their heads after a "potentially disruptive" solar storm smashed into Earth without warning.

The surprise solar storm hit Earth just before midnight UTC June 25 and continued throughout most of June 26. Scientists classified it as a G2-class storm, which means it was strong enough to create weak power grid fluctuations, cause minor impacts to satellite operation, disrupt the navigational abilities of some migrating animals, and cause unusually strong auroras.

The surprise solar storm hit Earth less than a week after a giant sunspot, known as AR3038, doubled in size over a 24-hour period and reached a maximum diameter more than 2.5 times the size of Earth. The giant sunspot sparked fears of a potentially damaging CME hitting our planet, but the spot eventually aimed away from Earth as the sun rotated. Scientists don't know if the gargantuan sunspot and the solar storm are connected.

SOLAR STORM FROM GIANT HOLE IN SUN'S ATMOSPHERE HEADED STRAIGHT FOR EARTH

~ *Newsweek, September 2, 2022*

Earth is expected to be hit by a moderate-strength geomagnetic storm in the coming days as solar wind escapes from a huge hole in the sun's atmosphere.

The U.S. National Oceanic and Atmospheric Administration's (NOAA) Space Weather Prediction Center (SWPC) warned that a G2-level geomagnetic storm was "likely" to occur. A coronal hole high speed stream is directly behind the expected G2 storm.

As the name suggests, this is a stream of high-speed solar wind that can interact with Earth's magnetosphere. As the streams of solar wind from coronal holes approach Earth, they catch up with and overtake the slower, ambient solar wind that already exists in the space between our planet and the sun. Intense magnetic fields can be produced at this interface between the fast and relatively slower solar wind streams.

The SWPC states that a G2 storm may involve changes to orbit predictions due to increased atmospheric drag, a fading of high-frequency radio propagation, possible voltage alarms in high-latitude power systems, and auroras possibly in states like New York.

EPIGRAPH

Evil exists. Evil hunts opportunities to infect humans.
Humans infected and overpowered by evil do horrible things.
∼ Newt Gingrich, Former Speaker of the House of Representatives

---

The greatest good you can do for another is not just share your riches
but reveal to them their own.
∼ Benjamin Disraeli, former Prime Minister of the United Kingdom

---

Farming looks mighty easy when your plow is a pencil
and you're a thousand miles from the corn field.
∼ Dwight D. Eisenhower, American President

Civilization begins with order, grows with liberty, and dies with chaos.

∼ Will Durant, American Historian and author of The Story of Civilization

---

Demoralize the enemy from within by surprise, terror, sabotage, assassination.
This is the war of the future.

∼ Adolf Hitler

PROLOGUE

Two weeks prior
The day the sun brought darkness
Harford House Motel
Harford, Pennsylvania

He was ostracized and shunned. Teased and ridiculed. A waste of space in the minds of some. Most avoided eye contact with the man while others chastised him for his perceived deviant behavior. "Get a job," they'd grumble as they passed him by. "Take a bath, somewhere. Anywhere."

He was frequently reported to the local police because ignorant passersby thought he threatened them. He was dangerous and unstable, they said, although he'd never raised a hand to anyone except in self-defense. And on those rare occasions, he'd shown remarkable restraint considering the verbal, emotional, and physical abuse he'd endured.

All in all, he was misunderstood.

Fred Stewart often had difficulty recalling his last name, frequently referring to the dog tags hanging around his neck as a reminder. Despite his memory lapses, some things remained fresh in his mind.

War. Killing. The loss of his brothers-in-arms. The abandonment of him, and other veterans like him, by his government and country despite their bravery.

Fred was a veteran of the War in Afghanistan. He was one of the last U.S. Marines who were flown out who wasn't in a body bag. During the disastrously mishandled departure from Afghanistan, thousands of refugees and U.S. personnel forced their way toward the Abbey Gate at the Kabul Airport. It was the only entrance into the airport that day, and the terrorist group ISIS-K knew it.

While his memory failed him at times, his dreams were remarkably vivid. The ball bearings flung in all directions by the explosive device detonated by a suicide bomber ripped through the Marines' body armor and helmets. Fred had lost an eye and nearly bled to death before being treated on the military transport. Although he'd survived the bomb that massacred nearly two hundred Afghans and thirteen of his fellow Marines, he barely endured the years that followed.

Wearing a black patch to cover the reddish eye socket, Fred frightened many. His Scottish heritage blessed him with fiery red hair. His handlebar mustache, which protruded past his cheeks and curled slightly upward, grew bushy over the years as his disheveled appearance took over his persona.

Like so many veterans, Fred was finding it difficult to cope stateside. He signed up for a few mercenary gigs in Ukraine and later in Moldova as Russia sought to reconstitute the former Soviet Union. He joined Taiwan's fight against China's multipronged invasion. It was a fruitless exercise as the People's Liberation Army forces crushed their defenses.

There, he had been wounded again and returned home. Or at least to Harford, Pennsylvania. He had no ties to the town other than some of his Marine buddies lived throughout the region. He parlayed his payment by the Taiwan government to purchase a decades-old Buick LeSabre.

He lived in the car for over a year, traversing the highways between the VA hospitals in Wilkes-Barre, Pennsylvania, and Syracuse, New York. He, like other disabled vets, learned how to game the system by visiting Veteran's Administration facilities in different states. He was able to duplicate his medications and receive benefits vouchers at both locations. There were several organizations in both cities willing to provide gift cards to those like him.

His frugal lifestyle, which revolved around free meals and living in his car, resulted in Fred becoming wealthy, in a way. His benefits checks were cashed, and the money hidden within the spacious confines of the LeSabre. Pharmaceuticals were accumulated, as were the gift cards. By the time Fred decided to take root in tiny Harford, he was loaded with necessities.

After a stop for gas at the Onvo Travel Plaza on Interstate 81, the halfway point between the two VA medical centers, Fred drove the short distance into Harford. In the center of town, he came across a long-stay motel that advertised weekly and monthly rates.

The Harford House motel was the former residence of a Hollywood actor who'd come to town with big dreams and a television production company in tow. He'd purchased a circa-1840 Greek revival home in the center of town along with several other properties. The actor-turned-restorer spent big bucks during the first year of production of the DIY television program. Homes falling in disrepair were beautifully restored to their former glory.

The show was a hit, and the actor invested more money in the projects that were in various states of completion, by design. Then, without notice, the network pulled the plug on the program and the restoration projects, leaving the actor without funding. The house of cards, consisting of multiple dilapidating homes and buildings in the process of being restored, fell apart. The taxman cometh first, followed by the mortgage holders. Soon, everything was seized, auctioned, and sold, including the magnificent Greek revival home.

The property changed hands twice. First, to a Realtor, who purchased it at auction, and then to a couple from New York, who had plans to create a bed and breakfast. The B & B was beautiful but remained mostly empty until they sold the property at a loss. An enterprising entrepreneur, a Patel from India, snatched it up and expanded it into a motel. However, this venture also floundered. When the actor was filming and restoring buildings, fans of the television program flocked to Harford to be part of the action. When the show died, so did the tourism.

Patel grasped at straws and began to rent out the property to short-term tenants that many viewed as transients. The once beautiful Greek revival became known as one of the seedy, no-tell motels where trysts occurred and drunks slept it off. Patel was able to pay the mortgage and hold off the tax collectors, but little more.

And then Fred moved in.

The main house was reserved for the motel's best clientele while the two recently constructed wings were rented out on a long-term-stay basis. Fred, using his VA housing voucher, rented a large room at the east end of the property. Yet he never slept there. Not even once.

He did utilize the bathroom and shower facilities. The rest of the motel room was dedicated to his stuff. Once Fred had a home, such as it was, he began buying necessities and storing them in the motel room. He continued to sleep where he was most comfortable—in his car.

For the better part of two years, people coming across his old Buick LeSabre in the parking lot thought he was homeless. His car was packed with various and sundry items, from clothing to cases of water, in case he had to move.

He was not homeless. He had a room. And an address where his government checks and other benefits were mailed to. When they arrived, he quickly cashed them with Patel for a five percent fee and hustled down to the Dollar General, where he'd fill his cart with a variety of necessities.

They called him a hoarder. Crazy pack rat. Doomsday prepper. Until the night the sun brought darkness.

Fred was sleeping in the front seat of his LeSabre, enduring his reoccurring nightmares of his deployment in Afghanistan. Only this time, the popping sounds in his head were all too real. Gunfire from his days in battle permeated his psyche. He tried to block it out, imagining Rice Krispies popping in a bowl of milk. Then the snaps, crackles, and pops grew louder, and one seemingly exploded over his head.

He awoke with a start to see sparks raining down on top of his LeSabre's hood. He instinctively reached for the .45-caliber pistol tucked under his seat.

But the apparent attack stopped, and silence surrounded him. And darkness. Except for the beautiful hues of blue and green that floated across the sky.

Fred stared in wonder as the quietness enveloped him. He tugged on both sides of his handlebar mustache and then gripped the thick hair on top of his head away from his scalp. It was the same unconscious action he took every time he woke up from a nightmare to confirm he was still alive.

He smiled. He knew what had happened. Fred Stewart might have been crazy, but he was crazy like a fox.

PART 1

Wednesday
Imagine the unimaginable.

CHAPTER ONE

Wednesday
Stanley's Farm
Harford, Pennsylvania, USA

Luke Cubbison lay flat on his back in a state of semiconsciousness. His brain tried to make sense of the feeling of his body snapping free, drifting upward, only connected by a fragile, silvery cord to his physical shell that remained in the field below. It was battered and broken, his right leg lying catawampus to his torso.

Inexplicably, Luke felt no pain. He tried to suppress any thoughts of death. To be sure, the stampeding cattle had hit him like a freight train. Yet he wasn't standing in front of the pearly gates or in that *other* place. He was still breathing. Living, albeit separated from his body somehow.

He was able to see his surroundings from his perch twenty feet above his body. Fire began to consume the bales of hay, its flames darting into the smoke-filled sky. Ashes and bits of burning grasses landed on the ground around his body, some singeing the hairs on his arms and peppering his face.

For a moment, he was mesmerized. It was if he had a seat at the top of an auditorium, watching the drama of a play unfold in which he was the star. His brain was doing a mighty good job of hiding the truth. On the one hand, he knew his mind and body were combined in their rightful places. On the other, Luke was firmly convinced he had a front-row seat to his demise.

The fire grew in intensity. The heat emanating from the compressed bales of hay began to scorch his exposed skin. His nostrils flared as the smell of burning flesh reached them. Was he burning to death? Was it something else?

Luke began to regain consciousness, and as he did, mind and body rejoined one another. That was when a wave of pain overtook him, causing him to let out an agonized, guttural scream.

All at once, his body began to shake and shiver despite the searing heat surrounding him. His right leg was broken and wouldn't respond to his commands to push himself away from the burning hay. He experienced blistering pain in his other leg, as his jeans had caught fire briefly.

Luke's eyes were wide with excitement and fear. The fire jumped from the large, round bales to the small barn near the fence. The structure never had a chance. The dry conditions and hot winds that had overtaken Eastern Pennsylvania the last several weeks contributed to the spread of the blaze. As the barn became engulfed in flames, the winds lifted the fire skyward and seemed to draw the burning hay with it.

Luke fought the pain and saw the destruction of the barn as the impetus to avoid burning to death. He rolled onto his belly and frantically tried to pull himself away from the intense heat with his arms. Clawing his way through the smoldering grasses, a stinging sensation ran across his body, causing him to oddly yelp in pain.

He rolled over to his backside in an effort to push away from the inferno with his good leg. He was making progress, a half a foot at a time, putting distance between himself and the barn. He glanced over his shoulder, squinting his eyes to determine his orientation in relation to the Stanley place. Then the walls of the barn succumbed to the fire and caved in. The heavy roof listed toward the source of the fire and began to fall toward Luke.

He drew all of his strength and pushed off the scorched turf with his left leg. Frustrated, he rolled over and clawed at the ground again, dragging his lifeless body toward safety. He caught a glimpse of the red, tubular gate that led to the next pasture. If he could only reach it, he thought, his mind struggling to focus.

Then the broad side of the barn slammed into the ground behind him. A beam from the roof's structure bounced off the ground momentarily before striking him in the back, knocking his chest flat against the ground. Once again, Luke was unconscious.

CHAPTER TWO

Wednesday
Stanley's Farm
Harford, Pennsylvania

As instructed by Luke earlier that day, Vida Khan, the Afghan girl who'd fled her family's compound in the next county, returned to the Yoder place to gather her things. The rest of the women and children, liberated from the men who'd exerted dominion over them, were busy going about their chores or playing in the front yard, an act of negligence that would certainly bring unwanted attention to them at some point.

Vida, the daughter of Jamal Khan, thought about her father and the Afghan men he was associated with. After they had been brought into America as refugees, they'd had an opportunity to remake themselves. Suddenly, they'd found themselves in a world without modern, electricity-dependent conveniences that truly made all men equal. Instead of coming together, they chose to carry forward old grudges and jihad, their religion's excuse for killing innocent people.

Vida wanted no part of that life or the abuses inflicted on young women like herself. So she'd fled. That was how she'd met Luke, a young man who was well mannered and stable. Luke had a family who would hopefully allow her to live on their farm. She'd work overtime to prove her worth and sacrifice everything to be under their protection.

Luke had cautioned her not to tell the other women at the Yoder place. This offer to join his family at Cubbison's Farm was for her only. Heeding his words, she surreptitiously slipped away, easing across the back of the Yoder property in the direction of the Stanley farm. Despite the setting sun behind her, she was able to see a change in the color of the sky ahead. If she were facing a sunset, she'd firmly believe that was why the sky was aglow. However, the black smoke accompanying the orangish sky alarmed her.

She immediately became concerned. "Luke! Luke." Struggling to hold onto her backpack, she raced through the tall grasses toward the source of the fire. The closer Vida got, the more she realized the blaze was emanating from the field where Luke was herding cattle.

Tears streamed down her face as she ran, praying to Allah for her new love's safety. Twice, she stumbled, her knees crashing hard enough on the ground to tear holes in her jeans. She regained her footing and ran toward the fire. Just as she approached the fence, the barn came crashing down in front of her.

The gust of wind brought a deluge of ash and soot toward her, knocking her to the ground again. She covered her face to avoid being burned by the intense heat.

"Luke! Are you there?" Her plea was full of trepidation.

When he didn't answer, she feared the worst. It was possible he was far away from the flames, leading the cattle through the woods as planned. However, something inside her compelled her to search for him. He was injured, and he needed her. She was sure of it.

When she reached the gate, the fire was beginning to cross the small field where the forty head of cattle had been held. The gate was hot to the touch, so she focused on unlatching it using two tree branches. Once it was freed, she covered her mouth and nose with her arm before entering the field.

Her eyes darted about as she called for him. "Luke! Are you here?"

She'd shout for him and immediately cover her mouth to avoid inhaling the toxic fumes. Her eyes began to water from the smoke. She called out his name again and began a coughing fit caused by inhaling the soot-filled air. She fell to her knees to regain her breath and orientation. That was when she saw the fallen beam lying across Luke's lifeless body.

On all fours, she rushed to join his side, screaming his name despite the smoke inhalation that inhibited her breathing. When she arrived at his unconscious body, she first placed her cheek against his mouth. His shallow breath on her skin gave her goosebumps and forced her to smile. He was alive.

Frantic, she wriggled low to the ground until she reached the end of the rough-sawn beam. With a grunt, she tried to hoist the end that had not been burnt but was unable to move it. She contemplated giving it another, more forceful effort. She grimaced as she visualized lifting the beam slightly only to drop it back on Luke's chest, causing him more harm.

Vida's mind raced. She needed to prop the beam up so that she could gradually elevate it without fear of it falling. Once again, she scrambled around in search of anything that might help.

Fallen trees. Fence posts. Firewood. Cinder blocks. Anything.

That was when help arrived. Vida heard voices in the distance. She screamed as loud as her smoke-damaged lungs would allow.

"Help!"

CHAPTER THREE

Wednesday
Stanley's Farm
Harford, Pennsylvania

For a few seconds that seemed like an eternity, John Cubbison pulled on the reins of his horse to bring him under control. The blaze that had engulfed the barn was spreading across the pasture toward the woods. His stallion was agitated and threatened to throw John out of his saddle.

John slid off his horse, and before both feet had hit the ground, his horse rose on his hind legs to perform an equine version of a pirouette. In a flash, he bolted back toward the trail and flew past the trailing Emma and Sam.

"John!" Emma shouted, her loud voice full of fear as she became concerned that her husband had been injured.

"Over here! Along the fence row. Stay left!"

Sam led Emma past the open gate blocked by several smoldering, half-burnt cows blocking the entrance. Some were already dead while others bellowed in distress. The sounds made by the dying animals broke down Emma, who'd thus far managed to maintain her composure. The shock to her mental state prompted her search for Luke to become frantic while the tears began to flow again.

"Luke!" John shouted again as he ran along the fence row, dodging fallen tree limbs.

"Over here!" It was a young woman's voice. "He's been hurt! Hurry!"

John picked up speed, his haste causing him to stumble over an unexpected rock beneath the tall hay. He fell hard to the ground onto his chest, causing his diaphragm to spasm. He fought to regain his breath.

Movement to his left caught his eye. Sam and Emma had directed their horses through the adjacent fields to reach the other gate. Sam knew the property better than anyone, as he'd befriended Gene Stanley decades ago. He was unaware, of course, that his old friend had been murdered by the men who had occupied the Yoder place.

"Where are you?" Emma shouted her question in response to Vida's pleas for help.

"By the gate!"

John filled his lungs with sooty oxygen and continued along the fence row, arriving at the open gate near simultaneously with his wife and father. They dismounted and joined John as they descended into the smoke-filled field.

"Call out to us so we can follow your voice!" John shouted.

"Bear left! Fifty feet. The barn fell on him."

"Jesus!" screamed Emma as she called upon the heavens for help.

John grabbed his wife's hand, and she in turn took Sam's. The three of them pulled their way across the smoldering field, following Vida's voice as she told them more about Luke's condition.

"He has a broken leg! A beam fell on him, and I can't move it alone!"

Seconds later, John emerged by her side and fell to his knees.

Distraught, Emma stroked her son's face and rubbed the sweat off his forehead. "Luke, wake up, honey. Can you wake up for me?"

"Sam, help me!" instructed John. He rushed around Luke's limp body. He was about to reach for the other end of the beam when Vida issued a warning.

"Careful! It's been burnt."

John was momentarily puzzled. Not at the prospect of handling the burnt beam but confused as to who the young woman was with the foreign accent.

He pulled off his shirt and wiped the volumes of sweat off his face to moisten it slightly. He prepared to lift the burning beam.

"Dad! On three!"

"Okay!"

John counted them down, and the two men jerked the beam upward. They moved laterally on their knees, carrying the heavy beam below Luke's extended leg, careful to avoid the broken one.

Emma shouted to the guys, "John, we have to get him out of here! He's having trouble breathing."

The group worked together. John lifted his son by the shoulders while Sam and Vida supported his legs. Emma held up his back, joining the others as they shuffled sideways toward the open gate. Moments later, they were in the middle of the field closest to the burned-out farmhouse, where the fresher air had an immediate, resuscitating effect on Luke.

He began coughing violently as he sucked in the oxygen. And then the excruciating pain of his shattered leg swept over him, causing him to pass out again.

CHAPTER FOUR

Wednesday
Stanley's Farm
Harford, Pennsylvania

"We need water!" exclaimed Emma as she looked toward the empty Stanley house. Evidence of the fire that had destroyed his outbuildings caused her to frown.

"I have some," said Vida. She rushed back toward the fire to retrieve her backpack before returning to Luke's side. She rummaged through her backpack until she found the partially filled bottle.

Emma took the water and poured a small amount into her cupped hand. She lovingly wiped her son's face with the moisture in an attempt to revive him. She glanced up at Vida and nodded, mouthing the words thank you.

"It's bad, John," said Sam as he gently examined Luke's broken leg. "We can try to splint it, but we've gotta find him a doctor. This could cause serious internal damage."

"What do we need?" asked John.

"Fence rails. Boards. Straight tree branches."

Vida interrupted his list. "There was a pile of picket fence pieces over near the trail to the other farm. I can get them."

"Who are you?" asked John.

"My name is Vida. I am a friend of Luke's. We were supposed to, um ..." Her voice trailed off before she exposed their plan for her to hide out until Luke could gain his family's approval to allow Vida to move to the farm.

"I'm John, Luke's dad. Thank you, and please go as fast as you can."

Vida dropped her backpack and began running. "I have some jeans and shirts in my pack if you need them."

Sam looked to John and tried to give him a look of encouragement. "We'll get him fixed up for now. However, he's gonna need a doc."

John, still shirtless, reached for Vida's backpack and retrieved one of her long-sleeve tee shirts. He ripped it until the sleeves were separated from the rest. She arrived seconds later, gasping for air until she broke out into a coughing fit. She knelt by their side and handed over the fence pickets.

"Thank you, Vida," said Emma, who reached out and touched the young woman's arm. "You're a godsend."

Vida nodded her appreciation as she tried to recover. She, too, had inhaled a lot of smoke in her efforts to save Luke.

John turned to Emma. "We need the truck."

She stood and nodded. "Vida, will you keep Luke calm when he wakes up. We don't need him to jerk around and hurt himself." Vida gladly obliged.

Emma fetched her horse and took off in a fast gallop toward the trail leading through the woods to their farm.

"How do you know my son?" asked John.

Having recovered from her coughing episode, Vida tried to explain how she'd met Luke and why he was away from home. She hesitated as she spoke, careful not to betray Luke's trust. She made no mention of his plan to bring her onto the farm.

"Luke told me that you were both away. Um, there are, um, were some men who took over the adjacent farm." She pointed over her shoulder.

"The Yoder place?" asked Sam.

Vida nodded. "I didn't know them, as they were killed before I arrived."

"Killed? What about the Yoders?" John's questions took his mind off his son's plight for a moment.

"I only arrived here a few days ago. These bad men came from the interstate after the power went out. They killed the Yoder family and the man who owns that house." She hesitated before continuing, "I believe they came to your farm to threaten Luke and his mother. I don't know all the details. It's just that, um, I believe Luke and, well, your wife killed them on the road."

John fell back on the heels of his feet and rubbed his hands through his hair. Sam, who'd been monitoring Luke's breathing, looked from John to Vida to the country road in front of the Stanley house. He turned to Vida.

"What was he doing in that field?"

"There were cattle penned in there. Luke wanted to bring them to your farm for safekeeping. He sent me back to the Yoder house while he did his work. Somehow, a fire must've started. I saw the smoke and came running to see what was happening. That's when I found him knocked to the ground."

John had more questions, especially about Vida's background. He wasn't very knowledgeable about the world's cultures, but Vida certainly appeared to be the same nationality as the men who attacked the armory the day before. There was plenty of time for conversation later. For now, he needed to help his son, who was beginning to stir.

"He's waking up!" shouted Sam.

Both John and Vida inched through the tall grass to study Luke's face. As his eyes opened ever so slightly, he first saw Vida's face. A smile immediately broke out across his face.

"Vida," he said in a barely audible whisper. She gently reached out and wiped the sweat off his forehead, feeling it for fever at the same time. She was relieved that it seemed to be warm from being exposed to the fire rather than hot from fever.

"You're gonna be okay, Luke."

He tried to nod in response as his eyes looked to his right. His lips quivered, and tears welled up in his eyes as he studied John's and Sam's faces. He lifted his arm slightly, but it immediately fell to the ground.

John grasped Luke's hand and gave it a gentle squeeze. "Hi, son. We're gonna get you fixed up."

"Cat? Matthew?" Luke whispered to his dad.

"They're fine. We're all good."

Sam intervened. "Luke, you need to save your strength. Emma's gone after the truck, and we're gonna try to find you a doctor. It's gonna hurt for a while longer."

"No problem," Luke whispered. "Pain means I'm still alive."

CHAPTER FIVE

Wednesday
Cubbison's Farm
Harford, Pennsylvania

Emma wasted no time racing down the trail leading to the family farm. She dodged wayward cattle like they were orange pylons on a road course. To their credit, the once frightened cows stood still, chomping on grass, seemingly uninterested in the horse and rider speeding by. Emma reached the clearing at full speed and found Matthew and Cat standing next to their horses. She was surprised to see them cradling rifles in their arms. Neither had shown a propensity to use firearms in the past. She'd later learn how times had changed them.

"Did you find him, Mom?" asked Cat, who was very close to her older brother. Although Luke and Matthew were twins, they were different in many respects. Cat had gravitated toward her brother Luke over the years.

"Whoa!" Emma pulled hard on the reins to urge her horse to slow to a stop. Both rider and steed were winded.

"Yeah," said Emma as she slid off her horse. She hugged her kids as she spoke. "He has a broken leg and inhaled a lot of smoke. We're gonna try to find him a doctor."

"Where, Mom?" asked Matthew. "Unless something's different around here, everything we saw was looted or abandoned."

"That's right, Mom," added Cat. "It's not safe, either."

Emma looked toward the sky and grimaced. She imagined her young daughter had seen a lot on the road, as had she and Luke.

"It's a bad break," she explained as she motioned them toward the barn. "I need you to help me with some things."

"Okay," said Matthew, who took the reins of her horse and led her to the water trough.

"Your dad wanted me to get the truck. I think Luke might be more comfortable in that car. How does it run?"

"Like a rabbit," said Matthew. "It might need gas, though. I'll have to raid the lawn equipment cans."

"Do it," said Emma. "I don't know what we'll run into in town, but if we're gonna lose a vehicle in the process, let it be the one that doesn't run on diesel."

"What can I do, Mom?" asked Cat.

"Follow me to the house. We need to gather some supplies and clothing for the trip. Also, I want to meet your new friends."

Cat led the way as the two Cubbison women marched toward the market. Asher and Lauren Doyle stood at the side, keeping an eye on the driveway while watching the three family members speak near the barn. They met Emma halfway.

Lauren spoke first. "Mrs. Cubbison, I hope your son is okay."

"Please call me Emma. He's pretty banged up and has a broken leg. We're going to take him into Harford to find a doctor."

"I'm Lauren," she said, extending her hand. She was surprised that Emma hugged her instead.

"Hi, Lauren. Thank you for helping my family."

The women shared a moment, albeit brief. It didn't have to be said. They were all family now.

"Emma, this is my husband, Asher."

The two greeted one another. The group made their way toward the house while Matthew jogged toward the 1969 Pontiac GTO they'd taken following the gunfight at the armory. The vintage muscle car waited patiently on the road near the Cubbisons' gravel driveway.

Asher peeled off and jogged toward the trail leading to the Stanley farm to assess whether the fire was a threat to the Cubbison property. The winds seemed to be carrying the flames north and west of the creek that bordered the two farms.

Lauren, who had some knowledge of first aid, helped Emma gather a few things for their trip. She suggested a blanket to keep Luke warm in case he went into shock. Advil and fluids were a must. They brought a change of clothes for everyone as well as ammunition for their weapons. Lauren and Cat couldn't imagine any threats existed around tiny Harford in rural Northeastern Pennsylvania. Emma, however, knew better.

Before she left, she issued some instructions.

"I'm going to insist Grandpa Sam return to the farm to stay with you guys. It seems like he's been through a lot. He's had his share of grief in recent years, and I don't want him exposed to any more. Besides, if that fire threatens the farm, you'll need everyone to fight it off."

"I'll take care of him, Mom," said Cat.

"We both will," added Lauren. "Sam is a very special man. He deserves all of our support."

Emma smiled and nodded. She wiped away a tear as she turned to Cat.

"How is Matthew holding up?" she asked.

Cat gave her a reassuring smile. "Mom, he has been amazing. Like a different person. Please don't worry."

Emma hugged her young daughter, who had apparently grown up quite a bit. She glanced at Lauren as she spoke.

"It appears all of you have worked together to protect one

another. Your dad and I'll get Luke fixed up and hurry back. I promise."

She glanced past her daughter toward the windows overlooking the event venue that had remained unchanged since the perfect storm. Beyond, the sun was beginning to lower toward the horizon, casting an ominous glow through the dark clouds of smoke.

CHAPTER SIX

Wednesday
Stanley's Farm
Harford, Pennsylvania

Logically, Emma made the right choice in risking the newly acquired Pontiac GTO to travel into town. It would be more comfortable for Luke than the pickup truck bed or even the front bench seat. However, as she traversed the field behind Stanley's farmhouse, she realized the vehicle was not made for the ruts in the ground. Over time, Mr. Stanley had driven his tractor in the same two grooves across the property. However, water runoff had caused dips and rises that aggravated the stiff suspension of the classic car.

Nonetheless, she managed to make her way to the trio monitoring her son. Luke was coherent again and writhing in pain. Vida knelt over him, whispering in his ear, a loving gesture that seemed to have a calming effect on Luke.

John rose out of his crouch to approach the slow-moving vehicle. He took over for a moment to turn the car around before they loaded Luke into it.

While Vida whispered words of encouragement to Luke, John, Emma and Sam stepped to the other side of the car to talk.

"We need to get going," said Sam with a sense of urgency. His eyes darted from John, the car, toward the setting sun. Then he watched the smoke float through the air toward Cubbison's Farm.

John took a deep breath and sighed. "Dad, I'd like you to stay at the farm and keep an eye on things. You've been through a lot and need to—"

"We've both been through a lot, son. I need to be there to help you."

Emma understood where John was coming from. "Listen, Grandpa Sam. We have a couple of new faces staying with us now. The Doyles seem like good people, but you've only known them for a short time."

"They saved our lives, you know, risked everything and gave up a lot. Emma, I trust them wholeheartedly."

She placed her hand on his shoulder. "I understand. However, they don't know the farm. Matthew and Cat are only marginally helpful in that regard. We still have things that need to get done, and you're best suited to oversee things."

Sam exhaled and nodded. Of course, they were right. He glanced back toward the car, where Vida was still talking with Luke.

"What about the girl? What do we know about her?"

"Nothing," replied Emma although it was clear she and Luke were close.

John added his thoughts. "She was there for him when he was on the edge of the fire. If she hadn't called out to us, we may have been too late."

Sam asked, "Is she alone? Do you think we should allow her on the farm?"

John replied, "She claims she's alone and not really part of the women and children at the Yoder place. She wasn't there at the time, but she was told their husbands and boyfriends, whoever they were, attacked you and Luke. Is that correct?" He studied her face. He hoped Emma wouldn't hide the truth from him.

"Well, not really. They came to the farm, twice, and demanded food. Even a cow."

"Did you give it to them?" Sam asked.

"Yes," she said sheepishly. Then, in a hushed tone of voice, she added, "Before we took it all back."

John looked into his wife's eyes. "What do you mean?"

Emma evaded his question. "John, I can explain all of this later. We need to go."

Undeterred, he persisted. "This will help determine whether we let this girl go with Dad to the farm. What happened?"

Emma took a deep breath and exhaled. She stared toward the road, wondering if the bloodstains still covered the pavement. In her haste, she'd driven the GTO past the proverbial scene of the crime and didn't pay attention.

"It happened over there. In front of the house. We gave them several heavy crates of food and a very difficult bullock." Her chin fell to her chest as tears began to flow.

"Honey, then what?"

"John, they'd keep coming back for more and more if we didn't do something."

Sam understood. He was blunt. "You had to kill them."

Emma nodded. "Only, they had two young boys with them. They had to witness the whole thing." She broke down crying in earnest.

John tried to comfort her. "It's okay. You're right; we can talk about this later. However, is there any reason to believe this girl is part of that group? She seems out of place from what I'm hearing."

Sam gave his opinion. "My gut says she is telling us the truth. Or at least most of it. Her backpack was full of clothing and water. She was leaving to go somewhere."

Emma wiped away the tears. "She helped Luke and won't leave his side. I think he'd vouch for her if he were up to it."

John turned away from them and took a deep breath. He placed his hands on his hips and spoke to Sam.

"Dad, this is all the more reason for you to stay. She deserves our protection. That said, we need to learn more about her background. Casually pry it out of her, okay?"

"I will."

Before the Cubbisons returned to the car, Vida spoke with Luke. She'd begun to fall in love with him in the short time they'd spent together. Adversity can be as powerful as Cupid's arrow. She promised him that she'd wait for his return in the Stanley house.

What she didn't say to Luke, nor would she immediately disclose to anyone else in his family, was that she recognized the classic Pontiac. She was no car expert; however, she was aware that a vehicle like this was very rare. It was her father's favorite car. That meant, she concluded, her father and Abdul had crossed paths with the Cubbison family members as they returned from New York.

Her mind was full of conflict. *What happened? And how did they take possession of the car? Did they have to kill to get it?*

CHAPTER SEVEN

Wednesday
Cubbison's Farm
Harford, Pennsylvania

Sam located his horse and shortly thereafter found John's. He was in no hurry to return to the farm because he wanted to assess the path of the fire and get to know Vida better. As he observed his surroundings, making mental notes of the heads of cattle milling about and the location of the fire, he spoke with Vida.

"I can't tell you how much our family appreciates you for helping Luke. He's a good young man."

Vida wanted to be conversational; however, she remained guarded. Especially in light of the Cubbison family's possession of the GTO. "He and I met by accident. I was traveling to my uncle's home near Rochester. I came across the women and children at the farm, who offered me a place to sleep. I hadn't planned on staying more than a day or two, when I met Luke."

"Tell me what you know about the men who were living there."

"All I can say is what I was told by Luke. The women took up with the guys for safety. They turned out to be jerks. The three women didn't really know about the men coming to your farm to demand food."

Sam was supposed to be tactful in his dealings with Vida. As they approached the clearing at Cubbison's Farm, he felt a sense of urgency. He assumed the role of interrogator.

"Do you know what happened?" he asked.

Vida shrugged. "Not really, other than what Luke told me. There was a confrontation between the men and your family. Luke didn't tell me much. I just know the men were killed."

Sam rested his hand on the pistol grip of his holstered sidearm. He had no reason to believe Vida was armed, but he didn't know for certain. The family could ill afford to lose one of their horses to a transient regardless of whether she'd helped Luke.

"You say you stopped by the Yoder place for shelter and were headed north toward New York, right?"

Vida nodded.

"Rochester's a long way," he added, observing her body language. Sam's tone of voice had changed. She tensed as she anticipated the next question. Should she tell the truth or lie? Sam continued with a logical question. "Where did you live?"

"Scranton," she lied. "It was no longer safe there. My father was abusive and left me alone. I needed to find family to stay with." Most of what she said was true. She could not let the Cubbisons know she was connected to Abdul Rahimi and his radical Islamist followers.

"Sam!" Asher yelled his name from across the field. He was making his way from the creek. "Is everything okay?"

Sam had more questions, but perhaps the interruption was for the best. There had been a noticeable change in Vida's demeanor at the end of their conversation. He sensed she was holding something back.

"They left for Harford to find medical help for Luke," he replied in a raised voice until Asher drew closer. "Has the fire jumped the creek?"

"Not even close. The winds died down as it got darker. I don't know if it will burn out, but the fire line appears to have some rocky terrain to cross over before hitting the farm."

"That's right," added Sam. "The creek isn't wide enough to stop a wildfire, but the outcroppings may slow it down. Rock doesn't burn. We're definitely gonna have to watch it."

Asher joined them and extended his hand to Vida. The two introduced themselves before Sam motioned toward the barn.

"Let me get these horses some water. Then we need to talk about where we go from here. I don't know how long they'll be gone. We need to talk about security, which will include keeping an eye on the fire."

"I can help," offered Vida. She desperately wanted to be accepted by the family. "I'm a good cook, and I also know how to work in the garden. I don't know anything about horses, and I've never touched a gun. Maybe I could be a lookout or something?"

Sam was touched by her offer. He, Matthew, and the Doyles were exhausted after their night fleeing the armory attack. He would consider assigning Vida to patrol the perimeter, without a gun, of course. The rest of them could take two-hour shifts to keep an eye on the farm and their new guest.

"Thank you, Vida. We could all use our rest this evening. Let's get you introduced to the rest of my family, including Lauren, Asher's wife. We all have stories to relay to one another, but I'm going to insist on waiting until tomorrow. None of us can afford an all-night session around the campfire."

She thanked Sam and began walking ahead toward the house. Asher immediately leaned into Sam and whispered, "She's from Afghanistan. So were those guys last night. Lauren is better with dialects than I am, so I'm going to defer to her assessment. I think I'm right, though."

Sam nodded and whispered back, "Her story is a little suspect. For now, let's keep an eye on her until we can learn more."

"Agreed."

"By the way, Asher, have you ever driven cattle?"

"Um, no. But I drove a Mustang once."

They guys, exhausted from their trip to the farm, shared a rare opportunity to laugh. These kinds of moments were few and far between in a post-apocalyptic world.

CHAPTER EIGHT

Wednesday
Harford, Pennsylvania

Emma settled into the backseat of the GTO and leaned forward to rest her forearms on the bucket seats. John eased the car out of the field and onto the highway leading into town. He was doing eighty miles an hour when he raced passed the Yoder house. A couple of the women and several children stopped playing to watch the vehicle speed past them.

"Arrrgh!" Luke exclaimed as his father had to jerk the steering wheel to the left to avoid a dead deer in the road.

"Sorry, son. I'm a little hyped up and didn't see it."

Emma reached around to feel Luke's forehead. The air conditioning of the GTO should've cooled down his skin that had been exposed to the fire.

"John," she whispered, "he still feels warm. Maybe with a low-grade fever."

"Don't we have a thermometer?" he asked.

Emma sighed. There were so many things she wished she'd had

to help treat her son. Like so many other families, the Cubbisons relied upon readily available medical treatment centers or even drugstores for emergencies.

"No, unfortunately. If I had known ..." Her voice trailed off as she touched her son's forehead again, hoping the minute that had lapsed might've made a difference.

John tried to reassure her. "Don't worry, honey. We'll get him fixed up."

He slowed as they entered a stretch of woods with several S-curves. He didn't want to jostle Luke unnecessarily. He glanced into the rearview mirror to catch a glimpse of his wife's face. He wanted to see her face as he asked a prying question.

"Um, Emma? Tell me about the shooting."

Emma slumped into the backseat and wiped away her tears. However, her sniffles betrayed her attempts to hide her emotional state from her husband. She still carried a lot of guilt for shooting those men on the road. Especially since there had been children in the line of fire who had to witness what had happened. In a way, the thought had crossed her mind that God was punishing her by nearly taking Luke's life in the fire.

She recounted the entire series of encounters from the beginning. "John, it didn't take long for those guys to come around making demands. They carried rifles and were very threatening. At first, I thought I could satisfy their demands with some of our inventory from the market and excess we could spare.

"Then Luke and I got to thinking about it. They'd keep coming for more until one night, they wouldn't announce themselves before they attacked us."

"You decided on a preemptive strike, so to speak," interjected John.

Emma began to sob as she buried her face in her hands. She'd prayed every minute for her husband to come home safely. The moment her family returned, Luke was almost killed. The happy reunion she'd imagined had become a fleeting moment in between crises.

"We had no choice. But ..." She paused to sniffle and wipe her nose on her arm. "Others would look at it as murder. Especially those two boys who were in the middle of it."

John was about to tell her what had happened with Matthew killing an attacker, when he spotted the sun shining on something metallic on the road ahead of them. He pulled the car to an abrupt stop and jumped out, dragging his hunting rifle across the seat with him. Leaning on the top of the door's window, he used the scope to get a better look.

"What is it?" Emma asked as she scooted forward in the seat again. She squinted to block out the last of the setting sun.

"A roadblock of some kind," replied John. He paused for a moment. "Only, it looks like motorcycles. You know, choppers. Not dirt bikes or the kind old people drive to tour the country. These are biker-gang style."

"Are they blocking the road?"

"Yeah. I see some guys milling around, smoking cigarettes."

"I don't like it," whispered Emma. She looked around the car in search of an alternative route.

"Me neither. We'll have to go another way."

John reentered the car, checked on his son, and slowly drove the car in reverse until he was around a curve. He stopped to think for a moment.

"The best way across the interstate is the next exit up by the Flying J and Burger King."

"What if they've done the same thing up there?"

John furrowed his brow. Then he sat upright in his seat. He did a three-point turn to maneuver in the opposite direction of the interstate. He explained their options.

"The Harford Road exit is one option. If I remember correctly, there is a gravel road that connects the rock quarry with Fair Hill Road on the other side. We'll use the underpass to cross."

"Won't the road be rough?" she asked.

"It's worth a shot. Blanding Lake Road dumps out right at the highway. We'll be sittin' ducks if there are more biker blockades."

John raced up the narrow, two-lane country road until he reached the entrance of the quarry. The chain-link gates were left open, and there was a smattering of vehicles strewn about, likely victims of the intense solar storm. It was getting darker now, and John had to slow down to find his way through the quarry complex to the back entrance.

It turned out his hunch was a good one. He navigated through the concrete underpass to the other side of the interstate with a minimal amount of added discomfort to Luke. Minutes later, they were on the road to Harford and approaching the county fairgrounds.

As the fairgrounds came into view, John had a thought. "This whole thing happened on a Friday night around 9:30. Do you know what was on the schedule at the fairgrounds that afternoon?"

Emma had to think hard. The family, typically without Matthew, frequently went to the fairgrounds for entertainment. Everything from rattlesnake shows to chainsaw carving demonstrations to rodeos took place on any given day.

"Friday nights, they usually have the rodeo in the main arena, followed by a band of some sort. Lately, it's been Dallas Carter." The band was well known throughout Northeast Pennsylvania, primarily playing hit songs from the nineties.

John slowed the car as the road opened up with fields on both sides. With dusk rapidly approaching, they'd be vulnerable because the car's headlights could give them away. John pushed the headlight knob firmly into the dashboard and leaned forward to focus on the road. "We're driving right past it. Let's stop by and see if there are any vets around."

He eased the car through the steel gates, which had been left open. Apparently, there had been a packed house that night, as the parking lot was full of now-inoperable cars and trucks. He drove deeper into the complex past the concession stand and toward the main arena. After stopping to assess their surroundings, he took a chance and honked the horn to garner attention.

At first, nobody approached them. He turned on the headlights. Then John stepped out of the car and walked around so he could be seen in the headlights. Nervous, he was startled when an older man emerged from behind a hay wagon.

"You need somethin'?" he asked casually.

"Yes, sir. My name is John Cubbison. I live—"

"Hey, John. It's Walt. Walt Harbin." Harbin was one of the managing members who operated the fairgrounds. He walked in front of the headlight's beam to be seen.

The two men embraced before John explained his plight. He asked about Dr. Caitlin Quinn.

"Yeah, CQ was here that night. She's always on call when there's a rodeo. You know, injuries are rare, but having her around is a must."

"She left, obviously," added John, looking around at the deserted complex.

"Yeah, they all did. Some hung around for a while, thinking the power would come back. Eventually, they all left, especially after some guys with guns showed up."

"What happened?" asked John.

"Kinda weird, actually. They were threatening, but they weren't. You know? They shouted instructions at people and waved their guns. But they never hurt anyone."

"What did they want?"

"Anything they could find in the buildings or in the vehicles. It happened two days after the lights went out. A couple of the guys thought about taking them on with their huntin' rifles, but within seconds, they had those red dot lasers all over their bodies."

"Like military?" asked John.

"Yeah, that's fair to say," replied Walt. "Rumor has it a bunch of those types are holed up at the Harford House motel. Folks say they've been gathering up supplies, food, weapons, and such."

John wandered away from Walt and looked toward town. "What about medicine?"

"Yeah. That too. They broke into CQ's vet truck and took out all the meds."

"Did she try to stop them?"

"Yup. She drew a handgun out of the holster tucked into the back side of her jeans. One of the guys smacked it out of her hand, and that was the end of that."

John sighed. He placed his hands on his hips and paced the ground next to the car. He had to get Luke some help.

"I'm gonna go see those guys about helping Luke."

Walt shook his head and furrowed his brow. "I don't know, John. Well, I suppose it's worth a try. Good luck."

CHAPTER NINE

Wednesday
Harford House Motel
Harford, Pennsylvania

Fred Stewart was a new man. It was as if the powerless world had cast off the doldrums that had plagued him following his return to the States. For the first time in his life, he was running shit, and it felt mighty fine.

When Patel, the owner of Harford House motel, left, Fred assumed de facto ownership. He was a firm believer in the axiom— possession is nine-tenths of the law. Unlike most people, he'd quickly realized the power was not coming back on. In fact, he somehow knew it would take years. After all, he surmised, most of those busted transformers were made in China. He doubted they were anxious to help out America by sending replacements. Heck, they were probably laughing at them.

Fred had studied history, both from a military perspective and from his genealogy. Like most Stewarts, he was a descendent of the Stewards of Scotland. After he looted the local hardware store, he officially renamed the Harford House motel to the House of Stewart. He took the only four cans of red spray paint at the store to write the new name across the once-pristine white façade of the main house.

Days after the collapse, two of his former comrades arrived at the newly designated House of Stewart. Fred set them up with their own rooms and tasked them with locating more of their brethren. In the first two weeks, every room was filled with former U.S. military personnel who'd engaged in mercenary activities alongside Fred in Eastern Europe or Taiwan.

When more of his former Marines arrived, he found lodging for them nearby on Decker Court and along School Street. The locals, fearful of the menacing-looking former Marines patrolling the streets with rifles, began to leave Harford. The town was gradually becoming deserted except for a handful of residents and Fred's compatriots.

A truce had been reached between Fred and the Warlocks, a group of outlaw bikers who'd occupied the Onvo Travel Plaza by the interstate. Both sides were heavily armed and capable of causing significant loss of life to the other. However, the leader of the outlaw motorcycle club agreed to stay east of the interstate, and Fred's people promised to remain to the west. The bikers were allowed to control the highway itself.

During the daytime hours, Fred sent out patrols to loot businesses, as well as abandoned farms and cattle ranches. He specifically instructed his people to avoid harassing the local residents. Further, they were instructed to avoid the use of force unless fired upon.

All of the former military personnel understood the importance of having well-defined rules of engagement, and none of them were interested in firing upon fellow Americans. Unlike the bikers, they were not killers for the sake of killing. If anything, they considered themselves to be patriots.

It was early evening, and Fred was holding court behind

Harford House, now the House of Stewart. The grills were fired up, and local beef was sizzling. Some of the men had found female companionship in the town and were enjoying the familial atmosphere that had been created through Fred's vision of life in a post-apocalyptic world.

A bottle of wine was passed around, although Fred didn't partake. Nor did he take the mind-altering drugs given to him by the VA doctors. Fred would deal with the nightmares of Afghanistan with a clear head, even if they drove him to madness.

He strolled through the courtyard, talking in a loud voice. "You had to wonder what people meant when they said *love of country*. I'd watch the fights between liberals and conservatives, both shouting *we're the patriots*. They both accused each other of ruining our democracy. In the end, it was the hand of God that brought the mighty U-S-of-A to her knees."

Fred didn't expect anyone to respond or chime in. They rarely did. They were more interested in eating the steaks and enjoying the companionship of the locals than discussing the politics of the day before the perfect storm hit. He continued his random musings.

"We should've focused on our own shit. All of the neocons who sent us off to war, meddling in other countries' affairs, abused their power. Think about it; we were sold a bill of goods to venture into the Middle East to begin with. Then they yanked us out without a plan. Meanwhile, NATO expanded across Eastern Europe while that thug Putin tried to slow them down by invading countries located on Russia's border."

"We're the good guys, and the others—Russia, China, Taliban— are the barbarians at the gate," one of his fellow Marines added.

"Exactly!" Fred agreed emphatically. "Now that the proverbial shit has hit the fan, is all that game-playing over? Do you think the politicians are finally ready to help the people who live in this country?"

A couple of the men began to laugh. "I haven't seen the FEMA trucks rollin' in with boxes of MREs."

"Yeah, we're on our own out here," said the other.

A third man strolled away from the grill and joined the conversation. "And I like it that way. Think about it. Fred's got us a sweet gig here. We keep the peace for the locals. We trade stuff for food. Everybody wins."

Fred smiled and nodded. He'd never expected the world to change as it had. Yet, somehow, his way of life was perfectly suited for the aftermath of the power grid collapsing. He'd brought together a good group of guys who were not opportunists. They were warriors who had survival instincts.

"Hey, Fred! We've got some folks who desperately need to see you. They need drugs. And guess what else? They have a car that runs."

Fred smiled. Of all the things he offered for barter, pharmaceuticals commanded the highest price. Like an operating vehicle, for example.

CHAPTER TEN

Wednesday
Harford House Motel
Harford, Pennsylvania

John and Emma stood in the entryway of the onetime opulent residence. After the furnishings had been removed by the Hollywood star who'd undertaken the renovations, the remaining shell seemed odd to most. There were doors installed several feet above the floor and a stairwell that led to nowhere. If a visitor didn't know the backstory, they'd think the prior owners had been building a carnival fun house, or that they were insane.

The present-day furnishings might've left a visitor with a similar opinion. Although the property had been converted to a bed and breakfast, followed by a motel room addition, it hardly resembled a business of that sort.

The reception counter was now designed for a watch station for the former military personnel who occupied the property. On the walls, patriotic symbols were abundant, ranging from a massive

American flag hanging from the ceiling to the Gadsden Flag, proudly proclaiming *Don't Tread on Me*, behind the watch station.

There were several artifacts hung on the walls or displayed on furniture throughout the lobby area and in the parlors that flanked the foyer. There were also dozens of handwritten quotes from the Founding Fathers as well as America's past military leaders.

A paintbrush had been used to inscribe *molon labe*, meaning come and take it, over a closet door. Other quotes dealt with the subject of tyranny. One in particular struck John. It was from former president Bill Clinton. *The road to tyranny, we must never forget, begins with the destruction of the truth.*

Emma leaned into John and whispered, "These people are crazy."

"Maybe, maybe not. It's hard to argue with any of these quotes."

Emma shrugged. "I just wanna get what we need and get out of here. Luke's fever has stabilized, but his pain levels have gone up. Advil isn't gonna help him."

"What do you think they're up to here?" John asked.

Emma glanced around and made eye contact with the two burly ex-Marines who held their weapons at low ready. Their expressionless faces gave her no clue as to what they were thinking.

"It's almost like they've created some kind of compound out of the motel. You know, a base of operations."

"To do what?" asked John. "We know they looted the fairgrounds. Thankfully, they haven't come our way."

"Yet," interrupted Emma. Then she thought for a moment. "I wonder if that biker roadblock applies to these guys as well."

John managed a chuckle. "I'd put my money on these guys over a bunch of beer-drinking, cigarette-smoking, overweight bikers."

Emma took a deep breath as she recalled the men she and Luke had killed. "I think a couple of the guys from the Yoder place were bikers. They fit the stereotype."

John wandered toward another wall leading to the back of the motel. The dimly lit room was illuminated by small battery-powered lanterns. It was darker here, so reading the inscription on the wall was more difficult.

He whispered, "The spirit of resistance to government is so valuable on certain occasions that I wish it to be always kept alive."

Emma was about to comment on the quote when a large, dark figure appeared out of an unlit hallway in front of them.

"Thomas Jefferson wrote that in a letter to Abigail Adams in 1787."

The man startled Emma, who shrieked. John instinctively wrapped his arms around her and pulled her behind him for protection.

They were face-to-face with Fred Stewart.

CHAPTER ELEVEN

Wednesday
Harford House Motel
Harford, Pennsylvania

Fred cleared his throat before continuing. "He also wrote it will often be exercised when wrong but better so than not to be exercised at all." He let out a hearty laugh and was joined by the armed men who remained standing behind the Cubbisons.

John tried to speak. "Um, we don't know much about that."

Fred seemed to ignore John as he continued. "You know, I agree with Mr. Jefferson. I like a little rebellion now and then. It's good for the soul. Kinda like a storm. I had no doubt a storm was comin'. I could feel it in the metal plate. Right here." He rapped his knuckles on the top of his head next to the black patch over his eye.

"Sir, we were told you might be able to help us," said John, trying to stick to the task at hand. Luke was hurting, and he needed to know if this crazy loon was going to be of assistance.

Fred huffed. He was used to commanding a captive audience who allowed him to espouse his worldview without them leaving.

They had to listen until they got what they wanted from him, or didn't.

"Follow me," he said brusquely. Then he shouted over his shoulder, "Have they been frisked?"

"Clear!" one of the men shouted back.

"You two aren't gonna be any trouble, right?"

"No, sir. We need help." Emma's voice reflected her motherly concern.

Fred led them into a candlelit room near the property's kitchen. It was small, containing only a rectangular dining table and chairs. Like the lobby, it was filled with patriotic memorabilia and handwritten quotes on the wall. There was also a map of Northeast Pennsylvania affixed to a bulletin board.

He motioned for the Cubbisons to sit while he took a seat at the head of the dining table. Beads of sweat appeared on his forehead as he leaned back in his chair. Like his guards, his face remained emotionless. He opened his arms wide with his palms faceup, a gesture encouraging John to speak.

"They tell us you might have what we need," John began before Fred interrupted.

"What's that?"

"Medicine. Painkillers."

Fred was curt in his response. "We don't sell to junkies, and you two don't look like you're hurting."

"No, wait. It's nothing like that." John tried to explain before Emma got to the point.

"It's our son Luke. He broke his leg. He's in terrible pain, and he has a fever."

Fred's eye grew wide, and he rolled his head around his neck. "What do you have to trade?"

"Trade?" Emma asked. "Well, um, we didn't think we'd need to trade—"

"Ma'am, you need to understand something. Nothing is free anymore. I am not a charity. I am not the government. Barter is the new way of doing business. If you have a need, then I will try to help you. If you have something I need, then we'll do business."

"We have a farm," said John. "We can bring you food. Vegetables from our garden. Herbs and spices."

"Good to know but not enough. You see, food can be regrown. Pharmaceuticals cannot. I need things that can't be reproduced."

Fred was angling to trade the medications for the car, which he'd confirmed to be a Pontiac GTO, one of his dream cars when he was growing up.

John and Emma were puzzled. They exchanged glances before John asked, "What do you mean?"

Fred leaned forward and rested his arms on the table. He studied the Cubbisons to assess their level of desperation. "Let me explain something. Our government basically left us behind in Afghanistan to be slaughtered by the Taliban and ISIS-K. My buddies got killed, and several of us suffered, too." He raised his eye patch to reveal the red socket where his eyeball once was.

"I'm sorry that happened to you," began Emma, averting her eyes from his injury.

"When I got back, like many of my fellow Marines, I was abandoned by our government. The VA was overwhelmed and treated my body but not my soul. Nobody would hire me. People mocked me. Pissed on me, literally. Called the cops on me. You name it. I gritted my teeth and endured it all.

"Now, things have changed. The people who treated me like shit are now begging me for help. I'm not an asshole. I'm a businessman now. I make deals that benefit me and the people I'm associated with. If we can't make a deal, you're free to leave."

John tried to control his anger. His son was hurting and in dire need of medications as well as a trained doctor, or veterinarian, as the case might be, to properly set Luke's broken leg. He knew Dr. Quinn's veterinary truck had been looted of its medicines, most likely by Fred and his men.

"We need two weeks of antibiotics and at least seven days of painkillers. Something stronger than Advil. Do you have these things?"

Fred leaned back and clasped his hands in front of his belly again. He simply nodded.

Emma balled up her fists and then relaxed her hands. She had to hold her tongue to deal with the man. She leaned forward and asked, "What do you want?"

Fred was blunt in his response. "The car."

John was incredulous. He waved his arms as he spoke. "You want a car that runs. After all that has happened. In exchange for a few pills. You've got to be kidding."

"That's my price. Take it or leave it."

"Come on, Emma. Let's go. We'll find help elsewhere."

John stood to leave, but Emma grabbed him by the arm. "Wait. Do you have a doctor here?"

"No."

"Do you know if Dr. Zimmerly is in town?" Dr. Daniel Zimmerly had a practice in Susquehanna, but his home was in Harford.

"Gone."

Emma continued the negotiations. Their options were severely limited. "Okay. Here's the problem. The only chance my son has is to get to the veterinarian's office to have his leg set properly. Then we have to get him home. We need the car for that. Can we take care of him and bring the car back?"

Fred continued to provide one-word, terse answers. "No."

John was still stewing. "You said you wanted the car. We're offering it to you."

Fred leaned forward and smiled, shaking his head as spoke. "I have no guarantees you'll be back with my end of the deal. So, therefore, we have no deal."

"I'll stay as collateral," Emma blurted out without thinking.

John's reaction was immediate. "What? Forget it. No, Emma. Let's go. We gotta get Luke to a doctor."

Emma had locked eyes with Fred. She exercised an enormous amount of self-restraint to keep from telling the man what she really thought. Fortunately, her experience with the four thugs who'd threatened her and Luke helped in this situation. She'd not only become a skilled negotiator but also a shrewd one as well.

"We'll take the car to the vet's office south of town to get my son's leg set. Then we'll be back for the meds. You can have your car, but we need you to drive us home."

"No."

John slammed his hand on the table. "Dammit, man! You said the car for the medicine. You said that!"

"We're not a taxi service."

"We only live a few miles from here," said John, waving his arm to point toward the east.

"Where?" asked Fred.

"Just east of here on State Road 547."

"No."

"Jesus! Why not?" John was losing it.

"We have a deal with the bikers at the truck stop. They stay over there, and we stay over here. It's a truce that's worked, and I'm not breaking it for you."

Emma tried to remain calm. "We know a way through the woods to avoid the highway. We'll show you."

"Do you have a gun?" Fred asked. "With ammo?"

"Yes, a hunting rifle."

Fred thought for a moment. He was fine with taking them back to their house. The car was invaluable. It was a terrific, one-sided deal for him. Yet, because these people were desperate, Fred tried to sweeten the pot.

"Okay, the gun and ammo will be payment for escorting you home. We'll be breaking our truce, so I need something to justify the risk."

John rose again with the intention of leaving, but Emma said, "Deal. We'll be back."

"But, Emma—" John began before she cut him off.

"No, John. This is fine. Luke needs our help now. Come on."

The two marched out of Fred's office without another word. John was still fuming, and Emma scolded herself for not keeping her head clear. She realized at the end of the bizarre negotiation that if Dr. Quinn had the medications they needed, this entire exercise had been a waste of precious time. Except they'd managed to learn a lot about a formidable adversary they might run across in the future.

CHAPTER TWELVE

Wednesday
Harford, Pennsylvania

John and Emma waited until they were in the car before they spoke about their encounter with Fred Stewart.

While John drove south of town, Emma explained her change of position. "If CQ has everything we need, then there's no need to deal with that guy. If she doesn't, then we still have our deal in place."

She gently rested her hand on Luke's forehead. He was sleeping, but his fever had subsided. Emma smiled as she turned to John.

"Makes sense," he added. "The whole thing pisses me off. However, we did learn something else."

"What's that?"

"There is some kind of unholy truce between Fred and his band of merry mercenaries and the biker gang at the interstate. We also know they've divided the county into a couple of territories. You know, east and west."

"That means we'll have to deal with more bikers making demands at some point," Emma added.

"Probably. But I'll take my chances with undisciplined bikers who are unfamiliar with the area over trained soldiers or whatever."

Emma jutted out her lower lip and nodded. "I've wondered why other bikers haven't moved in on the women at the Yoder place or made their way toward our farm. Maybe they're preying on inter-state travelers. It's easy, and they can stay close to home."

"Right. Their bikes don't work, and they have plenty of easy pickin's on the highway."

"Better slow down, John. I see the signs up ahead."

The wooden signs marking the entrance to Dr. Caitlin Quinn's equestrian facility were illuminated by solar-powered landscape lighting. The nearly two-hundred-acre farm included her personal residence, stables, a training facility, and her veterinarian's office. In addition to treating horses, she also saw small animal cases like family pets. She also treated local cattle, including the Cubbisons'.

John slowed as he reached her office, doubtful that she'd be there. Her home was farther down the gravel driveway past the stables. He imagined CQ, as she'd been known to her close friends since college, was complacent since her encounter with Fred's men at the fairgrounds. John wanted to be careful not to be on the receiving end of a nervous trigger finger.

He stopped a hundred yards short of her house and turned off the engine. He left the headlights on and immediately walked into the beams of light they emitted. With his hands raised high over his head, he slowly approached the front porch of the Indiana-style farmhouse.

"CQ! It's John Cubbison! I have Emma and Luke in the car with me. Can you help us?"

John stopped short of the steps leading up to her wraparound porch. After a moment of silence, he shouted her name again.

"Caitlin! CQ! Are you here? It's John. John Cubbison."

He waited.

"Hey, John."

Her strangely calm voice came out of the darkness to his left. John jumped a little and swung around.

"Shit, CQ!"

"Oh, um, sorry about that. I saw the headlights turn through the gate, so I grabbed my shotgun and ran behind the tractor."

Emma had crawled out of the backseat and ran into the head-light's beam. "CQ! Can you please look at Luke? He has a broken leg."

Dr. Quinn handed the shotgun to John and hustled toward the GTO. She briefly embraced her friend and mumbled, "Nice ride." Emma hurriedly explained what had happened.

"He's got other injuries like burns and bruises. Mainly, it's his broken leg that is causing his pain. He slips in and out of conscious-ness, which has concerned me, too."

Dr. Quinn briefly examined Luke's leg and also checked for a fever. She rose out of the front seat and hollered for John to bring the car down the hill to her clinic. Without hesitation, she began to jog down the gravel driveway without them.

Minutes later, with all three helping one another, they lifted a now conscious Luke out of the car and into an examination room. Dr. Quinn had the new, shielded Generac generators to provide power to the clinic in case of a power outage. The primary compo-nents within the generator's shell were sealed within a solid steel enclosure.

After the power was turned on, Luke was laid prone on a stain-less-steel surgical table. Dr. Quinn removed his pants leg and the makeshift splint. She left the room and returned with a MinXray portable radiography system.

John interrupted her. "Wait a minute. That works?"

Dr. Quinn responded, "I've only used it once since the power went out. I really don't know why it works while other stuff doesn't."

John was puzzled. He assumed all electronic devices had been ruined by the solar storm. "Where was it stored?"

Dr. Quinn pointed her thumb over her shoulder. "In the cages down the hallway. The man I bought the place from used to raise exotic birds. When I closed that part of the building in for storage, I kept the cages."

John wandered down the hallway and studied the rows of shelves with separate compartments. Each section was a perfect square with walls made from a fine metal screen mesh. He shrugged and returned to the examination room.

Dr. Quinn donned a protective vest and instructed the Cubbisons to leave the room while she took X-rays of Luke's leg. The digital radiography system transmitted an accurate view of the broken bones to a laptop sitting on an adjacent counter.

When she was finished, she turned the lights on and summoned the parents back inside. As she removed the protective vest, she relayed what she'd found.

"An MRI would tell me more about the other damage he sustained to nerves and tendons. The bruising makes it obvious he was trampled. Am I right?"

"We think so," replied John. "Luke hasn't been able to tell us much."

Dr. Quinn grimaced and nodded. "Well, I'll treat him as if he was. I'm pretty sure I see a bruise shaped like a hoof. Anyway, the first thing I need to do is perform a fracture reduction. We need to put the bone back in place so it will heal properly. I'll reset the bone by manipulating the broken ends into their original position. You know, to match up the way they were. Long term, he may suffer from arthritis in his leg, but that pales in comparison to the deformity if we don't set it properly."

"We understand," said Emma.

Dr. Quinn's demeanor changed. "Listen, you guys, this is gonna hurt like hell. An emergency room would probably use a general anesthetic to put Luke completely to sleep. I only have a hematoma block, which delivers a local anesthesia directly to the area around the fracture. If the nerves and tendons have been damaged, as I suspect, Luke's gonna feel it."

"What can we do to help?" asked John.

"Hold him down and keep him calm," she replied as she went to a wall cabinet to retrieve the medical supplies she needed.

Emma asked, "Do you have antibiotics and painkillers? We stopped by the Harford House and tried to trade that car out there for the meds."

"I have some. That guy sent his buddies to the fairgrounds, where they robbed my truck of all my large animal meds. I've got a lot of boarders in the stables that I won't be able to take care of without those drugs."

John thought for a moment. "Emma, if CQ has what we need to fix up Luke, why can't we give her the car. Let her barter with Stewart to get her medicines back."

Dr. Quinn raised her hands. "Hey, you guys don't need to pay for this. I'm glad to help."

Emma disagreed. "You're saving our son, CQ. It's the least we can do."

"No. No. I can't agree ..." Her voice trailed off as a thought came to her. "Okay, I do have a proposal. How about we make a trade?"

"What do you have in mind?" asked John.

As Dr. Quinn sterilized the skin around Luke's leg with iodine, she explained, "I have several horses that are boarded with me. It's more mouths than I can feed. I know you guys have your own horses, but could you use, um, maybe a few more?"

John and Emma looked to one another. He relayed his thoughts aloud. "Well, we do have those two newcomers who helped Dad and Cat."

"Yes," added Emma, addressing Dr. Quinn directly as she worked on Luke. "The Doyles. Plus the girl who helped Luke. Her name is Vida."

"She might not be staying," John quickly countered.

"I understand, but she might. A third horse would give one for each of us at the farm."

Dr. Quinn administered the hematoma block by injecting the anesthesia into the fracture area. This allowed the broken ends of the bone to be bathed in the anesthetic, which helped relieve the pain Luke would endure.

The prick of the needle brought Luke out of his semiconscious state. "What's going on?"

Dr. Quinn leaned over her patient. "Hi, Luke. Do you remember me?"

"Yeah. Of course."

"Good. I'm about to fix your leg."

Luke's eyes grew wide, and they began to dart around the room. "Aren't you gonna give me a stick or something to bite down on?"

Dr. Quinn laughed. "Well, I hope it doesn't hurt that bad, but, yeah, here's a towel."

Luke readily chomped down on the towel while his parents got into position. As she worked, Dr. Quinn explained the procedure.

"Luke, you're gonna feel some pressure in your leg and probably a crunching sensation. If you have pain, it's from the nerves and tendons that got trampled."

Luke nodded and mouthed the word *steer*.

Dr. Quinn continued. "Once the broken ends are held firmly in place, I'm gonna build a splint of plaster and fiberglass. It's gonna take a little engineering because I'm not used to human legs. No worries 'cause I can do it. Okay?"

Luke nodded.

Dr. Quinn got to work. The bones crunched. The nerves shot pain through his body, and Luke passed out.

An hour later, he was awake again, and an expertly modified cast had been fashioned onto his leg. For the first time since John had returned home from New York City, Luke smiled at him.

CHAPTER THIRTEEN

Wednesday
Quinn's Equestrian Center
Harford, Pennsylvania

"All right, how are we gonna get him home with his leg in a cast?" Emma asked a logical question that hadn't been considered when they agreed to trade the Pontiac for three horses.

"Actually, I thought about that while I was making his cast. Sometimes, when you're performing a procedure, your mind wanders."

"Great," quipped Luke. "Are my toes facing backwards?"

"Let's hope so, young man," said Emma. "Then you can kick yourself in the backside for frightening your mother."

After the group shared a laugh, Dr. Quinn explained what she had in mind. "John, I think you should lead Luke and his horse. We'll use leather straps to lift his leg into place so that it has some kind of support. It would become too heavy for Luke to dangle it as he rode."

"Makes sense," said John.

"I know it's late, and you're all tired. You're welcome to stay at the house until morning."

Emma smiled and thanked her. "If Luke is up for it, I think we'll be better to travel in the dark. It seems some people think they can steal from you without suffering consequences."

"You mean like Fred Stewart and his people?" asked Dr. Quinn.

"Yeah. And anyone else we encounter who might want our horses. I figure at night we'd encounter fewer people on the road."

Dr. Quinn checked Luke's fever one more time as she provided the Cubbisons a suggested route across the interstate. "Near normal. That's good news. Nonetheless, I've injected him with cefazolin for starters. It's a penicillin substitute commonly used for fractures. I gave you a dozen Tramadol for the pain. It's an opioid, so don't overdo it, okay?"

"Only if I need it," replied Luke.

"It's all I've got." Dr. Quinn patted her patient on the shoulder. "You take it easy while we get the horses ready. Along the way, if you are suffering any severe jolts of pain as the anesthesia wears off, I want you to stop and rest. Agreed?"

"Agreed. Thanks, CQ."

It took the group thirty minutes to pick out the best horses for the journey and future use. Dr. Quinn provided them the necessary tack together with the extra leather straps to support Luke's leg.

Soon thereafter, Luke was loaded onto his horse with the assistance of a wooden set of steps. He grimaced in pain as he swung his leg over the horse, but he soldiered through it. After their good-byes, the Cubbisons began their journey home.

While John knew the roads of Susquehanna County like the back of his hand, the trails and woods were another matter. They made a wrong turn here and there but eventually found their way by following their nose. The fire was still burning, and although they couldn't see it, they knew they were close to home as the rancid air invaded their nostrils.

John waited some time before he broached the subject of what had happened with the four men his wife and son had killed. It helped Emma to talk it out. She would continue to feel a sense of guilt for some time because she'd taken another human being's life. However, both Luke and John reminded her that it was necessary to protect themselves. All of them grimly acknowledged it wouldn't be the last time they'd have to take another's life to survive.

This conversation, and their shared opinions on the fate of the women and children left behind, led John to quiz Luke about Vida.

"Dad, Vida is from Afghanistan, part of a group of refugees brought here after we pulled out of their country. They settled over by Lake Wallenpaupack."

"Wayne County," John added under his breath. Wayne County stretched from the New York state line southward past Scranton. The fairly large lake was a popular recreational hangout for people in Eastern Pennsylvania.

"That's right," said Luke. "We've known that the Afghans were resettled all around us years ago. They've mostly stuck to themselves."

"Until we ran across some of them during the armory attack at Picatinny Arsenal in New Jersey," said John.

Luke scowled, slightly annoyed at his father's implication. "Dad, I realize it's a small world and all, but we don't know they're connected to Vida."

"I'm not saying they are, son. And certainly, Vida doesn't strike me as a terrorist. Maybe I'm just being overly cautious."

After a moment of silence between father and son, Emma spoke. "She seems like a nice girl, and let's not forget, without her, Luke might've, um, you know."

"She helped save my life, Mom. Let me explain why she was there." Luke stopped for a moment as he adjusted himself in the saddle. His broken leg was held firmly in place, which began causing his butt to get cramped. He continued. "She opened up to me about life as an Afghan woman. Her mother was beaten by her father regularly and allowed to be raped by her brother-in-law. She'd been beaten regularly by both of them and feared her time to be offered up to the uncle for sex was coming."

"Savages!" Emma said forcefully with anger in her voice.

"She'd been plotting an escape for some time," said Luke. "She has another uncle and cousins who live in the Rochester area. They love America and have done everything they can to assimilate. She kept in touch with them on a regular basis. Plus, her uncle in New York is her mother's brother."

"Is that where she was headed?" asked John.

"Yes. When the power went out, she decided to go for it."

"Rochester is a long way from here," said Emma. "It's not safe for a young girl. Especially a pretty one like her."

"I know, Mom. That's why ..." Luke's voice trailed off as he prepared to tell the truth about his plans for Vida. "She wouldn't be safe with those women at the Yoder place. They're irresponsible and will probably take up with the first set of men who come along and promise to take care of them. I asked her to hide out at Mr. Stanley's house until I could talk to you, and now Dad, about her coming to the farm."

"Oh," muttered Emma.

John hesitated before speaking, and an awkward silence hovered over the family as they crossed the field. Finally, he asked, "Son, what do you know about her father?"

"Only what little she told me. We spoke briefly, and I told her to gather her things. We were supposed to meet back at Mr. Stanley's house when everything happened. What she did tell me was that her father was a very big part of their community and would probably come looking for her."

"If they know she's close to her mother's family, they'll head straight for Rochester," added Emma.

Luke agreed. "That's what I told her. She wouldn't be safe there."

John threw cold water on the entire conversation. "If they look hard enough, they'll find her at our place. That won't go over well."

"Dad, I mean, she needs our help."

"We can't help them all," John said bluntly. "Especially those whose family is capable of—"

Emma cut him off. She gently pulled back on the reins to stop her horse. "John, we understand where you are coming from. We made the decision to say no to a bunch of hungry mouths just a couple of miles away from us. However, I think we owe this young woman the benefit of the doubt. She helped save Luke's life."

John spoke his mind. "What if she changes her mind and runs back to her father? What if she tells her entire community about what we have, and they descend upon us like locusts?"

"She won't do that, Dad!" Luke raised his voice slightly and immediately regretted it.

Emma tried to diffuse the potential argument. "Well, we've sent her to the farm with Grandpa Sam. In a way, our decision has been made. If she earns our trust and becomes a part of the farm, then we made the right choice. Regardless, by the time the sun rises tomorrow, she will have seen enough to tell her dad and the rest of the Afghans all about us. At this point, let's make her feel welcome."

"Fine," said John with a huff. "However, I think we need to adopt a trust but verify rule with any newcomers. The Doyles earned our trust and will be a great addition."

"Vida will be, too, Dad."

"I hope so, son."

They'd reached the highway in front of the Stanley place. A brief gust of wind swept the stench of burnt wood across the dried grasses. John turned his horse down the road, crossing the rise where the four men had been shot just days before.

The three of them found a new sense of urgency the closer they got to the front gate of the farm. The casual gait of their horses suddenly changed to a slow trot. They all worried that their farm was threatened by the fire. Their fears were partially correct.

PART 2

Thursday
Welcome to the neighborhood.

CHAPTER FOURTEEN

Thursday
Lake Wallenpaupack
Wayne County, Pennsylvania

Abdul Rahimi was stoic as he presided over the funeral preparations of the dead resulting from the attack on Picatinny Arsenal. Coping with the loss of a close friend and top lieutenant was difficult for Abdul. Jamal Khan had been like family dating back to their years of growing up together in Afghanistan.

As they were speeding away from New Jersey toward their compound on Lake Wallenpaupack, Abdul vowed to return to retrieve his friend's body. Khan had been shot in the head when they were surprised by gunmen during their attempted escape. His first inclination was to escape with the rest of his men and the large cache of weapons seized from the armory. After several miles of driving on multiple side roads, Abdul returned with a driver to retrieve Khan's body found lying facedown in the weeds.

In that moment, he closed his eyes, set his jaw, and vowed revenge against the infidels who killed his friend. But first, as the spiritual leader of his community, he must respectfully treat his fellow Muslim's body.

With his weapon drawn, he entered the motor home that had been parked near the back entrance to Picatinny Arsenal. Confirming it had been abandoned, he pulled the sheets off the bed and returned to Khan's body.

Ordinarily, he would close the eyes of his deceased brother as well as bind his jaw with cloth, but Khan's face had been obliterated. Abdul swaddled the body in the white sheets and hoisted it into the back of the pickup truck they'd driven. It was important that he return home to have Khan's body prepared for the funeral within twenty-four hours. His revenge would have to wait until his brother was sent to *Jannah*.

While Khan's body was being prepared for his funeral, Abdul led the Afghan community in the mourning process. Following prayer that early morning, the community drew together to support Khan's wife and his close friends.

Members of his family and Khan's wife participated in the Islamic tradition of washing their dead loved one. They used cloths to methodically clean his body, starting top to bottom and then left to right. This ritual was repeated seven times until his body was clean.

After he was clean, they shrouded his body in three white sheets and used four ropes to bind it together. They reverently followed the ritualistic process of preparing a male Muslim's body for his funeral and burial before taking it to a small cemetery located near the lake. Only a few people had died since their arrival in America, with Khan being the most prominent among them.

As the day wore on, the ritual was completed, and the community came together to console the family and one another. Abdul remained remarkably reserved under the emotional pressure of the day considering the great sense of loss he was feeling.

Yet despite his grieving for his friend, anger was building up inside him. Anger towards the Americans responsible for Khan's death. And anger at his friend's daughter, who had run away from her father and community, thereby shaming them all.

His eyes roved around the members of his extended family as they consoled one another. He balled his fists to the point his nails were drawing blood from the palms of his hands. Abdul Rahimi couldn't decide whom he wanted to hunt down first. The men who had killed Khan or his best friend's daughter, Vida.

CHAPTER FIFTEEN

Thursday
Cubbison's Farm
Harford, Pennsylvania

They needed a normal day. Or at least as normal as a day could be in a powerless world. From the moment the perfect storm hit, the Cubbison family, and their new acquaintances, Lauren and Asher Doyle, as well as Vida Khan, had battled all manners of threats. Now they were joined together under one roof at the Cubbison home. Emma was intent upon providing everyone a taste of Pennsylvania farm living.

After the long ride back from Harford on horseback that ended just after midnight, everyone had the emotional reunion they'd hoped for when they'd arrived the day prior. It was John who insisted the group get some rest. He reminded them there would be plenty of time to catch up and share stories after some sleep.

Matthew and Asher volunteered for the overnight security watch. Asher had been carefully monitoring the advancing wildfire while Matthew bounced from the front gate to the other most likely entries onto the farm. As the sun rose over Rock Mountain, the guys reconvened at the house and found Emma in the kitchen, preparing breakfast. The smell of coffee reached their nostrils the moment they opened the door.

"Coffee? Really?" asked Asher as he took in the aroma.

"Good morning, boys," greeted Emma, whose apron was covered with flour from making biscuits. "I fired up the generator to get the day started. We'll have biscuits and sausage gravy and, yes, Asher, coffee. How do you take it?"

Asher laughed. "You could pour it over my head right now, and I'd be thrilled. On the road, we drank everything from Capri Sun kid's drinks to warm sodas. How about you, Matthew?"

Matthew, who was not a coffee drinker, recalled sharing a beer with his father. It was a first among many others on the grueling adventure. "Not for me. I'd kill for a D-P." Matthew's favorite soft drink was Dr. Pepper.

Emma allowed a sly smile. She'd kept Luke's paws off the mini, seven-ounce-sized bottles of Dr. Pepper. It would be Matthew's welcome-back gift. There were two left, which she kept hidden in a cooler located within the market. Earlier, when she'd retrieved some sausage for today's breakfast, she'd grabbed a bottle for her son.

She reached into the refrigerator and held it high for her son to see. Matthew grinned ear to ear and nodded. "Just for you, buddy," she said. The two locked eyes for a moment, long enough for Emma to realize her son had become a man.

"You're the best, Mom." Matthew popped the top and took a long swig. He savored the twenty-three flavors in his mouth until he allowed it to ease down his throat. It was good to be home, he thought to himself.

"Hey, you guys started the party without me," said John as he entered the kitchen. Matthew and Asher gave him an update on their overnight patrols. They agreed to take a better look at the fire once the daylight allowed.

Within minutes, everyone in the house was awake and making

their way to the dining room. Luke had slept on the leather couch in the family room with his broken leg resting on an ottoman. He complained his back was stiff from sleeping awkwardly, but he had no complaints about the broken leg.

Vida was the last to emerge from her guest bedroom. She appeared shy and reserved that morning. She gravitated toward Luke as if he were a security blanket. She didn't shy away when addressed, but she didn't initiate conversation. Emma studied her demeanor and interaction. She clearly felt out of place and unsure of her future. Today, Emma would make Vida feel at home, and perhaps the young woman would open up about her family life.

After breakfast, everyone cleared their plates into a galvanized washtub. Vida volunteered to help Emma clean the kitchen and wash the dishes using the well water outside. With such a large group during mealtime, they both agreed it would take two loads in the dishwasher. Emma didn't run the generator long enough to finish one cycle.

John helped Luke back to the couch and urged everyone to join them in the spacious family room. He stood in front of the floor-to-ceiling stone fireplace while everyone got settled in. As he began, he made eye contact with the newcomers.

"It's ironic that the night of the solar storm, we had a houseful of people who were stranded. Honestly, I couldn't wait to send them home. Part of the reason was because of our concern for Cat and Grandpa Sam. But, also, because we had limited resources to share with others.

"That said, one of the things I realized on our trek to New York and back was that in order to survive, we were gonna need some help. The Lord blessed us with Asher and Lauren, who protected Grandpa Sam and Cat. And Vida, I cannot say enough how much I appreciate you staying by Luke's side to protect him from the fire. If you hadn't been there, we might not have searched that field looking for him. So thank you all, and welcome to our family."

The Cubbisons hugged the new additions. Vida began to shed a few tears as her fears of being expelled subsided. She was aware she'd still need to prove herself. However, she was up to the task.

John continued. "I feel like we need to do a reset to the day before Matthew and I left for the city. As Emma and Luke experienced, security has to be a top priority. People are desperate. Fathers like myself will do anything to feed their families. Mothers will fight tooth and nail to protect their children. Then there are the opportunists who are taking advantage of a world without law enforcement or rule of law. For them, morals and ethics are irrelevant. Its survival of the fittest. As a result, we have to change our way of thinking, too.

"When I think of Mr. Stanley, who lived on the adjacent farm, being murdered in such a sadistic way, it makes my skin crawl. And we don't really know what happened to the Yoder family, do we? All I know is that we can refuse to be victims of the heinous acts of desperate or lawless people.

"I want us to begin working in teams to keep our farm safe. We'll create a security patrol schedule based upon your regular sleeping habits. For example, Emma is an early riser, and Matthew is a late sleeper. I've thought about this, and I think I have a plan."

Emma raised her hand to get John's attention. "I'd like to be paired up with Vida. She expressed an interest in gardening."

Vida nodded in agreement. "That would be great."

"As a matter of fact, that's what I had in mind," said John. He turned to Sam. "Dad, you and Asher have a great relationship. Plus, you have the most patience to teach this city boy some farm livin'."

The two men, who were sitting next to each other, both began laughing. "I'd say we're a pretty good fit, wouldn't you, Grandpa Sam?"

"Yup. You're on my turf now. I hope you're ready to get dirty." The two men exchanged high fives.

John turned to his sons. "Boys, I'm gonna pair y'all together with a focus on security. For a while, Luke will be limited, but he's good with a rifle."

"No problem, Dad," added Matthew. "I can prop him up on the market's porch in a rocking chair."

"Whatever," said Luke with a laugh. "I dare anybody to come up our driveway when I've got them locked in my sights."

John smiled. He hoped his sons could mesh together as a team. They'd been polar opposites in their mindset for years. Maybe the end of the world as they knew it would change the dynamic between them.

"Despite Luke's injury, you two will be pulling the longest shifts. Matthew will be our rover, patrolling the perimeter of the farm, while Luke will remain stationary. Dr. Quinn said he had to remain in the long cast she created for six weeks. After that, we can come see her for a recheck and to remove the cast. Worst case is that she'll have to fashion some kind of brace or splint."

"I'm a fast healer," said Luke. "Three or four weeks. Tops."

"No, son," said John sternly. "Even once the cast is removed, your leg will still be healing. As it is, because of the circumstances, arthritis will be an issue for you when you get much older. In the meantime, we don't need another break. Got it?"

"Yes, sir."

John turned to Lauren. "I'd like you to hang with me. I'm gonna teach you every aspect of our farm's operations. You strike me as someone who pays attention to detail and is well organized. That's a great asset. Once you know the operations as well as the rest of the family, we can rely upon you in the event we have another incident that takes us away from the farm."

"Sounds good," said Lauren.

John surveyed the group for a moment, and then he spied Cat standing near the back of the room, looking forlorn. He smiled at her to reassure her that she'd not been forgotten.

"Daddy, what about me?" she asked. Her lower lip quivered slightly. The tough exterior she'd exhibited as they escaped from New York had disappeared as the realities of daily living set in.

"Come up here, Cat. I have big plans for you, too." Cat joined her father's side, and he immediately wrapped his arm around her shoulders to hug her. "Schools may be closed, but your education hasn't stopped. It's only changed."

"It has?" she asked, full of curiosity.

"Yes, ma'am. Tell us what your courses were about."

Cat thought for a moment and then started, "Well, I'm supposed to start the seventh grade, but I think the classes are similar. There's math, science, social studies, language arts, and gym."

"Okay," said John. "In this room, we have a lot of adults who've experienced all of these things, and they have certain expertise in others. For example, I can't imagine a better teacher of language arts than Lauren. She's a book editor, for Pete's sake."

"That's right, Cat. I had to study literature as well as build my own reading and writing skills over the years. I'd love to teach you that class every day."

"I'll take social studies," offered Asher. "I've always been a student of history, but more importantly, as a show writer for *Blue Bloods*, I had to keep up with everything from cultural changes to politics to current events to keep the show fresh."

"Wait, you write the *Blue Bloods* scripts?" asked Emma. "Somehow I missed that. Tom Selleck is so dreamy."

"Geez, gimme a break," moaned John.

"That sounds like fun, Asher," said Cat.

"I could handle the science and math classes," said Luke. "Especially since I'm gonna be laid up for a while."

"What about textbooks?" asked John.

Emma turned to Vida. "I know you were only at the Yoders' home for a short time, but did you happen to look in their children's bedrooms?"

"Yes. I slept in one of the bunkbeds of their daughters."

Emma turned to John. "The Yoders homeschooled their kids. I bet they have textbooks from several grades. If I remember correctly, their youngest was Cat's age, up to Jakob, who was seventeen."

"How could we get them?" asked John.

"I'll go," offered Vida. "They know me. I just need someone to help me carry the books."

"We'll go together," said Emma. "They'll be comfortable with me since I met one of the women on the road after the shooting."

"Sorry, Emma, but that's not a good idea," said Grandpa Sam. "I don't think we'll want them to connect you and Vida together. They might think they can all join us at the farm."

"You're right," said Emma.

"Let me take Vida on the wagon," said Sam. "It'll take a little longer, but we'll come in from one direction and leave through another. Then we'll circle back through the farms south of the highway."

"Solid plan, Dad. Take them a bushel of fruits and vegetables out of the garden in case they insist on trading."

Grandpa Sam gave him a thumbs-up.

John turned to Emma. "Instead of gym, we need to teach Cat how to handle a weapon. She knows the basics, but the more training she undertakes, the better she'll be able to defend herself."

Emma scowled but reluctantly agreed. Her young daughter had to grow up fast. "Okay. What about ammo? Do we have enough to practice?"

John sighed. "No, not really. We can run dry fire drills."

Asher leaned forward on his chair. "John, I learned from the armorer on the set of *Blue Bloods* that excessive dry firing can possibly damage the firing pins in some weapons. Especially the .22s. We used a Model 1911–style .22 on set, and the actors were constantly reminded to avoid overuse."

"I have to ask," began John. "Did you guys ever have live rounds on the set?"

Asher was emphatic in his reply. "Never. Never. Never. However, even so, all the actors were weapons trained, and it was their responsibility to clear every gun before they used it in a scene."

John smiled again. He was feeling good about their daily activities.

Luke raised his hand. "Dad, what about Mr. Stanley's cattle? I'd hate to think I got banged up for nothing."

"That's on today's agenda," he replied. He pointed toward Sam and the Doyles. "We're gonna assess the fire threat, and then these two are gonna get a crash course in driving cattle. Several didn't make it, but between what you moved already and the ones Grandpa Sam observed in the woods, we'll add at least thirty to our herd."

"Dairy?" asked Emma.

"Both," replied Luke. "Mr. Stanley had the steers separated from the cows. When the fire started, they broke out of their pen and trampled me. Mostly dairy, though."

"We still have enough beef in the freezers to last us into winter," said Emma. "Depending on the size of the steers, we could slaughter one every ninety days, give or take."

"And Sam and I will start hunting, too," added John. "Hopefully, the fires didn't run off all the deer and hogs."

"Son, we can expand our hunting to the south side of the highway," said Sam. "When Vida and I head to the Yoders' for the textbooks, I'll stop by our neighbors to the south and see how they're doin'. I'll try to get permission to hunt their property."

John was pleased with how the morning went, and as the light shone brightly inside the house, he realized they'd spent an inordinate amount of time without security patrols. It was this kind of mental lapse that could get them in trouble or killed.

CHAPTER SIXTEEN

Thursday
Cubbison's Farm
Harford, Pennsylvania

John and Sam led the Doyles along the creek that bordered their farm and the woods that separated them from the Stanley property. The fire had burned out, but there were numerous hotspots where smoke floated upward from the smoldering ground.

"A little rain would be nice," mumbled Sam as they dismounted near the newly constructed pond. He smirked and shook his head. The water level had dropped a foot since it had been completed two weeks prior.

"A lot of rain would be better," said John. "You wanna believe that the fire's burned itself out. Honestly, I don't know if it did. There's certainly plenty of forest to feed it."

Asher placed his hands on his hips. "You know, every year California has to deal with wildfires. Much bigger than this one, of course. I read the smaller ones can burn themselves out. They need oxygen and fuel to burn."

John added, "Mr. Stanley timbered this land years ago, pulling out all the pine trees. All that's left are beech trees and oaks. Maybe they don't burn as fast?"

"Beech trees are a very dense, hard wood," said Sam. "It's possible that between hitting the limestone cliffs and running out of fuel, the fire ran out of gas, so to speak. I don't know."

John gestured toward the horses and spoke as he mounted up. "Either way, we dodged a bullet although we need to keep an eye on these hotspots to make sure they don't flare up. Fortunately, we don't have any wind today."

"Are we gonna round up the cattle now?" asked Lauren. "Is it like on television?"

"Sort of," replied John. "The difference is we have to coax them out of the woods onto the trail. They can be stubborn. However, if they get spooked, nothing will stop them."

Sam chuckled. "It'll be a good learning experience for you. You two are still getting comfortable in the saddle. For today, stay calm and avoid any congestion on the trail."

"Dad, as I asked him to do, Luke moved our entire herd near the house. It was the only way the two of them could protect the livestock while we were gone. I noticed they have absolutely worn out the field already."

"I saw," added Sam. "We're gonna have to move them out and keep the steers separated. Cows that are nursing their calves get their own pen. The rest in the large field near the new lake."

John sighed as he looked across the fields of Cubbison's Farm. The expansive property had served his family well through many generations. Now he looked at it as being too big to manage and protect.

"We gotta do what we've gotta do," he began. "My chief concern is watching them. There are a lot of predators roaming around, both four-legged and two-legged."

Asher had a thought. "What if Lauren and I slept out here? You know, in a tent or something. We could keep an eye out while allowing the other security patrols, your sons, to focus on the front of the property where we'd most likely be threatened."

"We only have small tents," said John. "You'd be really uncomfortable."

"Let me work on that," said Sam. "If I remember correctly, the folks across the road had a small travel trailer he'd tow when he went pheasant hunting over in the Allegheny Forest. I'll ask about using it back here. The truck has a hitch, or we can pull it with the tractor, assuming it works."

"It does," said John. "We used it to move all the cars out of the way after the storm hit."

With their workday set, the four rounded up the remainder of Stanley's cattle and led them into the pen with the rest of the herd. John gave Asher and Lauren a detailed tour of the farm. Sam readied the wagon and sought out Emma, who was deep in conversation with Vida. He waited outside the kitchen door and eavesdropped.

"Did they threaten you?" asked Emma. Vida had opened up about her family and why she'd run away. As they worked around the house together, she'd made frequent references to her mother. It was clear that she missed her. Her father, not so much.

"We all knew what would happen to us eventually. Nothing changed when we came to America. Our customs followed on the rescue planes."

"Did you speak to your mother about it?"

"She would hush me. Warned me to never speak of such things. Only my aunt and uncle would keep me calm. We talked online."

"Your father didn't know about your conversations?"

"He would not use the computer. My father is a fundamentalist. Others in our community followed the teachings of the Quran that encourages us to seek knowledge. Most interpret that to mean by whatever means necessary, even if it meant going to China as the Prophet Muhammad taught."

"Did he drive a car?" Emma pressed their new houseguest. She was being considerate and respectful, but she also was trying to look for holes in Vida's story.

"Yes, but not the new cars with computers. He preferred vehicles with no frills. No computers. No power windows. The old kind." Vida caught herself, chastising herself for being too forthcoming.

Emma made a mental note of this response. It might not mean anything, but John had said the men they'd encountered were all driving older cars and trucks that had survived the electromagnetic pulse generated by the solar storm.

Emma didn't want to press any further. She glanced to her left and saw Grandpa Sam standing just outside the kitchen door. He must've been waiting until they finished their conversation.

"Okay," she began in a louder tone of voice. "Let's look at something positive, shall we? Have you ever worked in a garden?"

"Yes, all the time. It was one of my chores in our community. My mother loves to garden."

"Great! Let me show you mine."

Sam took that as his cue to enter the kitchen. He walked in, wiping his brow with a red bandana.

"Hey, Sam," said Emma. "I was just about to show Vida our garden."

Sam grimaced. "Well, we have an errand or two to run first. I wanna touch base with our neighbors about hunting their property and to see if we could borrow their travel trailer. Then we're gonna rustle up some schoolbooks for Cat."

Emma moseyed over to the kitchen counter. "I put together some canned goods and cereals. It looks different from what I sent over there before so they won't necessarily know it came from here."

Sam slung his rifle over his shoulder and adjusted his paddle holster. He reached for the box of food; however, Vida beat him to it.

"Let me, Sam. I'm actually pretty strong."

"Okay. You can set it in the back of the wagon, and I'm gonna fetch the binoculars."

Vida quickly scooped up the box and headed outside. The ruse had worked. Sam wanted a moment alone with Emma.

He leaned and whispered, "I listened into the tail end of your conversation. Do you believe her story?"

Emma nodded. "I do. I want some more time with her. I feel like there is something else. It has to do with her father, his brother, and a man she referred to as their community spiritual leader. She never mentioned his name, nor her father's name. In fact, she didn't mention anyone's name."

"Weird," mumbled Sam. "If she didn't plan on returning and if she never thought our paths would cross with theirs, why not use their real names?"

"That's what I mean. She is still very guarded."

Sam glanced out the window to confirm Vida was waiting for him by the horse and wagon. "Whadya think about going through her things? It wasn't much, but there must be something that could provide insight into who she is."

"Gee, Grandpa Sam. I don't know. That's so intrusive. I'd feel horrible if she knew."

Sam looked outside again and saw that Vida was heading back toward the house.

"Binoculars?" he asked.

Emma reached into the cupboard near the door. "Here. Be careful and don't sweat it. I do believe she's a good girl."

Sam shrugged and exited the kitchen. "Let's ride. First stop, schoolbooks."

CHAPTER SEVENTEEN

Thursday
Onvo Travel Plaza
Exit 217, Interstate 81
Harford, Pennsylvania

Since the 1960s, motorcycle gangs had been on the radar of U.S. law enforcement agencies as they began to engage in criminal activities across the country. After World War II, returning soldiers with few job options began to form motorcycle clubs to continue their *band of brothers* outlook on life. The first Hells Angels chapter was started in 1948. By the early eighties, a prerequisite to being a permanent member of the Hells Angels was a proven expertise in conducting profitable criminal activities.

Over the years, other gangs were formed, committing crimes from murder and extortion to sex trafficking. As the Hells Angels spread across the country, turf wars occurred with smaller gangs who claimed supremacy over a certain region or municipality. The sparring was not unlike inner-city gangs fighting over profitable street corners or city blocks.

Certainly, motorcycle clubs existed that had nothing to do with their criminal counterpart. They adopted an *easy rider* worldview, based on the famous 1969 movie by the same name. Bikers abandoned their possessions to enjoy the freedom of the open road. They even adopted an honor code of treating one another with respect and a commitment to help a biker in need. If in a club, there was a fierce sense of loyalty. A brotherhood that cannot be broken.

Most importantly, a biker cannot neglect his steel horse. Their motorcycle was their life, requiring constant care. Further, bikers strived to maintain their individuality by modifying their bikes in a unique way.

Now, their motorcycles had a commonality they never imagined. They were all dead.

Decades of technology had been incorporated into the Harleys and Indians they rode, making them just as susceptible to the devastating effects of an electromagnetic pulse as other modern-day machines.

The Warlocks Motorcycle Club ruled Eastern Pennsylvania, Delaware, and the Southern Tier region of New York State. Like so many other clubs that formed in the sixties, the Warlocks sought to establish a stronghold in areas underserved by the Hells Angels. Its rapid rise to power as a criminal enterprise earned it the designation by the U.S. Department of Justice as the first *one-percenter* outlaw motorcycle club in Pennsylvania. This moniker was created under the assumption that ninety-nine percent of motorcycle riders and their local clubs were not involved in criminal activities.

Jack Freeland walked out of the mobile home that had been the residence of the travel center's owner. There was nothing remarkable about the Onvo Travel Plaza located at one of the two Harford exits off Interstate 81.

Exxon gas. Truck parking. A Subway sandwich shop. Legal three-line slot machines. A store that included basic auto accessories, food, and live bait for anglers on fishing trips.

Freeland was ex-Navy, having served aboard the Aegis cruiser, the USS *Shiloh*. He'd patrolled the South China Sea and had received a medical discharge just before hostilities with China over Taiwan had begun to peak.

His greatest accomplishment in the Navy was making contacts with Indonesian producers of methamphetamines. Indonesia had become a major drug trafficking hub, especially into South and Central America. After Freeland was discharged, he followed in the path of his acquaintances aboard the *Shiloh* to traffic the fentanyl tablets using drug mules. The illegal aliens paid their way into the United States by stowing pills inside their bodies to evade detection by border patrol agents. Once they cleared a cursory intake process, the drug mules were released into America. From there, the drugs were turned over to bikers, who trafficked the pills around the country.

Freeland's operation became so profitable that he was welcomed into the Scranton-based Warlocks. In recent years, their trafficking of fentanyl in tablet form had increased exponentially. The logistics of his business operated flawlessly. Drug mules were recruited south of the border. They easily passed into the country. They were given free passage to their community of choice, namely Philadelphia, courtesy of the American government. They were met at the bus station by several Warlocks, who confiscated the drugs for distribution.

On the fateful day that the perfect storm hit, nearly fifty members of the Warlocks were rolling north on I-81 into their north-ernmost territory in New York. Binghamton, Ithaca and Cortland had craved what they offered. Addicts didn't care where they lived as long as product was available. They fled larger cities like Albany and Syracuse when word spread of the availability of the Warlocks' synthetic opioid nearly a hundred times stronger than morphine.

Everything was rolling for Freeland until the sun ruined every-thing. Half the club had traveled three miles ahead to the Flying J Travel Center at the next exit. His half of the riders had eased into the Onvo Travel Center and the Getty Fuel station across the road.

This was by design. Freeland wanted his bikers to ride in a pack too large to be tackled by law enforcement. However, when stopping for fuel and food, he didn't want all of his crew bunched together.

The sudden power outage caught the Warlocks off guard, just as it had the rest of the country. Freeland realized this was an extraordinary natural disaster when their bikes wouldn't function and their cell phones wouldn't power on. An EMP immediately came to mind.

When he had been on the USS *Shiloh*, the crew had been briefed on China's use of ship-to-ship electromagnetic pulse weapons designed to destroy electronics. The effects described by his superiors were identical to what they'd experienced that night.

Freeland wasted no time in responding to the power outage. First, he instructed his bikers to seize control of the two fuel stop businesses. Next, he chose two of his most athletic bikers, not an easy task considering their lives revolved around eating and drinking. He sent the emissaries to the next exit to advise his Warlock brothers of the situation. They, too, were to gain a foothold within the Flying J truck stop and surrounding businesses.

He was a crafty criminal. Without hesitation, rather than commiserating with his fellow bikers as to what had happened, he devised a plan on how to profit from it. He referred to it as shock and awe. He killed the owner of the Onvo and then marched across the street to murder the manager of the Getty station. If someone put up a fight or got too mouthy, they earned a bullet.

Freeland liked to kill. It was empowering. In the weeks after the power grid collapsed, he and his crew spread out in search of anything of value. At first, they walked the interstate, searching cars and abducting women for heinous levels of debauchery.

Some of the bikers ventured toward Harford, where they ran into a group of ex-Marines who chased them off with bullets skipping along the pavement. Freeland went into Harford himself on a scouting mission. That was when he had been taken at gunpoint to meet Fred Stewart.

The two men didn't like one another, but they weren't interested in mutual destruction through a prolonged series of gunfights. As a result, an agreement was reached establishing territories. The jarhead seemed content controlling the town and areas west of the interstate. Freeland was happy to take the rest. He chose to pick the interstate travelers clean first. The tractor trailer rigs that had been abandoned provided all types of nonperishable foods, so much so that they had difficulty storing it all at the truck stops they commandeered.

He'd sent a couple of his people to establish a roadblock up the hill just east of the exit. If they saw anyone, they were to seize them for interrogation to learn about the farms and ranches. After several days, he learned the farms were large and spread apart. It was deemed a waste of resources to go after crops that were dying on the vine and took days to bring back. Yet he saw these farms as an opportunity for something else.

His numbers were growing. The bikers were taking up with local women, and some had even forcefully convinced interstate travelers it was for their safety to become a biker's concubine. Their housing situation had become a problem.

For that reason, he decided he was going to take a few of his most trusted guys to explore the farmland east of the interstate. Naturally, he'd have the first choice of housing. A place that could be protected and where the bounty stolen from the tractor trailer rigs could be stored. Freeland was enjoying this lawless world. Now it was time to find a place to settle down.

CHAPTER EIGHTEEN

Thursday
Near Cubbison's Farm
Harford, Pennsylvania

Sam took a circuitous route to the pass by the Yoder house as if he were traveling from Harford. He hoped the misdirection would throw off the women and children who occupied the Yoders' home. His biggest concern was that the men killed by Emma and Luke had been replaced by a new bunch of thugs. He was pleased that the women were living alone, although just barely.

As he and Vida approached, a few members of the group were in front of the house. As they heard the horse's hooves clapping the pavement, they scampered inside. When Sam steered the horse and wagon down the driveway, curtains could be seen being pulled closed. They weren't fooling anybody, Sam thought to himself.

One of the young girls peeking through the curtains recognized Vida and shouted her name. Seconds later, all of them came pouring out of the house and raced across the dirt to greet the new arrivals. Sam was somewhat overwhelmed at how they threw caution to the wind in order to greet them. When they began peeking over the wagon's rails at the large box of food, he understood why. They were starving.

Vida was peppered with questions. Where did you go? Why? Did you see the fire? Can you spare any food?

Vida played the hero. She said she'd gone into town to find a place to live. She'd met this man, who agreed to ride out to give them what he could spare. Naturally, the women were already looking toward their next meal. They asked if he could bring more or, in the alternative, take them back into to town with him.

Sam lied and said he was going to see his old friend Mr. Stanley. When Vida had told him about his friend's death, he decided to provide Mr. Stanley a proper burial. That gave them cover for heading away from town.

Vida quizzed the women on whether they'd encountered any more travelers. They were happy to say they hadn't, although they planned on walking into town in search for food. They seemed encouraged by Sam and Vida's story. Sam knew it was a bad idea; however, it wasn't his job to dissuade them.

He turned the wagon around and began to head east back toward Cubbison's Farm. Just past the crest of the hill at Stanley's driveway where the shoot-out occurred, a long winding, gravel road led through a pasture and over a hill to the Ledbetter place.

Randy Ledbetter had inherited the property from his father-in-law as part of a divorce settlement years ago. His wife had been allowed to live on the farm for so long as she was alive. When she passed away, Ledbetter moved in.

Sam had said Ledbetter was a real piece of work on more than one occasion. The man knew nothing about farming or raising cattle and knew everything about burning through his life savings buying toys. A new truck was followed by a new car. A new fishing boat was followed by a new travel trailer. A new girlfriend was followed by another and then another. Soon, his property fell into disrepair; he sold off his cattle and didn't reinvest the money in calves. His crops withered, and his gardens became overrun with weeds.

So Ledbetter turned to the bottle. He was a prolific drinker, spending his days sucking down beers, and at night, he consumed the hard stuff. Eventually, booze wasn't good enough, so Sam had heard.

Because the man was unstable, Sam was cautious as he approached the four-car garage located at the front of the clearing where the residence was located. All of the garage doors were open, and the bays were filled with motorcycles, four-wheelers, and a fishing boat. The vehicles and the travel trailer were parked in the grass between the house and the garage.

The place was a mess but didn't appear to be looted. It was just the way the slob liked to live. Wherever he left something, it remained there until it was used again. Sam sat in the wagon for a moment and observed his surroundings. He was waiting for a half-drunk Ledbetter to emerge from the house or out from under a rock.

Instead, it was strangely quiet.

Sam whispered to Vida, "Wait here. If anyone shows their head, I want you to scream my name. Okay?"

She nodded rapidly, and then her eyes began to dart around the house. She was afraid although she didn't want to admit it to Sam. She was doing her best to make herself a valued member of their group.

Sam didn't offer her a gun. He still had trust issues. Plus, he wasn't sure if she knew how to handle herself. He approached the house cautiously, checking inside and around each vehicle. He saw that the front door was left open, as were most of the windows. The obese Ledbetter probably spent his days reeking of alcohol-scented sweat.

He slowly walked up the front steps onto the covered porch. The house was dark inside, as the windows with a southern exposure had their curtains drawn. Sam took a deep breath of fresh air. He didn't want to enter unannounced. So he chose to knock.

Using the back of his fist, he pounded the wall next to the open door and shouted, "Ledbetter! It's Sam Cubbison from across the way. Are you here?"

Ledbetter didn't answer, but his hunting dogs did. They rushed toward the front door, crashing into Sam's legs, causing him to spin around until he landed hard on the porch deck. Their eyes were wild, and their barking pierced Sam's ears.

Vida, who had a view of the porch from the wagon, saw Sam get knocked down. She came running.

"Sam! Are you okay?"

The dogs were still barking loudly but momentarily turned their attention to Vida, who was racing across the overgrown lawn. They ignored Sam for a moment, long enough for him to regain his footing.

"I'm fine. Ledbetter! Are you here?" he shouted over the dogs. Surely the man could hear the fracas.

The golden retrievers were now confused, as they didn't know which of the newcomers to approach. One sat down and began scratching behind his ear. Two ran back inside. The last two stood dumbfounded, trying to determine what to do.

"They're starving," observed Vida. "Look at how their ribs are sticking out."

Sam was focused on the threats that remained inside. He glanced at the dogs and saw they were in poor health. He held his hand up to indicate Vida should wait on the deck.

He allowed the barrel of his rifle to lead the way as he entered the house. The closer he got to a long hallway connecting the living area with the bedrooms, the worst the stench became. Two of the dogs were lying at the end of the hall in front of a closed door.

"Randy Ledbetter! It's Sam Cubbison. Can you come out?"

He focused all his senses on his hearing. He tried to make out any discernable sound—a groan, a shuffle, a bump.

Nothing.

He tried again. "Ledbetter!"

When there was no answer, he slid against the wall and reached out for the doorknob to the bedroom. He slowly turned it and gently pushed it open. The dogs crashed into the door and rushed inside. The smell of death rushed out.

Ledbetter lay in bed, partially clothed, dead. Apparently the high from liquor wasn't good enough. He'd turned to the needle and the spoon and a bad batch of heroin.

Sam turned and rushed out of the house, gagging and coughing from inhaling the stench. Vida quizzed him about what he'd seen, but Sam was unable to respond. Seconds later, the dogs inside the house began to howl, and the others joined in. It was a scene reminiscent of a horror flick.

After his coughing fit ended, Sam waved to Vida. "I think I have answers to my questions. Let's go."

Sam began to walk away, but she remained on the porch. "What about the dogs?"

"What about them?" he asked in return.

"Can't we at least try to feed them? Let me look for their food."

Without hesitation, Vida pulled her tee shirt over her mouth and nose as she entered the house. She made her way to the kitchen and found a closet with a large bag of Ol' Roy dry dog food. She tried to pull it out of the closet, but the dry, brittle packaging tore in her hands, and the food spilled all over the floor. At that point, she was lucky to survive the feeding frenzy.

All five of Ledbetter's bird-hunting dogs raced into the kitchen. They slid and stumbled until they were in the middle of the spilled dog food. They growled at one another, and their teeth gnashed. Vida was dangerously close to being bitten as she stood in the middle of them.

She hoisted herself up on the kitchen counter and slid along it with her feet drawn off the floor. As she moved away from the scrum, she knocked empty liquor bottles and beer cans onto the linoleum. Some of the bottles broke when they landed on top of one another. However, the crazed dogs were undeterred. She knew they shouldn't consume the food that fast after being starved; however, there was no stopping the feeding frenzy.

Vida walked briskly toward the front door, where Sam was waiting for her. As she did, she glanced into the dimly lit living room. A shotgun and a box of shells was sitting on the coffee table. She darted over to grab the gun and shells before she exited the house.

"I don't think he'll need this anymore, do you?" she asked with a grin. Rather than carrying it to the wagon herself, she presented the weapon and its ammo to Sam.

He gave her an appreciative smile and a wink. "You can carry it. Good find."

Vida had turned the corner.

CHAPTER NINETEEN

Thursday
Harford, Pennsylvania

The Pontiac GTO had become a problem for Dr. Quinn. Apparently, the vehicle's arrival had drawn more attention than she imagined. When the world was quiet, devoid of vehicles, roaring lawn tractors, and air-conditioning units fighting the heat, the sound of any operating machinery drew attention.

She was awakened that morning by someone pounding on her front door. She presumed it was one of her clients in desperate need of medical attention for their horse or other animal. Instead, it was a neighbor begging her to drive to Scranton to retrieve his daughter from college. Dr. Quinn was forced to turn the man away, which resulted in a barrage of threats and vulgarities hurled in her direction.

Once the neighbor had left, she fired up the powerful engine; the extraordinary horsepower was reflected in the rumble through the exhaust pipes. She drove it away from the clinic toward her house, where she stowed the car behind a barn.

This only served to alert others to its existence. Throughout the day, curious neighbors came to her home, inquiring about the sound of a truck or car.

Did we hear your car running?

Would you take us to this place or that?

We'll gladly pay for your gas.

Dr. Quinn knew it was a matter of time before the curious became violent. She had to get rid of the car before it got her killed.

She grabbed a shotgun from her gun safe and strapped a pistol to her hip. She doubted she'd survive a shoot-out with Fred Stewart or his men. However, the weapons might dissuade anyone she encountered on her way into town who might have designs on the car.

Her drive into the center of Harford was uneventful. That Friday night, most people were either at home or at the fairgrounds like she was. Stalled cars were few and far between, as were any pedestrians. Since the power grid collapsed, many people fled on foot to larger metropolitan areas in search of family or food. The others were afraid to leave the perceived safety of their homes. Also, a blanket of fear had covered the Harford community as Fred's men made their presence known.

Despite the rumors of Fred's activities, she'd not heard that his men had done anything to local residents. Certainly, businesses were broken into and looted. Stalled vehicles, like her veterinarian truck, were emptied of their contents. However, since Fred and his men had begun their patrols, she hadn't heard any reports of murders, rapes, or home invasions. It was if there was a new sheriff in town. It was a good thing since there was no sign of local law enforcement since the grid collapsed.

Dr. Quinn slowly entered the front parking lot of the Harford House motel. She was immediately greeted by four men wearing dark sunglasses and military-style clothing. She didn't absorb the details of their attire. Her eyes were affixed on the barrels of their rifles pointing at her chest.

After she slowly pulled to a stop, she stuck both of her hands out of the driver's side window. "Don't shoot! I'm here to see Fred about a trade."

"Keep your hands where we can see them, lady!" one of the guards shouted as he slowly stepped toward her. Dr. Quinn continued to stick her arms through the window until she was startled by the passenger door being slung open.

"Gun!" a man bellowed from behind her. She turned her body out of instinct. Within a second, the driver's door was pulled open, and she was dragged onto the asphalt, landing hard on her back.

Dr. Quinn groaned from the pain, struggling to catch her breath. Two guards rolled her onto her stomach to kick her legs and arms apart until she was facedown, spread-eagled. She'd never felt so vulnerable in her life.

"What's the deal, gentlemen?" asked Fred, who had emerged from the front of the motel.

One of his men responded without taking his eyes off Dr. Quinn, "Don't know, sir. She has a shotgun."

Another guard had patted her down and pulled the handgun from her holster. He held it up for the others to see. "It's an old Colt six-shooter. Haven't seen one of these in ages."

"It was my father's," mumbled Quinn, who continued to lie facedown on the asphalt.

"Did she come in here hot?" asked Fred.

"No, sir. Slow and steady. Immediately stuck her hands out the window."

Fred shook his head. Not everybody needed to be body-slammed to the pavement. "Help her up."

Dr. Quinn found her balance and took a deep breath as she wiped bits of asphalt and broken glass off her clothing. She glanced at the men around her, who'd lowered their weapons.

"That really wasn't necessary," she mumbled before making eye contact with Fred.

His face was emotionless, and his single eye studying her was intimidating. She chose to calm down rather than get manhandled again.

"I know this car," said Fred. "Where did you get it?"

"I'm Dr. Caitlin Quinn, the town's horse vet. I set the young man's broken leg last night."

Fred scowled as he looked from the car back to Dr. Quinn. "I thought they needed medications. They were supposed to come back to me after seeing you."

"I had just enough to supply them. Now I'm almost out of pharmaceuticals."

Fred placed his hands on his hips. They'd had a deal, and the parents broke it. He had to decide if the betrayal warranted repercussions. He focused his attention on Dr. Quinn.

"Why are you here?"

"You have something that belongs to me," she began in a stern tone. She was surrounded by men with guns. She had to let them know she meant business.

"We don't have any horses here, Dr. Quinn, medicine woman," replied Fred, drawing a chuckle from his men as he made a reference to the nineties' television show. The Western had aired on CBS for six seasons about the time Fred was growing up.

Very funny, Dr. Quinn thought to herself. *Like, um, one-eyed bandit. You don't think I've heard that a thousand times before?*

"I was at the fairgrounds that Friday night for the rodeo. They keep me on call in case an animal gets injured. Your men broke into my vet truck and stole the meds."

Fred stared at Dr. Quinn. He liked her because she didn't cower under the circumstances. He hadn't studied the medications in great detail because the vast majority of the labels indicated they were for equine and bovine use only. While he was sure they could be used for humans in a pinch, he didn't care enough to study on it.

"I cannot admit or deny that we are in possession of your drugs. However, even if we were, you can't just have them back. This is a trading post. We make deals."

Dr. Quinn expected as much; however, she feigned being incredulous. "Let me get this straight. You stole something of mine, and I have to trade you something to get it back."

Fred shrugged. "Pretty much."

Dr. Quinn sighed. "You made a deal to trade medications for this car. I want the same deal. You get the Pontiac, and I get back everything you took from my vet truck."

Fred jutted out his jaw and thought for a moment. He always tried to get a little more from a deal that had been offered to him. However, before he could speak, Dr. Quinn made an additional demand.

"Plus, you gotta give me a ride home." She paused for a moment. "And I want my guns back. You guys have plenty of your own."

Fred couldn't contain himself. He burst out laughing. A hearty, bent-over, genuine laugh that was infectious. His men began to laugh along with him although they kept a wary eye on Dr. Quinn.

Fred eventually regained his composure and nodded while raising his hands to shoulder height. "I give. I give. I haven't done anything nice for my fellow man, or woman, today. We'll make the deal, and I'll personally drive you home. How's that?" He was trying to contain his excitement over driving the car.

"Deal."

Fred issued his provisos. Dr. Quinn's guns would be locked in the trunk with her medications. She agreed that one of Fred's men would ride in the backseat to ensure there was no monkey business, as he put it.

As they loaded into the car, Fred said, "Nobody in town gets the details of our deal. Understood?"

"Sure," said Dr. Quinn.

"I don't want anyone to think that I'm going soft. You really took advantage of me, Dr. Quinn."

She raised her voice, albeit playfully. "I just traded you the only operating car in the county for my own medications that were stolen by your guys."

Fred raised his index finger and waggled it in front of her face. "Now, now, Dr. Quinn. We only took them for safekeeping."

"Huh? Gimme a break."

"No, it's true. Consider this. If we hadn't taken the contents of your truck to the House of Stewart, what do you think would've happened to them?"

Dr. Quinn hesitated. He had a point. "I would've come back for them."

"Maybe so. I'd bet you that some enterprising druggie would've beat you to it. He'd be out in the woods somewhere, shooting up steroids."

He was probably right, she thought. "Okay, fine. I won't tell anyone of your generosity." She shook her head in disbelief.

Twenty minutes later, Dr. Quinn had emptied the contents of the trunk and watched in amusement as Fred spun gravel all over her driveway until the rear tires caught the pavement, leaving two black streaks of rubber in a cloud of dust.

CHAPTER TWENTY

Thursday
Lake Wallenpaupack
Wayne County, Pennsylvania

With the day's funeral activities over, Abdul led his community in evening prayers before retiring to his home. He called in all of the men who had participated in the raid, which included his top lieutenants. After they shared words of condolences and memories of their fallen warrior, Abdul began the debriefing.

Despite the fact he wanted to probe the memories of his men as to the events surrounding Khan's death, he listened to each of them describe the role they'd played and recount their successes. The weapons and body armor secured from the raid would prove invaluable as they waged jihad against America.

Finally, they turned to the moment they'd encountered the motor home and the infidels they'd engaged on the service road. Without acknowledging it, Abdul knew he'd made a mistake by not killing all of the people they encountered during their escape from the armory. Khan had shot the woman in the back, likely killing her.

However, there were several others who would've been no match for his experienced fighters. He'd taken his eye off the ball, as the Americans say, and focused on escaping with his newly acquired weapons. That was when they had been surprised by the oncoming headlights.

It was naïve of him to think his operating vehicles were the only ones left after the solar storm. He should've also known that the people would be armed. Their shots had not only killed Khan but caused them to lose a valuable asset—the 1969 Pontiac GTO.

The men in the pickups described bullets flying at them from all directions. They exaggerated, of course, as they didn't want to admit to their leader they had been surprised by the unexpected counterattack. The soldiers at Picatinny Arsenal had been caught off guard and had been easy targets. The people who'd ambushed them on the service road as they exited had had the upper hand.

He quizzed his men about the shooters. They weren't soldiers. Nor were they law enforcement. They appeared to be travelers from the Winnebago. Or they were in the other vehicle.

He asked each of his men to share what they remembered about the vehicle.

Pickup truck. Very old style. Rounded fenders. Red. Wood slats.

Abdul, who'd been wandering the room, stopped to think. He stared across the grassy lawn leading to the lake. The full moon was rising and caused an eerie reflection on the water, which had barely a ripple of movement. The bits and pieces relayed to him by his men began to form a picture in his mind. Despite the frenzied sequence of events, he, too, could make out the details of the old truck. Including something the others did not convey.

"Cub. Mark," he muttered under his breath. In his mind, he sought guidance from a higher power. He shouted, "*Allah! Help me see!* Market. Cub? Cub Market?" He slammed his fist against the wall in frustration. He couldn't remember the entire logo painted on the driver's door.

He began pacing the floor again. His mind wandered to Khan's daughter. He would allow Khan's widow one day of mourning before he forcefully quizzed her about the whereabouts of Vida. Somebody knew something, and he'd demand answers. He was aware of an uncle in Rochester, New York. That was a logical place for the girl to be found. However, it was over two hundred miles, a journey of several weeks for the teenager.

Abdul decided to wait on retrieving the girl. He didn't want to expend resources and time hunting her down. The time would come when she would be taught a lesson by him and his men.

While still trying to recall the name on the side of the red pickup truck, he turned his attention to the next step in his plan for jihad against America. With the weaponry stolen from the armory, Abdul needed to bring other Afghan communities into the fold to bolster his fighting force. There were several others within Wayne County and in adjacent Susquehanna County. With more fighters under his control, he could expand his sphere of influence and systematically raid the surrounding towns and farms.

Also, his fellow Afghans needed to be fed and might require medical attention. He needed more resources. With his warriors wielding new firepower, they would scour the countryside in search of assets for his jihadist army.

Then he would seek opportunities to put the fear of Allah in the minds of all the infidels within his reach. Anyone who resisted would die.

Abdul's mind wandered, and an inner peace came over him. He caught himself managing a smile. Actually, they would all die. *Allahu Akbar!*

PART 3

Friday
Friend or foe?

CHAPTER TWENTY-ONE

Friday
Cubbison's Farm
Harford, Pennsylvania

It was the second full day at the farm since the travelers had returned from New York and Luke's broken leg had been treated by Dr. Quinn. While it was too early to say that the Cubbisons and their extended family had settled into a routine, they were certainly headed in that direction. Everyone eagerly performed their assigned chores without complaint.

Newcomers Asher and Lauren put in long hours and were genuinely excited about establishing an outpost of sorts on the back forty acres of the farm. They, along with Sam and Vida, had returned to the Ledbetter place that morning to retrieve the travel trailer. While they were there, they rolled Ledbetter's body in the swimming pool cover used in the winter to keep leaves out of the water. His corpse was too bloated and decayed to move without it. Despite the life Ledbetter led, Sam didn't think the man deserved to be gnawed on by any critters who got into the house. They dragged the body well away from the farmhouse next to a pond, where they set it on fire.

As for the dogs, Vida made a suggestion that earned herself an additional chore in the process. In Afghanistan, dogs were used as security for someone's property like an alarm system. Farmers would keep their dogs in pens and spread them out so they would bark if an intruder entered their property. Vida had overheard John and Sam lamenting how they couldn't guard the farm's entire perimeter for all hours of the day.

She suggested using the dogs as a form of perimeter security. John liked the idea and signed off on it. They would be spaced evenly apart along the farm's eastern fence line. Asher and Lauren could monitor the rear of the farm while living in the travel trailer. The roving patrols would watch the front and the woods separating their farm from the Stanley place, the direction intruders from town would most likely utilize.

Emma and Vida came up with a plan to use vegetables to create food for the dogs, including potatoes, carrots, beans, and peas. On occasion, Emma had to throw away some vegetables because they'd fallen off the plant before they were fully ready to eat. She'd create a meal that was far superior to the dry dog food from Walmart.

Cat took on an after-school project assisting her mom in removing heirloom seeds from the fruit and vegetable plants. Emma identified the plants that had grown beyond their maturity. She tasked Cat with removing the seeds and cleaning them in a bowl of water while separating them from the pulp. Cat learned how to differentiate between viable seeds and those that would not sprout, which floated to the top of the water.

However, they were not discarded. After meeting Fred Stewart in his barter outpost, she considered trading the floating seeds to him, especially since they were least likely to sprout. It was under-handed and a form of dirty dealing. However, that was the man she thought she was dealing with.

Once the viable seeds were dried, Emma provided Cat special

containers to keep the seeds airtight. After being labeled, they were taken into a root cellar beneath the house. The cellar had been used by generations of the Cubbison family to store seeds, canned jars of food, and as a place to safely hide during severe weather.

While Lauren and Asher set up their new camper, Sam and John rode through the woods toward the Stanley place.

"Dad, we got lucky. The fire seems to have burned itself out."

"God-watching-over-us lucky, in my opinion," Sam added. They rode another twenty feet before he pointed ahead. "Look, a straggler."

One of Stanley's cows emerged from the woods and stood in the middle of the trail, staring at the Cubbison men as they approached. They dismounted and slowly approached the cow. Sam handed his son the reins of his horse and walked ahead toward the cow, who remained still.

"Well, I'll be," he mumbled just loud enough for John to hear.

"What is it, Dad?"

"I think she's pregnant," he replied. "Maybe even close to her third trimester."

John tied their horses off to a tree and joined Sam in front of the heifer. He gently rubbed her forehead and scratched between her ears. Then he ran the palms of his hands along her belly.

"That's a bump, all right," said John as he patted the heifer's back.

"Could it just be distention from eating the underbrush instead of her normal feed?" asked Sam.

"Nah, Dad. Take a look. I mean, she's not heavily pregnant like they are in the third trimester. You know, a barrel with legs. But she's gettin' there."

"Do you wanna bump her to make sure?" asked Sam. An unreliable but often used test by cattle ranchers to determine if a heifer is pregnant is called abdominal ballottement, or bumping. If she's at least five months pregnant, it requires a trained touch by the rancher to feel for the fetus. Sam had learned the technique from his father and had passed it down to John. It was often used by the Cubbisons because they typically called Dr. Quinn or a veterinarian from nearby Gibson to do a farm call.

John shrugged and, without responding, placed his hand against the lower right flank of the heifer's belly. Then, with a short, upward thrust, he pushed into the cow's abdomen. He knew the results almost immediately.

"No doubt. There's a hard fetus in there. That means she's at least halfway through her gestation."

Sam took a turn at keeping the heifer calm. He retrieved the horses and suggested they lead the pregnant cow to the farm, where she'd be kept close to the house for observation. Then they'd determine if they needed to travel to Gibson in search of their regular cattle vet or seek out Dr. Quinn's assistance.

"John, she'll be fine here if you wanna check on things at Stanley's or the Yoders'," suggested Sam.

John thought for a moment and tried to study the sky through the tops of the trees. It was getting late in the afternoon, and he wanted to get this cow settled in.

"We'll get over here again in a day or two. I'm sure everything's fine."

Except everything was far from fine.

CHAPTER TWENTY-TWO

Friday
East of Harford, Pennsylvania

Jack Freeland and two of his fellow bikers began their casual stroll into the countryside that morning. They'd abandoned their signature leather chaps and vests as the August heat made the accessories unbearable to wear. Despite the circumstances, the men had feasted on packaged foods they'd pilfered on the interstate. None of them had shed any pounds during the apocalypse.

As they made their way down the highway, they stopped at the small farmhouses that dotted the landscape. In the first home they entered, Freeland was unfazed when they discovered an elderly woman lying on her couch, mouth agape, clutching a Bible. She'd been dead for several days.

On her kitchen table were several empty bottles of medicine from the local pharmacy. He knew very little about legal pharmaceuticals, but he presumed the medications were necessary to keep her alive.

The men rummaged through the kitchen. There was little in the way of food. Apparently, the woman had an affinity for baking, but without power, her dual range oven was of little use. She had a few hundred dollars in her purse and several items of jewelry on her nightstand. A .22-caliber rifle and a box of ammunition were stored away in a closet.

The rifle was a reminder to Freeland that the Warlocks only had a dozen handguns between them. Almost all of them were convicted felons. When stopped by law enforcement, the first thing they were subjected to was a pat-down search for weapons. It was an instant ticket back to SCI Fayette, considered to be the worst maximum-security prison in the state.

"It isn't much, but we'll keep it open as an option," Freeland told the other men.

"Everything's so spread out here," one of the men added. "We're brothers, and we should try to stick together. Living this far apart would be like splitting up the gang."

Freeland couldn't argue. He recalled surveilling the Harford House motel. Fred Stewart and his band of merry men had a centrally located stronghold in the center of town. It was easily defended and provided a haven where they could enjoy the cama-raderie established through the military. His bikers deserved the same; however, the town only had one hotel, and sleeping in the abandoned semis' cabs was growing old.

"Come on. We're just getting started." Freeland marched through the open doorway and looked across the open field. The sun was causing a galvanized metal roof to glisten in the distance. Just beyond that appeared another home.

"Where to, Jack?" one of his companions asked.

"There." He pointed toward the homes in the distance. If he couldn't have his own hotel, maybe he could string together several properties in a row. He handed the rifle and box of bullets to one of the bikers. "Load this thing. We might need it."

CHAPTER TWENTY-THREE

Friday
Yoder Place
Harford, Pennsylvania

Jenna and her daughters, Kay and Jewel, had stuck to themselves after Vida left without saying goodbye. They'd seen the smoke rising from the direction of the adjacent farm. The last time that had happened was when the men who'd taken up with the other women in the house had returned, bragging about how they'd killed the old man who lived there. Jenna had come to associate black smoke on the horizon as a sign of bad things to come.

She felt trapped with no good options for her children. The other women, including her sister, were irresponsible and flighty. When they were provided supplies and food from Luke's mother, they immediately squandered them. It was if they were waiting for someone to stop by and fill their cupboard.

Under the guise of taking her girls for a walk in the country, Jenna had kept them fed by entering abandoned homes, searching for anything edible. They'd explored the Ledbetter property before

Sam and Vida did. It was Jenna's youngest who discovered Ledbetter, and the vision of his lifeless body still haunted the child. Anything edible in the house was taken away and hidden in the man's garage. Each day, until the food was gone, the three of them would cross the fields without being seen by the other women. When the food ran out, they moved on to an adjacent farm.

The next small house had been abandoned, but at least nobody was dead inside. The home had little to offer in the way of food other than some stale cereal and a few canned goods. That lasted a couple of days. However, it was clean, and the open windows allowed some semblance of a breeze to cross through. This allowed Jenna's family to enjoy some alone time away from the others.

Now she found herself wondering where their next meal would come from. She was spending time in front of the house with the girls when, off in the distance, she saw several men walking down the road toward them.

"Come here, girls. Hurry!" Kay and Jewel ran to her side with looks of concern on their faces.

"What is it, Mom?"

"Do you remember how we talked about making a run for it?"

"Yes," replied her oldest.

"Now is one of those times. Okay?"

They nodded, and then Jewel asked, "Where will we go?"

That was a great question. Jenna didn't have a plan for that. "We'll figure that out later. Now, stay calm and quietly get your backpacks. Try not to wake anyone up. If they ask, tell them we're going on a hike. Okay?"

"In the dark?" asked one of her girls.

Jenna's mind raced for an excuse. "Um, tell them we're gonna camp out under the stars. Okay?" That was all she could come up with in a pinch.

They nodded and walked hand in hand briskly toward the house. Jenna took another long look at the men as they approached. They looked just like the last bunch who'd arrived at the Yoder place. She feared they would make the women completely dependent upon them, using force when they deemed it warranted.

Jenna debated what to do about her sister. She was, after all, family. She was also a liability to Jenna and her girls. Her younger sister would welcome the approaching men with open arms despite the threat they'd pose. Jenna would not take that risk with her kids.

She rushed inside and gathered her belongings, such as they were. Essentially, they had clothing and a second pair of shoes. They'd be traveling light, to say the least.

Minutes later, Jenna found her girls hiding near a small shed behind the house. She grabbed each of them by the hand, and they rushed toward the woods at the back of the property. They'd just reached the tree line when she heard shots fired.

At first, the popping sound resembled firecrackers. Her sister and the other woman in the house began screaming. Jenna felt horrible, fearful that her sister and her daughters would be harmed. Imagining all the ways the brutal men might torment her. She stopped momentarily and caught her breath. She considered going back to help, but what could she do except get herself killed.

Then she heard the shouts of the young boys whose father had been killed by Luke and his mother. The father was a piece of crap and deserved to die. However, she wished the young boys hadn't witnessed it. It had jaded them both. They tried to put on a good face, acting tough in their attempt to become the so-called men of the house. It mostly resulted in them bullying Jenna's kids.

What she heard next was enough to send her racing away and not looking back. Unlike the sounds of popping firecrackers, the next two gunshots sounded like cannon fire. It was followed by the wail of the boys' mother. The grief-stricken woman's cries were unmistakable. Jenna knew the men of the household had just been replaced by someone bigger and meaner.

CHAPTER TWENTY-FOUR

Friday
Cubbison's Farm
Harford, Pennsylvania

Luke was manning his post on the front porch of the market while Vida and Emma took inventory of their canned foods. With three new mouths to feed, Emma had to reconsider how much of her produce to can and how much to feed their growing numbers.

She symbolically patted herself on the back for religiously using Tattler canning lids and rings as opposed to the Ball jar brand. Emma considered herself a homesteader and prided herself on reusing and repurposing just about everything. She was a prolific canner, which required her to have an ample number of jars, rings, and lids on hand. For the products she sold in the market, Emma was fine using Ball jars, lids and rings. They were basically a single-use product for resale.

For home, she used the Tattler reusable lids and seals. They worked in the same manner as traditional metal lids only in two parts. Much like the Ball lids and seals that had been used for generations to the point of being considered an antique, the Tattler lids could be used indefinitely. Even the pliable rubber seals were capable of many uses.

"Okay, Vida, let's move on to the dried beans and corn," said Emma when she was suddenly interrupted by Luke.

"Gunfire! Small caliber followed by two shots from something much bigger."

"Which direction?" Emma asked excitedly.

"West toward the highway. Off in the distance but close enough to hear."

Emma turned to Vida. "Hurry, go inside and wake up John." He'd volunteered for the midnight-to-dawn watch. She yelled to Luke, "I'll find your brother. Where was he patrolling?"

"He went to the west pastures to give Asher a hand with the doghouses. Lauren took his shift along the creek."

Emma rushed out the back door of the market and retrieved her horse. Horse and rider galloped away from the house, leaving Luke alone at the front.

Luke rose out of his chair and cursed his broken leg. He needed to get to the cover positions along the driveway closest to the front gate. Without being discovered, he could get a clear shot at any intruders as soon as they approached.

He slung his rifle over his shoulder and used the hickory walking stick Sam had carved for him to use as a crutch. He awkwardly moved up the driveway, using the stick for support and swinging his heavy, cast-covered leg forward. He tried to minimize the jolt of pain that ran through his body by laying his foot down gently on the gravel surface. However, his adrenaline-filled body refused to move slowly.

By the time Luke got to his position and trained his rifle on the road near a clearing, he could hear excited voices near the house. A minute later, his father came riding up the side of the driveway until he pulled hard on the reins to stop his horse.

"Tell me what you heard," said John. His horse sensed the

excitement and refused to stand still. John fought the reins to keep from being spun off the stallion's back like a top.

"Three or four shots in rapid succession. Small caliber, Dad. Like a .22 maybe?" Luke thought he saw movement on the road, so he paused to search the area through his scope. It was nothing more than a crow taking flight.

"That's it?" asked John.

"No. Seconds later, two more shots. Maybe a shotgun or a .45."

Sam was the next to arrive. He shouted his question before they reached John and Luke. "Whadya got?"

John turned his horse toward Sam. "Gunfire. Two weapons. From the west."

"Let's take the fight to them, son," said Sam. "We'll take the trail through the woods and keep them from getting to our gate."

John glanced past the market. Emma was leading Asher and Matthew across the fields.

"Dad, where do you want the rest of us?" asked Luke.

"Have Asher and Matthew watch the front gate. I want you back at the house with Cat and Vida."

"Dad, I'm the best shooter—" protested Luke before John cut him off.

"You're not mobile enough to be front and center, son. Use the upper bedroom windows to watch for anyone who gets past us. Mom needs to cover the trail to the Stanley place."

"That's where you're going," said Luke.

"Yes. Just in case they get past us. Got it?" John turned to Sam and nodded his head toward the woods. The two were off in a flash, their horses sailing over the field as if their hooves never touched the ground.

When they arrived at the wooded trail, they slowed their pace to allow their horses to calm themselves. As they rode through the tree canopy, they discussed their options.

Sam spoke first. "Do we split up? One of us at the road in front of Stanley's and the other stays at the end of the trail?"

"I don't like it," replied John. "If either us has to back up the other, we'd have an open field to cross to give help."

"Okay. Then let's hold our position at the entrance to the trail. We'll have an open shot at anyone headed our way, and if we see them coming down the road, we can double back and warn Matthew and Asher."

"Even better, you double back, and I'll catch these guys from behind. We'll have them pinned down on the road."

They picked up the pace as the debris along the trail dissipated. They hadn't heard any additional gunshots, which meant the gunmen could be on the move.

Suddenly, John pulled back on the reins, causing the trailing Sam to almost run into his horse. He raised his hand, indicating Sam should stop as well.

"What?" asked Sam in a loud whisper.

"Somebody's coming. Quick. Get the horses into the trees."

John practically jumped off his horse and immediately pulled him between several mature oaks. Sam did the same on the other side of the trail. Both men took up positions away from their horses and readied their rifles as the sound of shuffling footsteps approached.

Seconds later, three distinct shadows appeared in front of them. John flipped off the safety on his rifle, and his finger slid onto the trigger. He was ready to fire.

CHAPTER TWENTY-FIVE

Friday
Cubbison's Farm
Harford, Pennsylvania

"Stop! Now!" John's voice boomed through the woods. The approaching silhouettes froze in place, giving him a better feel for who was approaching. Clearly, the adult was accompanied by two children, who immediately clung to the adult when he shouted his instructions.

"Please don't shoot us!" The woman's plea was genuine.

John and Sam broke cover near simultaneously. Sam asked, "Who are you?"

"My name is Jenna, and these are my daughters. There are men shooting at the house where we were staying. We ran out the back door." She was peppered with questions.

"Who are they?" asked John.

"How many?" asked Sam.

"I don't know," replied Jenna, her voice quivering. "I saw them coming up the road and told my girls to get their things. We aren't gonna be a part of that ever again."

"Whadya mean?" asked Sam.

"There were men who lived in the house for a while. They were horrible. They're, um, gone." Jenna's voice trailed off.

"Gone where?" asked Sam before John grabbed his arm.

He leaned into his dad and whispered, "She might be talking about the men Emma and Luke killed."

"They were shot," Jenna replied, confirming John's suspicions.

"What are we gonna do with them?" asked Sam.

John sighed. He glanced back toward the farm and then back toward the mother. He didn't see any indication that she'd been followed, but he needed to remain in place to make sure.

"Take them through the woods but only as far as the clearing. Emma should be there."

"Then what?" asked Sam.

John was stern in his response. "Under no circumstances are they to be allowed near the house. Especially with Vida there. If we're going to protect her, we don't need these former housemates knowing that she's under our protection."

"Makes sense," said Sam. He rolled his neck around his shoulders. "So what do I do with them?"

"We're not taking them in. They gotta move on, but first, we need to make sure these gunmen aren't gonna come any closer."

"They can have the Ledbetter place, at least temporarily," suggested Sam before explaining more. "He still has crops that can be tended to and a stocked pond for fishing. I know nothing about this girl and her kids. I do know they were smart enough to run from trouble. Maybe we could turn them into a neighbor and an asset rather than just three mouths to feed."

John laughed. "Sounds like you've got it all figured out. You can take on this project as long as it doesn't involve them coming to our place."

Sam slapped his son on the back and walked toward Jenna and

her daughters. They cowered away from him and were about to turn around when he spoke softly to them.

"Okay, Jenna. My name is Sam. I'm gonna take you through the woods, and then I think we have a place for you to stay. Maybe even long term. However, you're gonna have to work to survive. Do you know how to fish?"

"No."

"Um, how about a garden? Have you ever grown vegetables?"

"No, sir."

Sam sighed and shook his head in disbelief. John had referred to them as a project. He wasn't kidding.

Sam motioned for Jenna and her girls to walk ahead of him down the trail. He mounted his horse and stayed close behind in the event any of them caused trouble. As the clearing appeared before them, he saw Emma standing behind a tree with her rifle pointed toward the approaching group.

"Stand down, Emma. It's Sam."

Jenna's voice became excited. "Emma? Did you say Emma?"

Sam pulled the horse to a stop and turned in his saddle. "Yeah, why?"

"I met her on the road. Luke, too. They're very nice and tried to help us."

"Stay here," ordered Sam. He rode the last forty feet and dismounted before his horse came to a full stop.

"What's going on?" asked Emma.

"We're still unsure about the gunmen. Apparently, they're at the Yoder place." He pointed over his shoulder toward the trail. "There's a young woman with two daughters. Her name is Jenna."

"Kids named Kay and Jewel?"

"I dunno. She seems to know you."

Emma stepped past Sam. "She's okay. I don't think she's a threat." Emma began walking down the trail to speak to Jenna when Sam stopped her, speaking in a hushed tone of voice.

"Wait. John doesn't want her near the house, especially since Vida is hiding out with us."

"Are they supposed to sleep in the woods?" she asked.

"No. I'm gonna take them over to Ledbetter's. I'll get Asher or Matthew to help me get them set up. She can try to make a home there. Whether it's temporary or permanent will be up to her."

Emma nodded her understanding and left Sam standing alone. In the meantime, there was still a threat nearby, and the entire family would need to be prepared for what might happen next.

CHAPTER TWENTY-SIX

Friday
Cubbison's Farm
Harford, Pennsylvania

Sam and Asher escorted Jenna's family across the highway to the Ledbetter house. Emma took up a position at the top of the hill near Mr. Stanley's driveway. She was thoroughly familiar with this high ground, as it was the exact location where she and Luke had ambushed the last set of men who threatened her family. This time, there was no sense of guilt consuming Emma as she waited for the potentially dangerous men to appear. What she'd done then, along with what she expected might happen next, was necessary in this lawless world.

After an hour, Sam and Asher returned, and Emma waved to them to join her. She hadn't seen any sign of the gunmen, and the Yoder place was too far away to monitor any activity there except with Luke's powerful rifle scope.

They debated whether they should conduct surveillance to learn more about the men. Or should they rethink helping the women.

Jenna's sister and two children were among those left to deal with the shooters. After some conversation, they agreed to abide by Jenna's suggestion to take care of their own family, not hers.

"I'd feel better knowing what we're dealing with, wouldn't you, Sam?" asked Asher.

"Yeah, I would. That said, there's no easy way to sneak up on that property. The land around the house has been cleared. You might be able to dart from oak tree to oak tree without being detected. Then again, you might not. It would be you against three of them, if Jenna counted correctly."

Asher ran his fingers through his hair and wiped the sweat off his face with his tee shirt. He looked up and down the road. "All right. I can't disagree. How do we know Jenna isn't running a scam on us? I'm a New Yorker, and we're pretty distrustful of sketchy people."

"Emma?" asked Sam. "You've had prior contact with her. Has she changed from before?"

She shrugged. "Listen, my interaction with her lasted all of a hot minute. Like Asher, I'm pretty distrustful now. I don't know if Jenna is going to run down there in the middle of the night to report what she's learned today. I do, however, believe she'll be back to our place, looking for food."

Sam was quick to give his opinion. "That'll be on me. I'm gonna take a little time out of my day to make sure they get on their feet. I may be wrong, but Jenna seems to be willing to learn. She has a self-reliant nature about her."

"She proved that when she left her sister to the wolves," added Asher. "I'm just saying that was a bold decision that could be looked at two ways. Either she wanted to protect her own, as she said. Or she's disloyal to those around her."

"John was right to keep her separated from us," said Emma. "She needs to understand that she's on her own down there except for Sam's advice."

"I'll make sure she does," said Sam.

They stood side by side for a moment as the sun began to drop in the sky over Harford. Finally, Asher suggested they take off. He'd maintain a post at the top of this hill until somebody relieved him or called him back to the farm. Sam suggested to relocate one of Ledbetter's dogs up here. Their loud bark could be easily herd at the market, where one of them would be patrolling nearly twenty-four seven.

CHAPTER TWENTY-SEVEN

Friday
Yoder Place
Harford, Pennsylvania

It was almost dark when Freeland emerged from the bedroom where he'd held Jenna's sister at gunpoint for hours. She could be heard whimpering in the background as his heavy boots pounded the hollow wood floors in the upper hallway. As he descended the stairs to the foyer, he was careful not to slip on the spilled blood of one of the teenage boys who'd threatened him with a knife. His younger brother, whose body was still slumped over a sofa in the living room, had lunged at Freeland. He was unarmed, but in the moment, Freeland had shot and killed him with his .45-caliber handgun anyway.

He scowled as he caught a glimpse of the boy's corpse. "What's he still doing there?" he snarled at two of the bikers in the family room across the foyer. They had their legs propped up on the coffee table, smoking cigarettes.

One of the men pulled his feet off the table to sit up. With his cigarette dangling from his lips, he responded, "Yeah, shit. I forgot about that."

"I don't care what you do with it," began Freeland. "Dump it out in the front yard next to his brother. I can't think of a better *No Trespassing* sign than that. Am I right?" He began to laugh.

The bikers joined in. Both men stood to dispose of the body, but one whispered to Freeland first. He pointed upstairs to the bedroom where Jenna's sister was being held.

"Can I ...?" His voice trailed off without finishing the question. There was no doubt what he was asking.

"Nah. She and I have a good understanding. Leave her alone. Her kids, too."

"Okay, Jack. No problem."

The other biker turned and asked, "Are we gonna keep this place? It's in pretty good shape."

"Yeah, I think so," replied Freeland. "There's another one up the road that will work for us. The girl says it's empty."

One of the bikers seemed pleased with the news. "Great. We'll check it out in the morning. Which house do you want?"

Freeland took a deep breath and exhaled. "Mine's up the road a couple of miles except it's occupied."

The two men laughed. "Well, let's unoccupy it. Right?" They shoved one another.

Freeland remained serious. "It won't be that easy. Remember those guys who left the travel center on their own?"

"Yeah. They were riding Yamahas. They managed to push them up the hill and then ditched 'em."

"Should never have bought 'em in the first place," said the other biker. This caused more laughter between the men.

Freeland turned serious. "Those guys. Well, they decided to challenge this woman and her son who live on the farm up the road. It didn't end well."

"What happened?"

"The four of them got gunned down by Ma Barker and her kid."

"Jesus. Maybe we shouldn't—" The biker was cut off by Freeland.

"Their setup is sweet. Tons of food. Plus, I want it. We just need to check it out, that's all."

Both men remained silent, hoping Freeland wasn't going to instruct them to walk up to the woman's front door.

He continued. "Don't worry, I'm not gonna send you two. I'm gonna send the twit upstairs to check it out."

"What if she runs off or spills what she knows about us?"

Freeland sighed, somewhat angry at the bikers questioning his decision-making. He responded angrily.

"Then her kids are gonna freakin' die in the worst possible way. Very slowly."

PART 4

Saturday
Kick 'em while they're down.

CHAPTER TWENTY-EIGHT

Saturday
FEMA Disaster Recovery Center
Scranton, Pennsylvania

The world's terrorist groups weren't limited to one group, geographic area, grievance, goal, or methodology. They have committed violence for numerous reasons ranging from nation building or destruction, to freeing animals, to shutting down the flow of black gold by tormenting the fossil-fuel industry.

Despite their diverse goals, there was one commonality that united them—violence. Their strong ideological beliefs drove them to commit violence to accomplish their purpose. Oftentimes, terrorists would attack civilians to strike fear into a population. This method of psychological warfare impacted the victims, the bystanders, and all who viewed it through news reports.

Abdul Rahimi had not lost sight of the stated goal of his Taliban brothers, which was to disrupt the geopolitical makeup of the world. Certainly, he felt compelled to chase down Vida, the impetuous teen who fled her family and Abdul's control. All in good time, he was forced to remind himself. For now, it was back to business.

Rumors had reached their community that the U.S. government was organizing relief efforts across the country. Americans were flocking to FEMA's temporary housing facilities and supply distribution centers to help her citizens get back on their feet during the time of crisis. Moreover, the government wanted to instill a sense of hope in its population.

That wasn't what Abdul had in mind. He, along with other Islamic community leaders in the region, intended to establish a caliphate within America. In order to do that, pressure had to be put on the locals to leave.

Yesterday, he and his top scouts had traveled to the Viewmont Mall in the northern part of Scranton. They had avoided major highways that might be traveled by military vehicles hardened against the debilitating effects of the electromagnetic pulse. They'd walked the final three miles to the site in order to keep their trucks hidden from government officials and the locals. He'd also heard, and now confirmed, that FEMA and the Pennsylvania National Guard had been instructed to seize any operating vehicle for future government use in the relief effort.

The mall consisted of three large retail stores—Home Goods, Macy's, and JC Penney. Like the others stores in the mall, the government had a seizure order to take possession of the contents for redistribution. In addition to the retailers' products being packaged and distributed to the locals, FEMA handed out cases of bottled water, blankets, and ready-to-eat meals, or MREs.

The large parking lot allowed for dozens of FEMA trailers and housing units to be put into place. Interstate 81 bordered the southern boundary of the mall property and had been closed around Scranton so the military vehicles could travel easily from Philadelphia.

The first thing Abdul observed upon their arrival was the lackadaisical approach the Guardsmen took to securing the perimeter.

Most of them spent time chatting up the locals. Rarely were the guns held in even a low-ready position. Most kept them slung over their shoulder. Further, their backs were generally turned away from the streets leading into the mall parking lot. Their point of view was uniformly directed toward the activity around the shopping complex.

The men posed as refugees, spreading out among the crowd to walk through the lines of people, looking for supplies. They observed every aspect of the FEMA operation and then made their way back to a wooded area across from a bookstore to share their observations. While they spoke, they ate one of the MREs supplied by FEMA.

"The command post is outside the entrance to Dick's Sporting Goods," began Abdul, in his native language, Pashto. He'd shoved aside some pine needles and used fallen twigs to create an abstract of the mall's floor plan. "There is a perimeter road, and just outside of that to the west is the interstate."

One of his men pointed to the long branch Abdul used to indicate the interstate's location. "I took the time to walk up to the highway. It is clear to the south, toward Philadelphia. After the cloverleaf intersection, the vehicles have not been cleared. The road is not crowded with vehicles, and there are very few pedestrians."

"This would be our best escape route, no?" asked another.

Abdul thought for a moment and nodded. "We do not want to escape toward our community. We'll lead them in the opposite direction. Toward New York and to the southeast into New Jersey." In the back of his mind, he considered driving all the way to Rochester in search of Vida. Even if she wasn't there yet, he'd ensure that nobody would be waiting for her.

"What is our best plan of attack?" asked his top lieutenant, a man who could never fill Jamal Khan's shoes but who was capable nonetheless. This operation would test his mettle and determine if Abdul could make him a trusted advisor going forward. Abdul decided now was a good time to start.

"What do you suggest?"

"We have young men and women within our community prepared to commit jihad," he began. "Using our stockpiles of ammonium nitrate and the gallon bottles of nitro, we have the basic ingredients to create the kind of bomb that could destroy the infidels." Nitromethane, typically referred to as nitro, was a fuel additive used in vintage muscle cars to enhance their performance.

"We do not have diesel fuel," pointed out one of the men.

"Easily obtained," another countered.

Abdul said, "A single jihadist can carry up to thirty pounds of the explosive mixture. A detonation here would kill hundreds of the Americans, take out the command center, and reduce the mall entrance to rubble."

"Our young men will be suspect, especially wearing a coat in this heat," added one of the men. "I felt the eyes of the infidel soldiers on me. They had little interest in doing their jobs until I passed by them."

Abdul smiled. He was satisfied with the plan, one that he'd already had in mind. He was glad to see Khan's replacement as his number one pass this early test. He sat up a little taller as he spoke.

"Our women are warriors. They will be honored to serve Allah in this manner. The Americans look upon women as weak, gentle, and more peaceful than men. It is beyond their comprehension that Afghan women are capable of jihad. Soon, they will learn not to underestimate our will."

CHAPTER TWENTY-NINE

Saturday
Cubbison's Farm
Harford, Pennsylvania

Everyone on the farm had remained on edge throughout the night. The set of four murderous men Emma and Luke had extinguished had been replaced by a new bunch. By process of elimination, Vida led the family to assume the young boys were the likely victims of the gunfire. That morning at breakfast, the group debated taking the fight to the bikers rather than allowing them too close to the house.

Vida provided valuable insight into the minds of the women she left behind. She was made aware of Jenna's arrival in the woods. However, she was left with the impression Jenna and her daughters had been turned away. She was unaware of Jenna's presence in the farm across the road thanks to Sam's generosity and compassion. For now, because they were still wary of her, and Jenna, the group kept that information to themselves. As she spoke, however, Luke picked up insight to prove to his family that Vida was an ally.

"There are three women, the strongest of whom is Jenna. She is fiercely protective of her two daughters. As I learned from my conversations with all of them, Jenna never approved of allowing the other men to move into the house. Well, not that she had a choice."

"What about the other women?" asked John.

"Jenna's sister is weak. She doesn't have the ability or desire to take care of herself, much less her daughters. The third woman, who has two sons, is difficult to get along with. You have told us about gunfire. None of the women had guns. If the men used their weapons on anyone, it was likely the boys, as you believe, and perhaps their strong-willed mother."

John sighed and leaned back in his chair. He was tired. After the long, difficult trip home from New York, he'd hoped to allow his weary body some rest. Instead, he was faced with a battered son, a threatening fire, and now murderous thugs nearby. He relayed his thoughts to the others aloud.

"Part of me thinks we should take the fight to them. You know, catch them off guard."

Sam agreed. "My gut tells me they aren't in a defensive mindset. They are probably, um ..." His voice trailed off as he made eye contact with Cat. He chose his words carefully. "They're probably not expecting anyone to come after them."

"We know at least two of them are armed," added Emma. "And it's possible they have friends holed up somewhere else. If we allow them time to regroup, then we'll be facing numbers greater than ours."

Suddenly, Mathew burst into the kitchen and rushed into the dining room. "Somebody is approaching the front gate. A woman, I think." Without waiting for instructions, he ran back out the door with rifle in hand.

John pushed away from the table. "Emma, you're with me. Let's greet the newcomer. Sam, Asher, monitor the trail. Everyone else, protect the house and market. Let's go!"

Two of the dining chairs fell backwards as they hastily stood up from the dining table. John grabbed his rifle and leapt through the door, skipping the steps leading outside. Emma was hot on his heels, her rifle slung over her shoulder. She struggled to insert her paddle holster into her jeans as she jogged to catch up with John.

Cat and Vida hustled to clean up the kitchen and take their positions on the upper floor. Vida was tasked with moving from room to room, studying the fields surrounding the farmhouse through powerful binoculars. Cat had received substantial training using a .22-caliber rifle. Its feather-light recoil was perfect for young girls. While it might not have the stopping power of the adults' hunting rifles, it would certainly deter anyone from approaching the house.

With the house secure, Vida and Cat waited. Luke had maintained his position on the front porch of the market, while Lauren was sleeping in the travel trailer following a full night on patrol along with John. Sam continued to the trail while Asher raced across the field to wake up his wife. It was all hands on deck as the unfamiliar person approached the front gate.

Matthew carefully monitored her actions. A woman was attempting to push her way through the padlocked farm gate. She then struggled at first before stepping onto the rails with the intent to climb over it.

"That's close enough!" shouted Matthew, who hid behind stacked bales of hay. "Get down!"

John and Emma moved from one barrier to the next, maintaining cover as they reached Matthew's position. John kept an eye on the road and occasionally glanced back toward the market to confirm there wasn't anyone circling to their rear.

"Don't shoot! I need your help!"

"Who are you?" asked John.

"Beth! I'm staying down the street."

"What do you want?" John asked in a brusque voice reflecting his hyped-up adrenaline levels.

"My sister. She's disappeared with her kids. Have you seen her?"

"No!" said Emma.

John shot his wife a stern look. He wanted this intruder to hear from one voice.

"Emma? Isn't your name Emma?"

John took the lead again. "There's nobody else here except my family. It's time for you to leave."

"But Emma knows my sister. Her name is Jenna. She has two daughters. Remember? Um, is Luke here? He knows her, too."

John rolled his eyes. He was already concerned about how much this woman knew about his family. After studying her and her attire, he decided she was unarmed. Besides, he couldn't imagine her to be stupid enough to draw on him with three rifles pointing at her.

He broke cover and walked directly toward her with his rifle pointed at her head. "We don't know anything about your sister. Now, it's time for you to leave."

She hesitated for a moment. Her eyes darted from John to where Emma and Matthew studied her through their rifles' scopes. She nervously looked past them toward the market and its surroundings.

"Okay," she said barely loud enough for John to hear. She turned and began walking toward the top of the hill near the driveway of the Ledbetter farm. She glanced in that direction for a brief moment and then continued until she disappeared over the hill.

John cursed himself for not following Asher's suggestion and keeping someone posted at the top of the road. He'd been frustrated overnight as he saw how stretched the group was as they defended the farm. On the one hand, he needed another half-dozen people who could handle a weapon. On the other hand, with each new member of the group, he ran the risk of betrayal, which would put his family at risk.

Emma walked up to John as the woman disappeared. "John, that was too easy. I studied her face through my scope the entire time to get a feel for what her true intentions were. Sure, she might've been looking for Jenna. She also might've been lookin' around, too. Her eyes were shifty, you know?"

"She may have been gauging how quickly we reacted to her arrival," muttered John. "Recon, like in the military."

Emma took a deep breath to relieve some tension and exhaled. "If Vida's assessment of Jenna's sister is accurate, there's a good chance she was sent here to check things out."

John furrowed his brow and shook his head. "I can't believe that she'd do the dirty work for those murderous thugs. Seriously, just like that?"

"It's possible they threatened harm to her children," Emma responded. "But she didn't appear nervous to me. You were closer. What do you think?"

"Definitely shifty eyes," replied John, echoing Emma's assessment. "Either she was nervous or, as you said, she was checking us out. Either way, she's about to tell those guys a lot about how we deal with people approaching the farm."

"And here we are, knowing nothing about them."

John looked at the sky and rolled his head around his neck. He had to make a decision.

CHAPTER THIRTY

Saturday
Yoder Place
Harford, Pennsylvania

Beth arrived back at the Yoder place forty-five minutes later. She stopped to look around Mr. Stanley's farmhouse for any indication that her sister had been there. Although she had been forced to go to the Cubbison farm to gather information for Freeland, she was also curious to see if Jenna and her daughters had fled there. It was hard to tell if they were lying to her. It was near impossible who was telling the truth nowadays, she thought to herself as she walked through the big, empty house.

After rifling through the cupboards and pantry in search of anything edible, Beth left and made the lonely walk back to the house. At first, Freeland had been rough and threatening with her. He'd tried to break her spirit through his abusive actions and words. It worked, to an extent.

Beth had become jaded by past relationships, before and after the point when the grid went down. She seemed open to the abuse and rarely stood up for herself. If not for her children, she'd never have stopped at the Cubbisons' front gate. She'd be on her way to New York to start a new life.

She'd barely made it to the top step of the Yoders' porch when the door flew open, and a muscular arm grabbed her to pull her inside. The door slammed, and Freeland's hot breath was in her face as he bombarded her with questions.

She relayed every word that had been conveyed to her by the Cubbisons. She told him the details of their driveway and the barriers they'd constructed. She told Freeland there were only three people there. She assumed the unseen gunman behind the hay bale was Luke, who appeared to have let his hair grow longer. Then there was John and Emma, the parents.

"Just three? That's it?" asked Freeland.

"That's all I saw. I mean, it's a big place." She went on to describe the market and what she could see of the barn and the main house.

"What about horses? Cows?" he asked.

"I know they have both although I didn't see them this morning. I have no idea how many they have."

"Momma!" shouted one of her daughters, who came running down the hallway. The child had been crying and slipped away from the burly biker who'd been told to watch her.

"Come here, baby," she said, pulling away from Freeland to greet her child.

This angered Freeland. He snatched Beth by the arm and drew her close to his face. "We're not done!"

"I don't know anything else! That's all I saw!" Her voice quivered as Freeland intimidated her.

He grabbed her by the throat and forced her against the door. His face was inches away as he locked eyes with her. "You'd better not have lied to me. Do I need to remind you of what I'm capable of? That pile of dead bodies out front can get larger, and you know exactly where I'll start." He turned and stared down at the crying young girl.

Beth began to cry. "I swear. That's all I know. Please don't hurt my kids."

"You'd better stay in line," he hissed as he gave her one final shove against the door. He shouted to the other biker, "Let the other one go!"

"Go upstairs and get Blaze," he ordered one of his men. Blaze had been a longtime associate of Freeland's who earned his nickname because of his proclivity for committing arson. "We're about to make a move."

He ordered Jenna and her kids upstairs and told them to get in the bedroom with the door closed. He wanted to be able to talk without interruption. Once the four bikers were gathered in the living room, Freeland issued his instructions with a wary eye on the stairs.

"Here's the deal. I don't believe that damn farm is run by three people. Maybe they got separated somehow that Friday night, but I doubt it. That means there are either more family members or ranch hands. Maybe even the girl Vida they've talked about, plus Jenna, the sister. Either way, they've got horses and cows, and it's an operating farm with food. I want it."

"Let's do it, Jack," said Blaze.

"Right now sounds good to me," said one of the bikers, hitching his jeans up to his beer belly before they fell back in place.

"With what? That peashooter of a rifle and my .45? All three of them were armed with rifles. These country people have more guns than you can imagine. I want those, too."

"Our guys have guns," said the fourth biker. "The problem is they're all handguns. We need rifles."

"Slim has a shorty," added the other. Shorty was slang for a sawed-off shotgun.

"Yeah, I remember," said Freeland. He wandered into the foyer for a moment, looking upstairs to see if there were any ears eavesdropping on their conversation. All was quiet except for the sniffling of the kids. He hated wimpy kids.

"We'll have to go up to the Flying J to get him," said Blaze.

Freeland nodded.

"What about the jarheads in town? Maybe they can hook us up with an AR or AK?"

"We don't have anything to trade," replied one of the bikers. "We've kinda gone through the food from the Sysco rig. We've got cigarettes, but I think the guys would rather starve than give up their smokes."

Blaze added, "Fred Stewart ain't gonna give up a long rifle for a case of cancer sticks. We have to promise him something much bigger."

Freeland had a vision, one that didn't include raiding passersby as they trekked up the interstate. Internally, he called it his Green Acres plan. You know, goodbye city life, Green Acres is the place to be. He'd talk to Fred personally about a trade.

CHAPTER THIRTY-ONE

Saturday
Lake Wallenpaupack
Wayne County, Pennsylvania

After morning prayer, Abdul and his men got right to work. The bombmakers convened in a barn and closed out the prying eyes of their families. Abdul interviewed the proposed women who'd carry the explosives strapped to their bodies. One young girl who was very devout stepped forward. In fact, she'd been dreaming of the day that she could honor herself, and Allah, by performing the task. Her family was proud of her decision and worked with Abdul to create a ruse that would catch the infidels off guard.

Just a few months ago, one of the women in the community had given birth. She was slightly heavier than the young volunteer, which suited their needs perfectly. She'd worn a maxi dress of loose-fitting jersey material designed for Muslim women who were late in their pregnancy. With this dress, the women came up with a plan.

They would use a slightly stuffed pillow to wrap around the explosives to emulate a baby bump. With the sewn-in pockets on the side, the girl could easily approach the target and detonate the bomb before drawing attention. The scheme was brilliant because a pregnant Muslim would never be considered a threat, not to mention she would be unapproachable by Guardsmen for fear of being labeled an Islamophobe.

Throughout the afternoon, many of the women in the community descended upon the young girl's home to express their gratitude and pay their respects to the family. She was making the ultimate sacrifice for Allah and in the war against the American infidels. The other young women vowed to honor their family when the need arose.

Meanwhile, the bomb makers studied the pages of a three-ring binder containing the contents of *The Anarchist Cookbook*, a book written in the early seventies used by leftist revolutionaries in America to create explosives. They were careful not to make a mistake as they created the perfect concoction and poured it into containers. Throughout the day, without the detonators in place, they called in their young jihadist to put on the vest.

She gave them feedback on how it fitted her body and whether the weight was too much to carry. Once they came up with the perfect balance of explosive capability and weight, she was required to walk two miles to determine if she could handle the load. She brazenly faced the men and told them she could handle more. The strength of *Allah*, she said, made her body stronger. So they added more explosives.

Once the delivery mechanism, the young woman, and the explosives were ready for deployment, Abdul led the entire community in prayer. That evening, he convened his men to discuss the logistics of their plan, which would commence in the early morning hours the next day.

Similar to before, they'd enter from the east of Scranton. Two of the men would escort their jihadist to the mall, where she would join the line of refugees looking for their share of the FEMA supplies.

Based on their reconnaissance, they determined she'd arrive near the command center just after nine.

The significance of this was not lost on Abdul. He made a mental note to speak with the young girl before she set out on foot to complete her mission. He fumbled with his watch as he spoke with his lieutenants. He'd tell her the precise time to fulfill Allah's wishes.

9:11 a.m.

CHAPTER THIRTY-TWO

Saturday
Cubbison's Farm
Harford, Pennsylvania

"We're gonna be stretched too thin," said John as he paced the living room floor. Throughout the day, conversations were held among the group as to whether they should eliminate the threat that existed just a couple of miles away from the farm. He'd already agreed to send Asher and Lauren to observe the Yoder place from atop the hill near Stanley's. With the binoculars, they could maintain a safe distance without being seen. If the men decided to make a move on the Cubbisons' farm, Lauren could easily ride her horse back to the house to warn everyone.

Luke was the most vocal proponent of a preemptive strike. "They'll never see it coming, Dad. Just like before. I'm not saying it was easy to take another person's life, but all I could think about was what if they came back in the middle of the night when we weren't watching."

Emma agreed, adding, "And what if his bunch recruits more gunmen. We don't know anything about them."

John wasn't against the idea. Mainly, he was playing devil's advocate. "Taking that as true, murdering these guys might infuriate their friends. That means we'll really be facing a dang swarm of yellow jackets."

"Better on our terms rather than theirs, John," said Emma. John studied his wife. She'd clearly gotten over any remorse for killing the first group of men.

"Dad, what do you think?" John asked Sam.

Sam sighed. "I do believe putting eyes on the Yoder place is a good idea. It's not likely these guys know the woods and trails well enough to find a back trail onto our farm. That said, if they put their mind to it, they could find a way. Here's the thing. We're going to be facing these kinds of threats for so long as the power grid is down and society has collapsed. There'll be no respite. Each situation will be different, and I suspect this won't be the last time we have a discussion in this living room about how to prepare."

"At least we have the time to discuss options," said Emma. "Next time, we may not."

John wandered toward the living room window that looked across the lawn toward the market. He noticed dust flying up from the dirt path running parallel to the driveway.

"We have a rider!"

Sam joined his side. "It's Lauren. She's got the palomino." The golden-colored horse with its white mane was unmistakable.

Emma was the first person out the door to greet her. "Is everything all right?" she shouted to Lauren as she rounded the market in a hurry.

Out of breath, Lauren tried to respond. "There are four of them, but three just left towards town." She dismounted, and Emma handed her a bottle of water. Lauren gulped it down as she tied her horse off near the water trough.

"Four? What did they look like?" asked John.

"Asher saw them first. He described them as bikers. You know, beer guts. Jeans. Longish hair."

"So three of the four left?" asked Emma.

Lauren nodded. "The fourth man was holding a rifle. He stood on the front porch for a minute, looked around, and then went back inside. Asher studied the house for a little longer and followed the men as they walked out of sight. That's when he sent me to let you guys know."

Luke had hobbled to the doorway to listen in on the conversation. "Dad, this is our chance. We can take out the one guy and free the women."

John spun around. "To where? We'll free them and then what? Bring them here? Send them to Ledbetter's?"

"Scranton," said Sam.

"Why?" asked Emma.

"Wait, that makes sense," interrupted Lauren. "If the government is trying to make any kind of relief effort, the larger cities would be addressed first. It doesn't make sense to send FEMA or DHS resources into the countryside."

"Right," said Sam. "Either way, we'll tell 'em a white lie. They're like mice to a snake for us. Snakes always hang out where the mice live. Get rid of the mice, you get rid of the snakes who feed on them."

"That's thirty miles," said John.

"I know, but it makes the most sense for them," said Sam. "We'll direct them along the back roads to avoid running into more of these biker types, as Asher described them. They could find a place to stay at Thorn Hill Lodge or some of those small motels near the Elk Mountain ski area in South Gibson."

"They'll have options," added Emma, placing a positive spin on the relocation plan.

John began pacing again. He was tired of pacing. They all looked to him to make the final decision, a role he was glad to play, along with the burden of its consequences.

"Fine. We'll hit him just after dark."

"I agree, son," said Sam.

"All right," began John. "Let's sit down with Vida and get an exact floor plan of the Yoder house. I wanna know where the women and children would be sleeping or locked up. Where would this lone biker be located in the house? Are there any blind spots?"

"All good points, Dad," said Luke. "From what I remember, the back of the house is best. There are a couple of sheds and a garage to use as cover. There are only two entrances and exits. The front porch and the rear door leading into the kitchen's mudroom."

"Let's get saddled up," said Emma.

John gave his wife a look. "Wait? What?"

"Yeah, let's not waste any time. I think we should get into position now so we can hit the house when it gets dark."

He nodded his head to the right. "Can I talk to you for a minute?"

"Um, sure," she replied with skepticism.

They strolled away from the group, who began talking amongst themselves. John explained his reasoning for the private conversation.

"We shouldn't both go. It's the same principle as the trip to New York. One of us. One parent needs to stay home for the benefit of our kids. Asher, Sam and I can handle this."

Emma placed her hands on the back of her hips and stretched her shoulders. She tried to make her argument. "I can keep the women and children calm. We don't want them coming back here. Plus, I can have your back."

John took his wife in his arms and held her. He whispered in her ear, "I'll be fine. Listen, I want to trust Asher's interpretation of what he saw. However, I also know that there are many ways to circle back to the farm. This could be a trick, and we have to be prepared for that. I need you and the boys to protect the farm and each other."

Emma sighed. John was right. "I'll worry."

"I'm glad. It proves that you do, in fact, still love me."

She playfully swatted his chest. "I was talking about Grandpa Sam. Young studs like yourself are a dime a dozen."

"Hey!" exclaimed John as they shared a laugh. They hugged and then walked arm in arm to rejoin the group.

"We're ready," said Sam. "Lauren is gonna join Asher. He'll signal us right after twilight. We just gotta decide who's gonna watch the front and who is gonna bust in the back door."

"You're out front, Asher," said John. "We'll take the back door."

"I think I'm gonna take my shotgun," said Sam.

"Good choice. Just remember your scatter. There are women and children in there."

Lauren took off in a flash. As her horse disappeared from sight, John turned to his family and Vida.

"This could go sideways. We all need to be prepared for them to sneak up on the farm or, later, as we suffer the repercussions of our attack. Are we sure about this?"

"We're all in, Dad," said Matthew, the first time he'd spoken that afternoon. John studied his son's face. It was the same look of resolve Matthew had had after he killed the man who tried to attack John.

"Okay, let's get our guns and horses ready."

CHAPTER THIRTY-THREE

Saturday
Harford House Motel
Harford, Pennsylvania

Freeland, Blaze, and another biker made the two-hour trek into Harford to meet with Fred Stewart at the Harford House. He walked at a much faster pace than he preferred in order to arrive before sunset. It was dangerous enough to break their truce while armed and encroach upon Fred's territory. To do so after dark would most likely result in one of those *shoot-first-ask-questions-later* bullets between the eyes.

He and his men walked onto the parking lot with their hands raised high over their heads. As expected, a swarm of armed guards converged on them. Red laser dot sights danced around their chests.

"I'm Jack Freeland. I need to talk with Fred."

The guards remained focused on the newcomers and ignored his request. "We know who you are. Slowly, remove your weapons and lay them on the ground."

Freeland and his men complied. They immediately raised their hands above their heads again, although they were getting somewhat perturbed at having to follow orders.

"Now, will you get Fred? I have a proposed trade."

The men didn't respond although one of them stepped a few paces backwards and disappeared into the lobby. Moments later, he returned and addressed Freeland.

"Only you. And I'll need to pat you down."

Freeland rolled his eyes but walked forward to succumb to the pat-down. The guard didn't have his heart in it, searching Freeland just enough to confirm there wasn't a gun or knife hidden in his clothing. Freeland's best weapons were his muscular arms and strong hands capable of choking a man in seconds.

As soon as Freeland was escorted into the lobby, he was met with more armed guards and dozens of candles illuminating the once opulent home. Now it smelled of stale air and sweat. He was led down a dark hallway to a room where another armed guard patted him down. Finally, he was allowed to meet with Fred.

"Sit down, Freeland. This'd better be good." There wasn't any animosity between the two leaders of the groups who occupied Harford. However, each felt compelled to show they were strong, so they adopted a somewhat different persona than usual.

"I'll get right to the point, then," said Freeland. "We need guns. Ammo, too. Rifles. And I don't mean the kind kids shoot at squirrels or hunters chase down deer with. I'm talkin' ARs, AKs. Battle rifles."

Fred studied Freeland for a moment, waiting for the punchline. Surely, the man was kidding or out of his mind. A moment later, he burst out in a hearty laugh. His condescending laughter aggravated Freeland, so he continued.

"This is a legitimate request and offer to make a trade."

Fred raised his hands in front of him as he slowly controlled his incredulity. "Freeland, why in the hell would I trade guns, especially battle rifles, to men who could use them to kill me? Hmm?"

"I'm not gonna use them against you."

Fred leaned back in his chair and laughed again. "Said the Taliban to Washington!"

"You're not my target," Freeland insisted. "I'm going to disclose to you what our intentions are and how to make this trade work."

Fred waved his arms across the table that separated them. "Good luck," he said sarcastically.

"First of all, I only need three rifles. I'd prefer them to be the same platform. Two magazines for each and at least a hundred rounds for each weapon."

"You're out of your mind!" Fred slammed the palms of his hands on the tabletop. "I think we're done here." He began to stand, but Freeland continued.

"Hear me out. I need them because of what I have to trade."

Fred erupted with laughter again. Now he was enjoying ridiculing Freeland. "Let me guess. You're gonna give up your M1 Abrams."

"No, actually. I'm giving up our territory. I'll trade you the entire stretch of interstate we've secured and the two truck stops at each exit. We're planning on moving into the farms east of the highway."

Freeland had the former Marine's attention. Fred was aware of the foot traffic making its way from Scranton to New York and vice versa. There were opportunities to scavenge the tractor trailer rigs with his newly acquired transportation. He could also lie in wait for other classic car owners who dared cross through Susquehanna County near Harford.

"When do you want to make this trade?"

"Right now. My people are prepared to pull out of the Onvo at Exit 217 tomorrow. We can turn over the next exit at Harford Road in a couple of days after I take care of some business toward Gibson. At that exit, you'll have the Flying J and the Holiday Inn Express. We're holding the Pennsylvania State Police building as well. We just can't breach it, but you might have the equipment to do it."

Fred began to contemplate the possibilities. He was certain the staties had an arsenal and ammunition inside their facility. He could make up for the traded weapons and then some. Both men sat quietly, the intensity of the standoff causing the temperature to rise in the windowless room. Finally, Fred made a decision.

"Screw it. Here's how this will work. Tomorrow morning, I'll deliver your arsenal to the Onvo. I want all of your people gone except for you and two others to carry your end of the bargain."

"I don't know. What if you don't show up?"

"Gimme a break, Freeland. Of course we're gonna show up. If we don't, your fat bikers can come right back to their truck stop home again."

"Fine! What time tomorrow?"

Fred wasn't gonna wake up early for this jackass. "Nine o'clock or so. I'll get there when I get there."

Freeland stood and attempted to shake hands with Fred. Fred looked at him and smirked. He'd let Freeland venture out into the farmland to clear occupants out of the way. Once they were nice and comfy and spread out, he and his trained devil dogs would eliminate them.

CHAPTER THIRTY-FOUR

Saturday
Yoder Place
Harford, Pennsylvania

Asher and Lauren maintained watch over the Yoder place from a distance atop the hill. John and Sam rode across the field behind the burnt ruins of Stanley's place, keeping the tree-line fence row between them and the Yoders'. They tied their horses off near the gate leading behind the farmhouse. Then they waited for Asher's signal.

The sky was completely devoid of clouds that evening, and the setting sun resembled a giant orange ball disappearing over the horizon. By agreement, once the sun set completely, during twilight, Asher would confirm to the others that none of the bikers had returned to the Yoder place. Using their highest-powered flashlight, he would turn it on for five continuous seconds to indicate they were ready to proceed. Rapid flashing meant to abort the mission.

While they waited, John and Sam discussed the possible scenarios they'd face when they arrived at the back of the house.

"What do you remember about the house, Dad?"

"It's a simple farmhouse, typical of what was built in the 1800s before being expanded to the rear. Of course, back in the day, the kitchens were separated from the main structure so they didn't burn the place down by accident."

"I've never been inside, but it seems fairly small. Maybe two thousand square feet?"

"That's right," said Sam as he gave John the visual. "Entering through the front door, there is a small foyer. More of a hallway, really. To the left is a formal living room coupled with a dining room. To the right is a family room and a utility area just beyond. The addition at the rear is just one story. There's a mudroom and another activity room where Mrs. Yoder taught her kids."

"What about upstairs?"

"Four bedrooms, one in each corner of the house. The parents had one, as did Mrs. Yoder's elderly mother. The kids split the other two. Boys in one and girls in the other. They lived frugally, John." A wave of sadness came over Sam as he considered their demise.

"I knew them to be good people," said John as he consoled his father. "Justice was administered by Emma and Luke. Now we have to do our part to save these women."

Sam sighed. "Son, how many times are we going to risk our lives for others? I wanna believe that karma is at play here. You know, one day somebody will come to our defense. Unfortunately, everybody who approaches our farm is a taker."

John furrowed his brow and slowly nodded in agreement. "I'll be honest, I expected this sort of crap in New York. I don't want to talk about it in front of Asher and Lauren because that is their hometown."

Sam interrupted him. "Trust me, they understand. Asher said more than once that the goings-on in New York gave him plenty of story ideas for *Blue Bloods*. And you know, Lauren is an editor specializing in those end-of-the-world disaster stories. Thinking back on the novels she'd read, she said most authors diminished how bad it could be."

John rose from his crouch to get a look at the sun disappearing over the trees. He saw the faint glow of a lantern or candlelight emanating from the upstairs bedrooms. He opened his eyes wide to determine if Asher was signaling them yet. Sam stood to join him.

"Here's the thing that worries me. Our three most immediate neighbors have died or were murdered. We haven't even reached out to the folks back toward Gibson. Truthfully, I thought we were far enough away from the interstate to avoid desperate killers or thieves. I was very wrong."

Sam stood to join his son. "Maybe the dangerous situations we faced in New York prepared us for what we're seeing now. All of us have become hardened as we've encountered violence. Even Cat and the boys. They've been forced to grow up quickly."

"Too fast," added John. He thought for a moment. "One person still hasn't witnessed or participated in the violence—Vida. I know she was running from a culture that was abusive to women. However, would they force her to pick up a weapon? I don't know if their religious beliefs would allow that."

Sam shrugged. "I didn't see any women among that bunch at the Picatinny Arsenal."

"Granted, I wasn't taking inventory, and it was dark, but you're right."

"John, at some point in time we're gonna have to trust her. She did notice that shotgun I missed at Ledbetter's. She could've easily left it behind, snuck back over there later, and attacked us. Instead, she retrieved it and offered it to me first thing. I let her take it to the house, but she hasn't asked about it since."

"I appreciate that, and she has yet to do anything to betray our trust. But does that mean she won't pick up a rifle to defend our home? We need capable shooters. Heck, I've even trained Cat on the .22."

"Let's get through tonight and see what develops. Tomorrow

let's talk with Emma outside of Luke's earshot. He's smitten with the girl and isn't objective."

"Good idea. Like Cat, we could start her off with a .22."

Sam nudged John's arm and pointed back toward the hill at the front of Stanley's property. The flashlight shined bright and steady. They were ready.

CHAPTER THIRTY-FIVE

Saturday
Yoder Place
Harford, Pennsylvania

Asher gave Lauren a long, loving hug and kiss. She admonished him to be careful, fighting back the tears to remain strong for her husband. She also reminded him not to trust the women. After hearing the details of Beth's visit to the farm earlier, she became suspect. It was possible, in her vulnerable state, Beth had already fallen under the spell of her captors.

Lauren had studied the psychological phenomenon known as Stockholm syndrome while she was editing a nonfiction book for Random House. The condition occurred when someone held captive developed positive, and even romantic, emotions for the person who was holding them against their will.

Rather than feeling fear and disdain, the vulnerable hostage either became sympathetic toward their captor or appreciative for being well taken care of. Lauren believed, based on her conversations with Jenna, that Beth had a history of taking up with abusive men, therefore making her susceptible to Stockholm syndrome.

They told each other how much they loved the other before Asher began the brisk walk down the hill toward the Yoders' farmhouse. He kept a keen eye out in the dimming twilight for the return of the three bikers who'd left hours earlier. Any glimmer of light, whether from a flashlight or the glowing red cherry of a cigarette, would encourage him to run toward the back of the house to warn John and Sam. At this point, he could ill afford to use the flashlight for fear of giving away their approach.

The sun had begun setting at around eight o'clock. Last light was closer to 8:20. The men agreed to begin their advance inside at exactly 8:30. They'd even synchronized Sam's old pocket watch with Asher's self-winding Seiko.

Asher's biggest concern, as he'd learned from interviewing members of law enforcement, was friendly fire. Especially in a building with no power, shadows moving through a hallway could be mistaken for the target. A nervous trigger finger could easily result in a deadly accident.

Once inside the house, Asher would guard the front door, escorting out any of the hostages and preventing the gunman's escape. At the rear, John would lead the way, sweeping through the house in search of the hostage-taker while Sam secured the only other exit leading through the kitchen.

Asher used the ambient light from the moon to check his watch. The second hand ticked down until it was precisely 8:30. He took a deep breath and made his way up the steps to the front door, keeping his back pressed against the wall. With his free hand, he reached over and turned the doorknob to ease it open.

It was locked.

"Seriously?" he mouthed the word to himself. Of all the contingencies they'd discussed and he'd considered on his own, somehow the fact the gunman would lock the door hadn't crossed their minds. He sighed as his eyes darted up and down the front porch in search of options. He even looked for a key under the dusty coir mat with the faded word *Welcome* written across it.

He reached on top of the porch light for a key. Nothing. Then he cursed the change of events and took up a position on the ground, using the three-foot-tall porch as cover. All he could do was wait and be prepared to shoot only the bad guy if he exited.

Sam gave John the signal indicating it was time to enter the house. They'd taken a moment to look inside the windows at the rear and found the rooms to be empty. The candlelight was still emanating from the back bedroom, which Sam believed to be the master.

John pulled open the screen door and handed it off to Sam. Sam found the rusted hook affixed near the bottom of the door frame and carefully eased the hook into the eyelet screwed into the siding. John tried the handle. Like the front door, it was locked.

"Locked," he said in a loud whisper to Sam.

Without hesitation, Sam reached down and pulled up his right pants leg. He retrieved his prized hunting knife made by Morakniv. Sam traded places with John and used the sharp tip of the carbon-steel blade to jimmy the latch bolt. The doorjamb had deteriorated over time, making the wood soft. He easily popped the bolt, and the door pushed open slightly.

Both men held their breath as they listened for any signs of activity. The door creaking open was louder than the act of breaking in. After a moment, they were satisfied.

It was John's foresight that saved his life that evening. He turned to Sam and whispered, "If this door's locked, the front might be, too. Go see if Asher made it inside. If not, tell him to wait. I'll make my way to the foyer and open it before we try to go upstairs."

"I'm on it. Be careful, son."

John nodded and entered the mudroom. He was careful with every step to avoid kicking anything in his path. A misplaced empty can of vegetables could careen across the brick kitchen floor. It would be loud enough to garner the attention of the man holding the women and children upstairs.

There was very little light finding its way inside the house. In that moment, John wished the aurora would return, although in the weeks prior, he'd cursed its very existence. At least the hues of blue and green would provide him some light inside the unfamiliar house.

First, he made his way toward the foyer, clearing the dining room and formal parlor as he did. There were no signs of life except for a wayward mosquito that buzzed around his ear. John thought about smacking it into oblivion but feared the contact with his face might be noticed.

Asher was nowhere to be found, so he assumed he was still outside. Just to make sure, he moved quickly across the foyer into the family room and pointed his gun into every corner of the room. He called out Asher's name in a loud whisper, but there was no response.

Keeping a watchful eye on the stairwell and the landing at the top, John felt his way back to the front door. He fumbled around for the handle. The old door was still equipped with a mortise lock, a throwback to the nineteenth century when the home had been built. This modernized version of the original had a small toggle that slid up and down to engage the lock. Holding his gun in one hand pointed toward the top of the stairs, John slowly turned the knob, listening to every creak and click as if it had been amplified by a megaphone.

The door popped open, and a rush of fresh air entered the damp, humid farmhouse. Asher was just outside the door.

"Sam gave me a heads-up," he whispered to John before entering. "The upstairs rooms toward the front of the house appear dark. The windows are open on all four of them."

John opened the door a little wider and motioned for Asher to enter. Once he was inside, John slowly closed the door until it latched. He tapped Asher's arm and pointed up the stairs and to the right. Asher, who'd been briefed by Sam outside as to the possible location of the man with the hostages, nodded his understanding.

The two men began to ascend the stairs. By the time John hit the fourth of the eighteen stairs leading to the landing, the creaks and cracks of the old nails connecting the treads to the stringer began to groan under his weight.

"Shit!" he uttered a rare expletive under his breath.

"Movement," said Asher as he tapped John on the backside.

An upstairs door opened, allowing the candlelight to wash the landing. A man called out, "Jack, is that you?"

"Yeah," said John in a husky tone of voice. He began marching upstairs with a purpose. Asher, who was lighter on his feet, was hot on John's heels. By the time John grabbed the top newel post, the gunman had slammed the door shut and was cursing them.

"Bullshit! I don't know who you are, but I will kill you!"

Neither John nor Asher responded. They focused their efforts on getting into position. Asher ducked into the doorway leading to the bedroom across the hall from the master while John pressed his back against the wall with his gun trained on the closed door.

Across the hallway, Asher also pointed his weapon at the door.

Unexpectedly, the gunmen shouted, "Come here, you little shit!"

The doorknob turned, and the door flew open. A young girl ran out of the room and crashed into Asher. The gunman fired wildly toward the girl, barely missing her and grazing Asher's shoulder. Asher spun around and fell to the floor with the girl next to him. The child began to wail from fear.

John didn't hesitate. He moved quickly in front of the partially opened door and kicked it hard with his boot. The force of the door crashing into the wall behind it sounded like an explosion. The hostages shrieked and cried out. The gunman panicked and fired at the door rather than the opening.

Concerned an errant shot might kill one of the hostages, John bum-rushed the shooter, slamming the barrel of his rifle into the man's chest. The man fell backwards, crashing into a chest at the foot of the bed before twisting into a rocking chair. The force of the impact dislodged his rifle, which flew across the room and landed near a fireplace.

In a flash, Beth leapt for the weapon. Her nervous hands searched the dark floor before she found it. Then she immediately turned and pointed the weapon at John.

"Wait!" John said, holding his hands away from his body.

She didn't.

Beth pulled the trigger three times, finding her mark just once.

CHAPTER THIRTY-SIX

Saturday
Yoder Place
Harford, Pennsylvania

Sam took on the task of watching both exits to the home. He walked briskly back and forth along the east side of the house, alternating between the front and back doors while keeping an eye on the candlelit bedroom above him. When the first shots were fired, he didn't hesitate. Running through the tall grass, his shotgun leading the way, he slammed his shoulder into the front door, sending it flying inward.

He stopped to point the barrel into the two front living areas until more shots rang out. The noise was deafening in the quiet house. Sam rushed up the stairs with the shotgun pointed toward the landing. He had to keep his wits about him to avoid shooting the wrong person. If the gunman showed up, Sam would take him out.

"Stop shooting! Enough!"

It was John's voice.

"Girls! This way!" Asher was shouting instructions from the other bedroom.

By the time Sam hit the landing, he was somewhat out of breath, but his adrenaline willed him forward.

"Beth, go in the other room!" John was yelling at her. The other woman had already raced through the doorway and onto the landing, nearly smashing into Sam in the darkness.

When Sam rounded the corner and entered the master bedroom, he saw why Beth was unresponsive. She stood dumbfounded in front of the fireplace. Her arms were dangling at her sides as if they were barely attached to her body. Her index finger allowed a .22 rifle to hang on by the trigger guard. On the floor was a blood-soaked body of a man writhing in pain. He'd been shot in the chest just above the heart.

"Beth," said Sam in a calm, grandfatherly voice. "Honey, it's over. You're safe. Okay?"

Sam handed his shotgun to John.

"Momma? Are you okay?" one of her girls asked meekly from across the hall.

Sam's calming voice coupled with the sound of her child asking for her caused Beth to relax. Then she began to sob. She dropped to her knees and allowed the gun to hit the area rug. Sam moved quickly to scoop up the weapon, and tucked it under his armpit. He consoled the young woman and helped her to her feet.

"Let's go see about your kids," he whispered into her ear. "It's over."

She stopped and began to shake her head violently from side to side. "No! It's not over. They're coming back. More of them. Maybe all of them. They're all coming back!"

Beth began wailing and shaking uncontrollably. While John watched the bleeding gunman, Sam helped Beth out of the room and into the arms of her children. They held each other tight until the other woman who'd endured the ordeal joined them. She'd lost her husband and two sons since the perfect storm had upended their lives. Beth and her kids had become family to her.

Asher, whose shirt was bloodied, whispered to Sam, "Can you help them outside? Let them know what our plan for them is. I have a feeling we'll need to have a conversation with this piece of crap before he dies."

Sam nodded and began gently guiding the hostages toward the stairwell. All of them were whimpering or crying, but they were gladly cooperating in order to get away from the shooting.

Asher entered the room and kicked the shooter's leg.

"Arrggh!"

"Good, he can still speak. Sort of." Asher chuckled, his humor odd under the circumstances. "Come on, pal, up you go."

Asher grabbed the man by his injured shoulder and pulled him upright. Then he body-slammed the man against a dresser near the bed. He slapped him on the chest with both hands to ensure he wouldn't fall over. It also had the added effect of causing the man to scream in pain.

"Tell us what she was talking about," Asher hissed. He'd written many scenes in which a perp was practically tortured into admitting guilt or revealing facts about his fellow criminals. He'd always wanted to play the scene out in real life. "Talk, dammit!" he angrily yelled in the man's ear as spittle flew out of his mouth.

The man began to laugh, a heinous, sadistic chuckle that further enraged Asher. Asher drew his right arm back and punched the man's gunshot wound as hard as he could. The look on the man's face spoke volumes. His mouth flew open, and his eyes grew wide. However, he was unable to emit a sound. The force of Asher's blow must've rammed the bullet fragments into multiple nerves in the shoulder as well as broken already damaged bones.

"Nooo!" the man shouted finally, blood suddenly oozing out of his mouth.

"Tell us what they're planning!" Asher shouted again. He drew his arm back, but the man begged him to stop.

"Okay. Okay. Stop!"

"Talk!"

"He went back to get the others. They're coming to take the farms. But they needed ..." His voice trailed off as he began to lose consciousness.

Asher shook the man and then slapped his face to revive him. "Needed what? Wake up, dammit!"

The man's eyes popped open. He managed a grin, allowing blood to pour through his mouth onto his chest. Internal bleeding was about to kill him, and Asher wanted more answers.

"Guns." The man began to chuckle and broke into a coughing fit. "You're all dead."

Then he died first.

Asher had dropped to one knee. Exhausted, he allowed his chin to drop to his chest as he thought of the man's words. He regained his composure and looked back at John.

"She was right. This isn't over."

John sighed. "Figured as much. We probably don't have a lot of time." He reached out to hoist Asher up.

"I'll do it. I got hit on the left shoulder. No big deal, but it burns."

John pulled the flashlight from Asher's waistband and illuminated his injured shoulder. His shirt had been torn open, and a hunk of skin was missing. It was burnt from the heat of the bullet passing through it.

He shone the light on Asher's face. "Can you make it back to the farm on your own?"

"Yeah," he replied. He grabbed a dish towel off the fireplace mantel and folded it over. Then he applied pressure to his wound. "You guys need to be quick about it."

John sighed as he led Asher toward the stairwell. "We're gonna have our hands full. Tell everyone to be ready, and don't shoot us when we return through the trail."

The two men joined Sam and the others at the front door. The women thanked John and Asher for their bravery. They were receptive to Sam's plans for them. They thought they were safer on the road alone than remaining behind to fend off Jack Freeland and his men.

CHAPTER THIRTY-SEVEN

Saturday
East of Interstate 81
Harford, Pennsylvania

By the time Sam and John had reached the intersection of Upper Podunk Road, the country back road running south and parallel to the interstate, the women and children were complaining of being tired. It was if they'd forgotten the ordeal they'd just escaped from and the bravery of the heroes who accompanied them to safety. The trip to Scranton was actually thirty miles, two full days of walking for them. Sam lied and said it was a day's journey. He was fearful that if he told the truth, they'd cling to the Cubbisons and never leave. He was probably right.

After they said their goodbyes, John asked Sam if he was up to walking a couple of miles toward the interstate. He wanted to get a look at the intersection and the two fuel centers where the rest of the bikers had been living. At that hour, they should be asleep, so the guys could get a close look unnoticed.

Sam was all for it, especially after John described what he'd seen when they had been rushing Luke into town. They had barely rounded the curve when they saw the bikers milling about, ostensibly operating a roadblock.

Sam knew of a trail just past Blanding Lake Road that led to a mud bog many of the local teens liked to drive their four-wheelers and dirt bikes through. It was perched high on a hill overlooking the travel plaza and the entire interstate exit.

It took them nearly an hour to get into position above the Onvo facility. As expected, there was little activity at that time of night. To get an idea of how many bikers they might have to face, they moved through the trees along the hill and counted the motorcycles. Naturally, they acknowledged there could be others who'd joined them, such as stranded truckers or people who were walking along the highway.

"John, forget about anyone they recruited into their biker gang. Assuming we've taken out that guy plus a couple killed by Luke and Emma, that still leaves three dozen bikes with riders down there. We can't fight off those kinds of numbers."

"It is what it is," mumbled John. He pointed his thumb back over his shoulder, indicating they should start walking back to the farm. By the time they retrieved their horses and rode through the woods, it would be at least another hour or more. Plus, John had an idea that might buy some time. Father and son assessed their options as they walked.

"The guy said they needed guns," began John. "There's only one place he could get them quickly that I can think of."

"There weren't any gun stores in town," Sam said facetiously.

"Exactly. Besides, they had a deal with Fred Stewart to stay out of Harford. That's what got me thinkin'. This bike gang leader may have come up with a trade. You know, something of value that he had, like drugs, in exchange for weapons."

Sam looked over his shoulder as if the threat they faced grew in stature. "How many guns did Stewart have?"

"I can't say. He might not even make the deal. It's like I

discussed with Emma before we left for the city. We would never consider trading our guns or ammo unless absolutely necessary."

"All right, that makes sense," said Sam. "Most likely, even if he could make a swap, it probably wasn't enough for all of his biker buddies. A few at best, don't you think?"

"I hope that's the case. We've got to devise a plan that gives us the upper hand and keeps them as far away from the farm as possible. Let's assume these guys are criminals and thugs. Fine. Let's even assume that they've shot and killed people before."

"Maybe," said Sam. "Murderers or even convicted violent felons aren't necessarily roaming the streets. I'd bet most of them don't even have handguns much less trained with them. I just visualize a bunch of drunks out in the woods getting stoned and firing at empty beer cans."

"Right," added John. "And most likely, they've never been shot at. If we could pick a few off before they get past Stanley's farm, we might send them running back to the truck stop. Whadya think?"

"What if they come through the woods?" asked Sam.

"I don't know, Dad. It's possible. I just see these guys as a bunch of arrogant pricks who think they can march right up and take what they want. They prey upon the weak and vulnerable, like the women and kids at the Yoders'."

The two men walked quietly for several minutes before Sam broke the tense silence. "It's our family's home, son. And it always will be. I'll die before I give it up."

"Me too, Dad. Me too."

PART 5

Sunday
Hold Down the Fort.

CHAPTER THIRTY-EIGHT

Sunday
Onvo Travel Center
Harford, Pennsylvania

Freeland arrived back at the Onvo Travel Center around two that morning. A notorious night owl, he decided he deserved the extra sleep that Monday morning, allowing himself to get rested for his big day. Although Fred Stewart had scheduled the delivery of the weapons at nine, he expected the man to be late as a callous show of superiority. Freeland would do what it took to get the weapons. However, he vowed to show that one-eyed bandit who was really running shit someday soon.

His crew had gathered all the small propane tanks they could find from motor homes and campers on the interstate. Portable grills were placed under the canopy leading into the travel center's store. Every morning, a campfire coffee pot brewed coffee stolen from a Starbucks delivery truck. It was the highlight of the day for most.

Fred had instructed Freeland to empty the travel plazas of his men before his arrival. Freeland stubbornly did not. He had no intention of vacating their stronghold until the weapons were on the property. As he sipped his coffee and stared down the two-lane road leading into Harford, he glanced at the old Timex he'd found on a dead trucker. It was nine o'clock, and there was no sign of Fred.

He rolled his eyes and stepped to the side of the travel center to relieve himself. As he was finishing up, excited voices from the other bikers grabbed his attention.

"Gotta car coming from town."

"Sweet goat!" Goat was a common nickname for a classic Pontiac GTO. Very few people outside Detroit knew that the acronym GTO actually stood for *gran turismo omolagato*, an Italian phrase loosely meaning street-legal, competition-ready touring car.

Freeland hastily yanked up his zipper, catching part of his briefs in the process. He cursed profusely as he rushed into the parking lot to see for himself. Now he had another incentive for obtaining the weapons from Fred. He wanted that car.

"Boys! Move out like we discussed. Carry what's not tied down. We should have time to come back to get the rest, but take what's most useful to us first."

Like busy ants building a colony, the still-out-of-shape bikers gathered their belongings, which were more voluminous than when they'd arrived at the Onvo. The sight of the burly men bugging out into the countryside was comical. Yet they were remarkably efficient. By the time Fred eased across the interstate overpass, most of the men were trekking up the hill.

Freeland stood in the middle of the parking lot with his hands on his hips. He didn't expect to be ambushed by Fred. Nonetheless, he eased his hand onto the grip of the .45 tucked into his jeans. The heavy weapon bulged slightly and would've been noticeable to the trained eye. Its booming sound when fired was unmistakable.

The GTO slowed to a stop well short of the travel plaza entrance. With its powerful motor idling, the exhaust sounded like a guttural growl of an unseen beast in the jungle. The sun reflected off the windshield, making it difficult for Freeland to see the occupants.

He was becoming increasingly nervous. What were they doing? He glanced over his shoulder at the three men he'd assigned to carry the new weapons and ammunition. They, too, fidgeted in place.

"Jack, what's the deal?" one of them asked.

"I dunno. Just be ready."

"They'll cut us to ribbons if they want to."

"Shut up," ordered Fred. Then, with conviction, he added, "Today's not our day to die."

Maybe. Maybe not.

CHAPTER THIRTY-NINE

Sunday
Harford House Hotel
Harford, Pennsylvania

Fred Stewart and Jack Freeland held a mutual distrust for one another. In their limited dealings, the two men constantly questioned each other's agendas and truthfulness. While Freeland's request for weapons appeared to be reasonable, Fred was concerned the man was giving up too much for three AK-47s. Especially the rifles Fred was going to deliver.

Years ago, the Pentagon had issued a directive preventing military personnel stationed abroad from returning stateside with captured weapons. During the chaotic escape from Afghanistan, many of the Marines carried their assigned M27 automatic rifles, which were based on the AR-15 platform. A few in Fred's unit had gathered up the dead Taliban fighters' AK-47s as they hustled onto the military transport in Kabul. These weapons had found their way back to the States in duffel bags.

He happened to have three of the rifles that Freeland sought.

While he had more of the 7.62 x 39 rounds, he held them back for future trade potential. This type of ammunition was not as prevalent in the U.S. because the AR-10 and AR-15 weapons platforms dominated most gun collectors' safes. Also, the AK-47 was notorious for having a low muzzle velocity, and the weight forced the shooter to use a looping-like trajectory to hit their target.

These AK-47s had not been maintained since their return to the States. He couldn't guarantee they wouldn't jam or misfire. He seriously doubted Freeland and his biker buddies were capable of clearing a jam, especially in the heat of battle.

All in all, Fred was comfortable leaving these weapons in the hands of their chief rival, knowing they'd be no match for the firepower of his men.

That morning, he awoke early and refreshed. He was anxious to make the deal and take the GTO for a ride up and down the interstate to survey his new territory. He expected much of the highway had been picked clean by the Warlocks' group of vultures. However, there might be some valuable items that were too heavy yet capable of being loaded into the trunk of the car.

He was also especially interested in the condition of the Pennsylvania State police station at the Harford Road exit. That had the potential to yield a treasure trove of assets for his group. After he made the trade with Freeland, he'd head up the highway a few miles to ensure the other bikers were vacating his exits. Then maybe he'd cruise down to Scranton to determine if there was any ongoing recovery effort.

Fred was also keenly aware that he'd be leaving the motel, the House of Stewart, with a smaller than necessary security detail. While he doubted Freeland would be so bold as to conduct a surprise offensive on the motel, he had to consider the possibility. Based upon their reconnaissance of the biker group, as many as sixty men and women were divided between the two exits. Should Freeland decide to attack the motel with a show of overwhelming force, his men would have difficulty defending their stronghold despite superior weaponry and training.

The night before, after the deal had been made, he'd sent a patrol into the night to shadow Freeland and his men as they returned to the travel plaza. His scouts had returned just before dawn to report there was no indication Freeland was going to attack the motel. Nonetheless, Fred established an extended perimeter, giving his best shooters the ability to snipe the bikers as they approached.

Some might call Fred paranoid. He preferred to call it managed paranoia. Since the grid had collapsed, he'd moved quickly to reestablish himself as a functioning member of this new society. For years since they'd pulled out of Afghanistan, he'd suffered emotionally. Now that he was living his best life in a lawless world, he didn't plan on giving it up.

After they arrived at the travel center, Fred was perturbed to see bikers still packing their gear and milling about.

"I told him to be gone, not half-ass gone!" exclaimed Fred as he slammed the steering wheel. "We outta just light him up to teach this bunch a lesson."

For several minutes, he allowed the GTO to idle as he observed their surroundings. In that brief time, the bikers continued to leave the two fuel stations to join their companions who were trudging up the hill. Fred wasn't in the best of shape himself. However, he couldn't help laughing at the bikers toting their gear up the hill, stopping periodically to rest.

"Could you imagine those fat-asses marching to the rifle range at Pendleton carrying a hundred-pound pack, and then trudging across the sand dunes?"

The former Marines laughed.

"They'd be facedown in the sand after two minutes."

"Hell, most of 'em couldn't hoist their pack."

"Yeah, they'd be looking around for a motorcycle with a side car."

Fred got a good laugh and then noticed Freeland beginning to pace back and forth. By this point, most of the bikers were gone except for a few standing behind their leader. He took a deep breath.

"All right, boys. Weapons hot. Secure the perimeter and make sure this guy hasn't planned anything stupid. He'll probably draw a gun, but he's not stupid enough to shoot it."

Without turning off the car, Fred and the man occupying the passenger seat simultaneously forced open the doors. They quickly took defensive positions behind the doors with their weapons trained on Freeland and the nearby buildings. A second later, the two men in the backseat rolled out of the car and darted to the sides, their weapons scanning the buildings and the bikers walking up the hill, who'd suddenly stopped to observe the activity.

As expected, Freeland fumbled to draw his sidearm. Fred shouted his warnings in a full-throated, menacing tone.

"Don't do it! We're just clearing the perimeter!"

"We had a deal!" Freeland shouted back.

"We still do. Let us do our jobs, and then we'll do business."

Fred raised his left hand over his head and motioned for his men to split up. One rushed across the street toward the Getty Oil station; the other ran towards the parked tractor trailer rigs in search of hidden threats. The third ex-Marine ran past Freeland and his three men, his eyes darting between the group and the travel plaza building.

After a few minutes, shouts of *clear* filled the air. Fred placed his rifle on the front seat of the car, turned off the motor and removed the keys. He walked around the car and popped the trunk. Then he shouted to Freeland, "Send them over! One at a time!"

It took a few minutes to empty the trunk of its contents. Freeland, annoyed at his treatment by Fred and his men, didn't try to shake hands like he had the night before. Instead, he snarled, "It's all yours."

Freeland walked away backwards, not breaking eye contact with Fred. In his mind, the two would see each other again at some point. When they did, he'd have an army of well-fed, well-rested killers to do battle.

CHAPTER FORTY

Sunday
Viewmont Mall
Scranton, Pennsylvania

Nadia stood proud as the men prepared her vest. Unlike many women born into the Taliban, she was not being coerced into the act of terror by a domineering husband or father. Her motives were personal, however.

All of her brothers had been captured or killed by the U.S. forces in Afghanistan. Two of them were too young to be fighters. Their crime was playing in the fields outside Jalalabad in the easternmost province of Nangarhar. Nadia had witnessed the explosive device dropping from the sky and raced to warn her brothers. The device detonated and killed thirty pine nut harvesters as well as wounding forty others.

She longed for the opportunity to make the Americans pay for their crimes. She, like most female suicide bombers, was misunderstood. American media attempted to make excuses for their actions because of their gender. Their motives were not ideological, many pundits would argue. Other experts argued the women didn't really want to die but were forced to sacrifice their lives by overbearing male influences.

Nadia strongly believed she was making the greatest sacrifice, her life, for altruistic reasons. She was a soldier every bit as much as those who wore a uniform. Combatants on all sides of the War in Afghanistan were willing to lay down their lives for a cause they passionately believed in.

One by one, the men who led her to the outskirts of Scranton to commit jihad stopped by to praise her for her actions. She'd be remembered by all who waged war against the infidels. She would be praised and rewarded by Allah, they said.

Then the time came for her to act. As the men moved away to their assigned posts, far away from the blast zone, Nadia moved toward the designated entrance to get her share of FEMA supplies. She adopted an exaggerated waddle, impersonating a woman in the late stages of her pregnancy. She held her hands under her belly for added effect, which also served the purpose of carrying the extra explosives she'd requested the day before.

Once she was in line, the Americans, mainly the women around her, attempted to make casual conversation with her as they shuffled closer to the mall entrance at Dick's Sporting Goods. Naturally shy, she had no difficulty avoiding eye contact and the brainless conversation about her baby. She'd never had a child, although she anticipated the usual inquiries.

How far along are you? Do you know if it's a boy or girl? I bet you're ready after carrying your baby for so long. What's your due date?

During her relatively short time in this country, she'd learned Americans seemed to have a *right to know*. They'd question and quiz you until they got answers. However, if the tables were turned and they were interrogated about such a private matter as having a child, they'd likely get offended and declare the questioning to be rude. Her inner thoughts and observations of the people around her only caused her disdain for the infidels to grow, and bolstered her confidence in carrying out jihad.

As she drew closer to the Dick's Sporting Goods sign over the boarded-up entrances, she noticed a large gathering of soldiers near two white trailers. They were drinking coffee and munching on pastries while only a handful of others were handing out boxes of food and water. The dichotomy between the haves, in this case the government and military workers, and the have-nots, the commoners in line who were all but begging for basic sustenance, only enraged her further. The least these officers and high-ranking officials could do was enjoy their coffee and donuts behind the trailers, she thought to herself.

Then she smiled. Her eyes lit up. She almost laughed out loud as she visualized the looks on their faces when she shouted *Allah is the greatest* before detonating the improvised explosive device.

She inched closer, one shuffled step after another. There were no impediments to her carrying out her task. No forced reasons for her to pause and change her mind. She was getting closer and closer to her target.

Finally, she was in front of the table, waiting to be given a few morsels of food. She froze for a brief moment, garnering the attention of two men wearing suits near the tables. One provided her a toothy grin and a wink. He would be one of the first to die. Nadia set her jaw and then raised her head to the sky.

"*Allahu Akbar!*"

CHAPTER FORTY-ONE

Sunday
Viewmont Mall
Scranton, Pennsylvania

In the still of the morning in which only the steady hum of military generators filled the air, the massive blast reverberated throughout the bedroom communities located north of Scranton. The massive blast broke windows and caused some elderly residents to suffer deadly heart attacks. Those who didn't run for their lives away from the blast were frozen in place, suffering from shock. This was the reaction Abdul expected.

During his days in Afghanistan, he'd witnessed the aftermath of bombings initiated by the Taliban as well as those directed from above via American drones. The reaction was uniform regardless of circumstances. People fled, willing to knock over the elderly or the young. Others immediately suffered from intense psychological trauma that was debilitating. Confusion, fear, and disbelief caused them to freeze, nearly oblivious to their surroundings. Something, whether a fleeing victim or the screams of agony from their fellow man, would snap them out of their temporary paralysis.

He'd counseled his men this would be the case, and they were prepared for the aftermath. Because they knew what to expect, they shielded themselves from the blast. Then they moved quickly to their assigned targets around the mall's perimeter. One team of four was tasked with stealing a tractor trailer rig full of water and food supplies located at the outskirts of the mall parking lot. The day before, Abdul had noticed that the drivers left the diesel rigs running in order to operate the refrigeration units on the trailers.

Four men descended upon the EMP-hardened military rig guarded by a lone soldier who stood in abject disbelief as to what had happened. One of Abdul's men easily slipped behind the young man and slit his throat with a serrated knife. He rolled the body under the trailer without being observed by a single panicked person fleeing the mayhem.

After stealing his weapon, two of Abdul's men jumped into the cab and began to drive off. At first, they slowed for the fleeing Americans. Then they hammered down, as they say, plowing through the crowd. The sounds of bodies being crushed as they raced onto the roadway gave the men great joy. Soon, the truck was maneuvering around stalled cars, heading toward their community.

Abdul led a team that had their sights on a series of military trailers used to store weapons at night. They'd noticed that the soldiers traveled to the mall aboard two-and-a-half-ton M35 cargo trucks. Upon arrival and check-in, they were issued weapons out of these trailers.

Located on the back side of the mall from the blast, the National Guardsmen manning the weapons arsenal would not have been injured. They also were wholly unaware this was a coordinated attack. Once again, as instructed, Abdul's men used their training and stealth-like ability to maneuver to kill the armed guards with their knives. He'd instructed his people to avoid using their guns unless absolutely necessary. Gunfire would alert the surviving soldiers to adopt a defensive position. At this point, Abdul presumed, the soldiers would be focused on helping the injured and searching for their comrades.

Throughout the next hour, while panicked locals ran away from the bombing scene and surviving soldiers tried to help the injured, Abdul's men made multiple trips into the staging area around the mall parking lot in search of weapons, medical supplies, and food.

Four of his men had been tasked with relocating their pickup trucks on the interstate at the south side of the mall. They were to guard the vehicles as they were filled. Soon, Abdul advised his men, additional military personnel and first responders would descend upon the area to help the injured. Two of the trucks would head east on the interstate before making their way back to their community. He would lead two trucks north on Interstate 81 before turning back east. Any witnesses or pursuers would be confused in the middle of the chaos and therefore not be able to identify the details of the Afghans' escape.

Remarkably, Abdul and his men were able to scour the staging area without being noticed. Or, if they were, people had more important things to do than deal with the looters, as they were perceived. In fact, his group was not alone in picking up supplies of value. As time wore on, opportunists like themselves descended upon the mall to view the carnage and enrich their own cupboards.

He called an end to the frequent runs onto the mall property. His men were exhausted, and the pickup beds were full. He praised his brothers for their efforts and sent them all on their way just as a caravan of military transports began to head toward the mall from Interstate 84.

Abdul drove away slowly. He had one armed man sitting on the bench seat with his weapon ready to shoot through the open passenger window. Two men sat in the back, the buttstocks of their rifles lying on top of their thighs, keeping a watchful eye for any pursuers.

He planned on driving fifteen miles or so to the north, turning east before he reached the small town of Harford. His limited knowledge of the area required him to find roads headed eastward through the mountains and farms until they found familiar surroundings in Wayne County.

After they reached a less congested area in the neighboring bedroom communities, Abdul breathed a sigh of relief. There was no sign of any vehicles pursuing the two trucks, and his men's menacing looks deterred any pedestrians from attempting to steal the spoils of their victory. He raised his left arm out the window, indicating his intention to stop. He suddenly slammed on the brakes as an approaching vehicle in the southbound lane of the interstate caught his attention.

A car was weaving in and out of the stalled cars. The vehicle slowed. The driver, a man with one eye, stared across the grassy median at Abdul, who glared back at him. Abdul's face contorted as anger welled up inside. It was Jamal Khan's GTO, and Abdul had found his murderers.

CHAPTER FORTY-TWO

Sunday
Interstate 81
North of Scranton, Pennsylvania

"Hold on!" Abdul shouted as he pressed down hard on the gas pedal. He put a death grip on the column shifter as he worked his way through the gears. At the overpass, he turned the truck hard to the left, nearly throwing one of his men onto the pavement. He looked down the southbound lanes to confirm the Pontiac was still there and that he hadn't been mistaken. He was certain and willing to abandon the weapons and supplies they'd obtained to avenge his top lieutenant's death.

The GTO had slowed after he'd made eye contact with the driver. Curiosity had forced him to take notice of the two pickups. Abdul sped down the entrance ramp, jerking the steering wheel back and forth to avoid broken-down vehicles. Even if he pushed the truck to its limit, he would never catch up to the much quicker Pontiac muscle car. He needed Allah, and luck, on his side.

He decided to take a chance. The other pickup traveling behind him was much faster. He stuck his arm out the window opening and waved them alongside. He looked for a stretch of the highway where they could pull next to each other.

"Go after them! I will wait on the highway for them to return!"

"Praise Allah!" yelled the driver. The other three men in the truck began pumping their rifles into the air. Ordinarily, they'd be squeezing the trigger, sending the bullets skyward, to celebrate. They'd learned ammo discipline since the solar storm's arrival in America.

The driver lurched forward, driving the more powerful eight-cylinder truck in pursuit. Soon, he was tearing down the open stretch of highway back toward the massive cloud of debris and smoke emanating from the bomb site.

Abdul pulled off the next exit and stopped the pickup just beyond the overpass. He grabbed his rifle and instructed his men to join him by the concrete retaining wall overlooking the northbound lanes. He took a deep breath and gathered his thoughts. He closed his eyes to ask Allah for one more victory on this day.

Fred and his men were enjoying the carefree ride down the interstate. The disabled cars were spread out and allowed him to navigate easily between them. On one occasion, he hit a hundred miles an hour in the car that had been around for nearly six decades. When he saw his passenger leaning his hand on the dashboard, preparing for impact in the event of a wreck, Fred let off the gas.

He was enjoying himself. It was a good trade, and after he discovered the state police offices were undisturbed, he felt like there would be a hidden treasure in the deal. They had just passed the exit where the Onvo travel center was located when one of his men pointed out the smoke rising in the air in front of them. His interest was piqued, so he picked up speed as he raced toward Scranton.

Then he saw the vintage pickup trucks across the median.

"Check it out, boys," he said, pointing toward the northbound lane. "Look at 'em sitting on the edge of the bed, rifles propped on their thighs."

"Are we back in Kandahar?" asked one of the men from the backseat.

Fred slowed and leaned on the driver's door to get a better look at the two trucks and their occupants. "Those truck beds are filled to the brim. I see boxes of MREs, meds and maybe ..." His voice trailed off as he stretched his neck as the trucks continued driving northbound.

"I saw long guns stacked in the back of both trucks," said the front-seat passenger. "These guys made a helluva haul from somewhere."

"Middle Eastern, am I right?" asked Fred as he picked up speed and continued driving toward Scranton.

"No doubt about it," replied his front-seat passenger.

"Absolutely," added one of the guys in the backseat.

Fred gave his side and rearview mirrors another glance before picking up speed. The closer he got to Scranton, the more congested the road became, and the plume of smoke rising skyward became darker. They began to hear sirens.

"This has to be a bomb," opined one of the men. "Or a hella-big fire."

"Bomb," said Fred. He leaned forward to look through the top of his windshield. "Look at the debris floating with the smoke. The superheated air is dragging lightweight material upward with it."

"The road's blocked ahead," said his passenger. "This may be our last off-ramp to head back the other way."

Fred nodded and pulled off the interstate, driving along the shoulder to avoid the stopped vehicles that had been stranded at the traffic signal. He made a left across the interstate. That was when he noticed they were being followed by one of the pickups.

"He took the exit," said the driver calmly. He leaned out the window and shouted to the men in the truck bed, "Get ready. That is brother Jamal's truck. We have found our killers!"

"Do we shoot them?" the man sitting behind the driver asked.

"Disable the car," the driver responded. "Their lives are not ours to take. They belong to Abdul."

When the pickup reached the top of the overpass, the men in the back began firing on the GTO. Bullets skipped along the pavement with only two jumping upward to embed in the driver's door.

"What the hell?" Fred shouted his question. "I'll kill all those bastards!"

Just as he finished his threat, the trunk was riddled with bullets.

"Jesus!"

"We can't get a shot at them from back here!"

As mad as Fred was at the unprovoked attack, he began to think of the GTO as one of his most valuable assets. Regardless of the shooters' motive, which, he assumed, was commandeering his car, he needed to avoid a confrontation and focus on getting the GTO returned to the Harford House in one piece. He relied on the speed and maneuverability of the car to avoid their pursuers.

Fred pushed the limits of a safe speed as he weaved in and out of the stalled traffic. The car's steering was sluggish at the high rate of speed, but his driving served to put a considerable distance between them and the trailing pickup.

"Where did the other guys go?" asked the man in the passenger seat. "There's no doubt they were together."

Those were his last words. The windshield exploded into a thousand bits of glass as a high-powered round burst through it and into the man's shoulder.

"Holy shit!" shouted Fred as he began to steer the car back and forth as they sped under the overpass. He flinched as several rounds from the shooters overhead ricocheted off the fenders and pierced the hood.

"Let's kill these mothers!" yelled one of the rear-seat passengers.

His hands were covered in blood from trying to stem the bleeding of the injured man.

Fred's eyes darted from the rearview mirror back to the highway. The pickup was on the move, racing down the exit ramp in pursuit. They almost collided with the other truck while giving chase at a high rate of speed.

They were approaching the Lenox exit, the last one before reaching Harford. Because of a large creek that ran underneath the interstate at the intersection, the northbound lane's exit ramp did not match up with the corresponding on-ramp like most rural interchanges. He did not want to draw these crazed Middle Easterners directly to the motel, so he tried to lose them.

Fred whipped the wheel to the right at the last moment to exit. At the high rate of speed, the men in the backseat were thrown toward the left, as was the unconscious man, whose head and shoulders landed on the center console. Fred shoved him back upright with his right forearm.

"Buckle him in!" he shouted to his guys. "And hold on!"

He waited until the pickup drivers approached. Fred sat near the overpass where the drivers could see him. He lifted his arm high into the air and flipped them the bird. Then he sped off toward the county road up ahead and found his way to the back of a convenience store that had a good view of the on-ramp past the creek. Fred hoped he was right.

After turning the motor off, he ran around the front and slipped between two broken-down cars. He waited and listened. He raised his body to get a better look. Then a broad smile came across his face.

The two pickups had reversed their course and came driving down the on-ramp. They turned on the country road directly towards his position. This was when Fred held his breath. He wanted them to believe he'd sped off in another direction toward Kingsley. He wouldn't know whether they'd bought his misdirection for sure until they passed him and didn't return for several minutes.

With his men hiding behind a dumpster at the convenience store, rifles at the ready, Fred walked into the parking lot to listen. In the new quiet, the sound of the vintage pickups could be heard from a considerable distance, even if idling. He waited and listened for several very long minutes until he was satisfied the ruse had worked. Minutes later, he fired up the engine, cursing the sound of its power, and slowly drove to the on-ramp. His man needed a doctor. His revenge on the gunmen could wait.

CHAPTER FORTY-THREE

Sunday
Cubbison's Farm
Harford, Pennsylvania

Cubbison's Farm was bustling with activity as everyone prepared to be attacked. As soon as the family was reunited, they moved a picnic table in front of the market to go over their plans. Sam retrieved a copy of a plat map showing the boundaries of the farm and its relation to other homes. He was making notes on the plat, including approximate distances and the location of trail entrances, to provide an overhead visual of their vulnerabilities.

"Obviously, we expect them to come at us from the front," began Sam as he flattened the plat map on the table with the palms of his hands. "We've made good use of this hill overlooking the Stanley and Yoder properties. It also provides us a clear line of sight toward Harford." He had Emma retrieve four Ball jars from the market to hold the plat map flat on the table before continuing.

"I think we have a couple of options. One, leave it as it is but position one or maybe two shooters in hiding to pick them off as they approach. Or, two, block the road with stalled vehicles to provide our shooters protection and to slow their advance if they happen to have operating vehicles."

"Do motorcycles still run?" asked Emma.

"I don't think so," Sam replied. "Most of the bikes have all the electronic bells and whistles. Like cars, they're probably fried."

"Plus, if they worked, we would've seen them by now," added Matthew.

"Good point," said John, nodding his head in approval. "Same applies to cars or trucks. My guess is that those guys have been holed up at the interstate for some time and have decided to branch out. When the four of them arrived at the Yoder place, they saw how good farm life could be."

"Better than sleeping in a truck stop," added Sam.

John stood up from the table and looked toward the road. "That's right. They left one man behind to guard the women and children while the others returned to bring the rest of their group."

Luke was leaning on his hickory stick, staring toward the road. "Do you think they took the time to check out their surroundings? If not, there's a good chance they don't know whether the road was blocked or not."

Sam replied, "I believe they went for their fellow bikers and planned on doing that later. I vote for blocking the road to provide our shooter protection."

"Who do you think that should be?" asked Asher.

"Me," Luke quickly replied. "I'm the best in the family."

John turned to face his son. "I can't argue with you. However, you're not mobile. If you get overrun ..." His voice trailed off without stating the obvious result.

"Dad, I can pick them off one by one. Heck, I can even turn them back and maybe end this whole thing before it starts."

John played out another scenario. "What if they come at you from the sides? Through Ledbetter's fields or even the woods to your right."

"I'll take the Cushman," Luke argued.

"John, I've spent a lot of time on that hill, and I'm aware of your concerns. What if I spot Luke and even assist him? If it gets too hot, we'll haul our cookies back to the farm in the farm cart," Asher said.

Sam was nodding his head. "I'd personally feel better about that."

Luke made a suggestion. "If I take the matching Remington 700s, Asher could keep the magazines full so I wouldn't miss a beat."

"Mom?" asked John, knowing that Emma would have to sign off on putting her injured son at risk.

"Reluctantly, yes. But only because I know Luke and Asher have level heads. No risks. You guys aren't fighting this battle alone."

"I have another thought," interjected Sam. "If it makes sense to take the fight to them before they reach the farm, shouldn't we do something similar at the trail that opens up behind Stanley's house? It's the only other logical point of entry to our farm."

"I like that, too, Dad," replied John. He pointed to the plat map and traced his fingers along the drawing as he spoke. "If we take up positions in the trees along the fence line, not only could we keep them from coming at us along the trail, but we could protect Luke and Asher from being caught off guard through a side attack."

"If we get overrun, we'll have our horses to retreat quickly," added Sam.

"May I add something?" asked Lauren.

"Sure," replied Sam.

Lauren approached the plat map. "Granted, my experience in all of this is coming from the perspective of the authors' books I've edited. Believe it or not, I read them for fun as well as to suggest corrections. Anyway, one author wrote extensively about creating booby traps in the woods for people approaching his property. He called them force multipliers."

"What does that mean?" asked Cat. She and Vida both were involved in the meeting but remained in the background.

Lauren responded, "From what I gather, in the military, a force multiplier is something that gives the soldiers an edge. For example, a machine gun might be a force multiplier as opposed to a regular rifle. Or having security cameras on your property might be a force multiplier for a single Ring doorbell."

"Like the dogs," added Vida.

"Yes, exactly!" exclaimed Lauren. "We don't have enough people to patrol the east side of the farm. The dogs act like a security alarm to warn us of somebody approaching."

John stepped up and studied the plat. He turned to Matthew and Luke, who stood together. "Boys, you know these trails at the back of the property near the creek bed better than any of us. Do they lead to the Yoder place?"

Matthew answered, "Yeah, eventually. When we were kids, we used to cut them out and keep them cleared. We kinda stopped when we got older although I used them more than Luke."

Luke laughed. Now that they'd advanced to the same level as adults, he could tell on his brother. "Yeah, Mathew escaped his chores to meet up with his buddies through those trails. Right?"

"Shut up, or I'll break your other leg," Matthew said playfully. Then he became serious. "Listen, if they search long enough, they can find the trails at the back of the Yoder house. I don't think they'd know where they lead, though."

John looked to Vida and Cat. "Can you two go with Matthew to reposition the dogs near these trails?" He glanced at Matthew and pointed to the plat where Sam had marked the entrances.

"Yes, Daddy," Cat replied for both of them. She and Vida had become close since they'd spent so much time together in the house.

"Good," said John with a smile. "Now, let's get back to these force multipliers Lauren mentioned. Are you suggesting we use them along the trail?"

"Yes. Let me just talk off the top of my head. First off, you'll want to keep your horses on this side of the booby traps. If you are outnumbered, make an easy way back to your horses through the trees."

"Okay," Sam interjected. "Tell us what you remember about these traps."

Lauren took several minutes to describe the two traps that came to mind. The guys agreed they had the materials and ability to build them, if they had time.

It was John who noticed the shadows were starting to grow longer, meaning nightfall would soon be upon them. He sent Luke and Asher to take up their positions on the hill. Sam followed with the farm truck to tow the smallest and lightest of the abandoned vehicles into position. Matthew, Vida and Cat moved some of the dogs to the west boundary of the farm along the creek bed.

John took Emma and Lauren to build the booby traps as well as to monitor the fields behind Stanley's farmhouse. John had never heard of a force multiplier before, but he sure wished he had a couple of dozen of them.

CHAPTER FORTY-FOUR

Sunday
Cubbison's Farm
Harford, Pennsylvania

John was deep in thought, contemplating what he and his dad had to undertake at the Yoder place on their way home. It was a compassionate gesture on the one hand and a form of subterfuge on the other. He hoped it had the desired effect.

He led Emma and Lauren through the woodsy trail. The two women chatted about life on the farm and how it differed since the apocalypse was upon them. Other than the threats of violence, Emma said tending to the gardens and livestock wasn't that different.

John could only think about the security of his family. During his entire life on the Cubbisons' homestead, he couldn't recall a single event where their life or property had been threatened. The only criminal act was that of an innocent child occasionally dipping their hands in the jars of jellybeans Emma sold by the pound in the market.

No cattle rustlers. No tools stolen. No wayward hunters pursuing deer at the back of their land. Heck, even the foxes stayed out of the henhouse.

He firmly believed the family, with their new additions, could survive and thrive in a powerless world. But as was often the case in normal times, other people got in the way. The seclusion of their farm from big cities, or even the small town of Harford, was a blessing and a curse. The farms were spread apart in the area east of the interstate. Their three most immediate neighbors were all dead. He'd been too preoccupied with the threats they faced to travel east toward Gibson to check on those residents.

Now, with the possibility of a swarm of angry bikers headed their way, he had to figure out ways to compensate for the lack of warm bodies on his side of the fence. Lauren's suggestion of installing a number of improvised defense strategies acting as force multipliers was a good one. However, he wished he had more time to create more of them around the farm.

Like others around the country similarly situated, John thought of all the countermeasures he could've had available had he just prepared for the collapse. Battery-operated driveway alarms might've survived the harsh effects of the EMP. They could warn of approaching intruders or vehicles. He was familiar with caltrop spikes, a medieval tool often made from twisted rebar. They could be hidden under leaves in the road to flatten tires of approaching cars or motorcycles. They could be buried in the trails to deter riders on horseback from encroaching upon their property. He would've invested in those HESCO barriers utilized by road crews to line highways during construction. His tractor could've moved them to block the road that Luke and Asher would be guarding this evening.

All of these measures might've been ridiculed or mocked by others. Today, they would've been envied.

"Okay," said John, forcing himself to focus his thoughts on the task at hand while letting Emma and Lauren know it was time to get to work. "Let's set up the first obstacle."

"Actually, it'll be more than an obstacle for the first couple of guys who make the mistake of coming this way," added Lauren. "John, find us a fallen tree with good, firm branches. Cut it down to about five feet and leave the branches intact except for twelve inches."

"Why's that?" asked Emma.

"We're going to suspend the log above the trail using the nylon rope. It will be slung over a strong branch like, um, that one." Lauren directed their attention to an oak tree that had branches hanging over the trail. "Using this steel wire we found in the barn, we'll stretch it across the trail to create a tripwire. When they head this way, they'll run across the wire, releasing the log overhead. Not only will the impact of the log swinging down knock them flat, with a little luck, they'll be gored by the spiked branches."

"Stuck like chuck," said Emma with a laugh.

"Exactly," said Lauren.

Emma and John worked on finding a fallen tree that would fit their needs. It required them to work with a two-man crosscut saw to create the proper length. Then, with John's knife, he whittled the branches to create the spikes.

After the log was set, the three of them quickly moved away from the device for fear of triggering it by accident. Lauren explained the next step.

"Once that thing is deployed, hopefully taking out at least two of them, they'll be wary of moving forward. To give them incentive to enter the woods, let's take the cut limbs off the log and create a somewhat obvious punji stake trap."

"Punji snake?" asked a confused Emma.

"Stake," Lauren replied. "We'll stick them in a low-lying part of the trail, like this one, with the spikes sticking up. We'll create a trip hazard using rocks covered by leaves. If they see all of this, then they'll avoid the trail and fight their way through the woods and underbrush. If they don't, then they'll fall on the punji stakes and, as you say, get stuck like chuck."

"The woods will be hard to move through," observed John, pointing to the dense thickets of thorns and saplings.

"Exactly," said Lauren with a smile. "That's where you farmers have a great security tool and didn't realize it. Barbed wire is not just for penning up your livestock. It can tear a man up who unknowingly runs into it. We'll take that roll you have, stretch it, and then bunch it up on both sides of the trail through the undergrowth. Not only will it injure them, but it might also send them back the other way to avoid whatever we've set up as traps."

John was concerned about the time. He sent Emma to the trail's entrance at the Stanley place to watch for the approaching bikers. While Luke and Asher would be able to see them coming while they got their blockade set up, without communications, there was no way to immediately warn John and the women short of opening fire. After Emma took off, he worked with Lauren to string the barbed wire, and asked about additional options.

"What else have you got in your bag of tricks?" he asked.

"Well, another one, if we have time, is to create nail strips. Pretty simple, actually. If you have any long nails, we can hammer them through a thin board or even some sheetrock and bury them under leaves near the end of the trail where it opens up into the farm. You'd want to do this last, after you and Sam retreat on the horses. These guys could run over them and puncture the soles of their shoes. If they trip and fall on them, it'll hurt a lot worse."

John was impressed. "And you learned all of this from reading books."

Lauren smiled and nodded. "I'll be honest. Some of these apocalyptic stories are really out there. You know, zombies, space aliens, supernatural beings. Others are frighteningly realistic, based on plausible scenarios."

"I feel like we're living in a movie," added John.

"Listen, bad things happen to good people all the time," Lauren said after taking a deep breath and stretching her back. "If we're smart, work hard, and stick together, we'll come out on the other side of this."

CHAPTER FORTY-FIVE

Sunday
Little Meadows Stables
Harford, Pennsylvania

Dr. Caitlin Quinn was tending to the horses in the stables when she heard the distinctive roar of the GTO coming toward her property. Her veterinarian clinic had a circle drive entrance off the remote county road. The large Dutch barn to the rear was built next to Polk Pond, a freshwater lake created mostly from rainwater runoff. It bordered the adjacent cattle farm.

She took a deep breath and silently cursed. She'd made a deal with Fred although she wasn't completely comfortable dealing with the man. He held a grip on the Harford community through intimidation and an economic stranglehold. By raiding and looting the few businesses in town, Fred had established a monopolistic barter market, giving him the upper hand on any trades.

She hoped he was simply joyriding through the countryside, but her gut told her otherwise. He was either coming to retrieve the equine medications he'd traded, or he wanted to steal her horses. Either way, Dr. Quinn was prepared to make a stand.

She rushed to the office located at the entrance to the stables and grabbed her hunting rifle. The sound of the powerful car's exhaust indicated the car was slowing near her entrance. Dr. Quinn ran across the lawn toward an oak tree. The multiple branches sprouting upward provided good cover as well as a resting spot for her rifle, allowing her to adjust her sights.

As expected, the car turned into the driveway and roared to the front of her clinic. Fred and another man poured out of the driver's side door. Through her scope, she could see another man slumped over in the passenger seat.

She relaxed and then rolled her eyes. She'd had more human patients than animals since the collapse. Another man emerged from the backseat to help carry the unconscious victim toward her clinic entrance. Fred found the door locked and began pounding on it, shouting her name repeatedly while nervously looking around.

Dr. Quinn was still obscured from view behind the tree. If she had a killer's instinct, she could have easily shot Fred and the other two men in the back before they could realize where the shots came from. However, that was not her nature. She was a healer. If her failure to shoot the unwanted guests resulted in being robbed or even losing her life, so be it.

She shouldered her rifle and began walking briskly toward the new arrivals. The amount of blood on the man's shirt led to the logical assumption she'd be dealing with a gunshot wound. It would be another first in her career. Setting Luke's broken leg was the other.

"What've we got?" she asked. It startled Fred. He swung around and pulled his pistol with remarkable agility. Dr. Quinn immediately raised her hands.

"Are you nuts?" he snarled.

"Sorry," she said unapologetically. Inwardly, she laughed at the fact she'd scared the badasses. "Are you gonna put that away?"

Fred hesitated and then holstered his sidearm. "He's been shot in the shoulder. You gotta fix him up."

Dr. Quinn retrieved her keys from her pocket and opened the door. "I'm not a doctor, Fred."

"You're all we've got," he snapped back.

You've got that right, she thought to herself.

The door swung open, allowing sunlight into the darkened space. She turned on a couple of battery-powered lanterns that flanked both ends of the reception counter. Her clinic smelled musty from lack of air circulation. It didn't matter how well she cleaned it, there was always a lingering smell of animals.

The men followed her inside, waiting for her instructions. Instead, she stood staring at them with her hands on her hips. She took a bold risk.

"Gentlemen, before I turn on the generator and get to work on your friend, we need to discuss payment."

"Are you kidding me?" Fred was incredulous. He drew his weapon again and pointed it at Dr. Quinn.

"What are you gonna do? Kill me?"

"Yeah! Fix him up!"

Dr. Quinn didn't back down. "You made the rules, Fred. Remember? Everything is about trading. If you kill me, then he'll probably bleed out and then so will the next guy who gets shot. And the next one might be you."

Fred thought for a moment, then lowered the gun. "Fine! What do you want?"

Dr. Quinn didn't have an answer because she had no idea. She pointed toward her patient. "Let's see what I have to deal with here, and then we'll have a conversation. I promise you that I'll be fair, a lesson you need to learn. Now, take him into exam room one while I fire up the generator."

The men walked past Dr. Quinn's outstretched arm pointed toward the last room on the right. Without another word, she made her way to the back of the clinic to turn the power on. Suddenly, nervous perspiration appeared on her forehead. For all of her moxie, she'd better make sure this guy stayed alive, or Fred would kill her.

When she returned, the men had placed the gunshot victim on the same table she'd used to treat Luke. The plight of the Cubbison family had weighed on her mind since they left her facility that night. She also remembered how Fred had treated them so callously in their time of need. The wounded man was fortunate she didn't have the same attitude towards life.

Dr. Quinn donned sterile gloves and placed a headlamp on her forehead to provide additional lighting. She began her examination while the men stood back, allowing her plenty of room.

"Fellas, if you're gonna hang around, I'm gonna put you to work."

"Okay," said one of the men who regularly patrolled with the injured man.

As she spoke, Dr. Quinn ran through the five critical factors to assess the condition of her veterinarian cases. She referred to them as the A-B-C-D-Es.

"Just in case he goes into shock, I need one of the horse blankets out of the stables. The clean ones are stacked near the office. Please don't startle the horses."

"On it," the man responded.

Using a tongue depressor and her fingers, she checked his airway for obstructions or blood. She listened to his breathing through her stethoscope.

"In the hallway behind me, I've got plastic jugs of purified water. Get me a couple of gallons and two stainless-steel trays located on the shelf above them."

Fred nudged the other man and pointed toward the door at the back of the examination room. He was now alone with Dr. Quinn.

She felt the man's hands, which were warm to the touch. Visually, his skin color wasn't blue or pale. She placed two fingers on his wrist.

"He's got a strong pulse."

"He loved to run," said Fred in a soft voice.

Dr. Quinn looked up to study Fred's face. He appeared genuinely concerned for the man. She ran her hand along his neck and under his back, checking for other injuries besides the gunshot wound that might disable her patient. Finally, it was time to focus on the wound itself to determine how much his body had been exposed to trauma.

"Fred, will you help me roll him over? I need to check for an exit wound."

Fred joined Dr. Quinn on that side of the table. She used scissors to cut the man's shirt off. It fell to the floor in a bloody heap.

"He's lost a lot of blood. I'm not set up to type his blood or run a transfusion."

"What's that mean?"

"It means I'm gonna have to monitor him constantly," she replied. "Now, let's get him on his side."

They turned him halfway onto his side. Dr. Quinn leaned closer to his back to make sure she was correct in her assumptions.

"Okay. Good. Through and through. Ease him back down."

"That is good, right?"

"Better than me digging out fragments," she mumbled. She glanced behind her and noticed the man standing with the jugs of water in one hand and the pans in the other. "Set them on the table, please. Also, I need you to check the seat back where he was located. I need to see the bullet."

He darted off while Dr. Quinn began to clean the wound. She shouted after him, "Don't wipe it off! I need to check for bone fragments!"

Thus far, her patient had not gone into shock, but she was concerned that the fourth man had not returned with the horse blanket as she requested. She was wary of them being on her property unattended. Were they petty thieves, picking up anything of perceived value? Were they assessing her assets to determine whether she was worth killing to take what she owned? These were not the kinds of things that needed to be running through a doctor's mind when treating a patient whether it be an animal or a human.

With Fred's help in positioning the man's body, Dr. Quinn finished cleaning and closing the exit wound. She began work on the entry wound next.

"I got the bullet. It looks good as new." The man handed it to Dr. Quinn for examination. She studied it closely and nodded. She handed it to Fred.

"Two-two-three," he mumbled before shoving it into his pocket. The Remington round, one of the most commonly used cartridges, was used in both hunting rifles and AR-15s. From his recollection, the barrage of bullets had come from semiautomatic AR-15s. "My guy is gonna want this."

"Fine," said Dr. Quinn. She noticed the other man had arrived with the blanket. She addressed his tardiness. "What took you so long?"

"Um, I was checking out the horses."

"Are they more important than your buddy going into shock?" she asked angrily.

Fred intervened. "Guys, give us the room, please."

The two men exited, leaving Dr. Quinn alone with the unconscious man and Fred. She pulled off the examination gloves and dropped them onto the bloodied pile of gauze. She took a deep breath and exhaled as she leaned over the patient for a final look.

"This could have been a lot worse," she began. "The bits and pieces of windshield on his clothing could've entered the wound along with the bullet. Unfound foreign objects cause internal bleeding and infection. He's gonna need some of those antibiotics you've got stashed away."

"I'll give them to him. Just tell me—"

"No, Fred. I don't think you understand. He's gonna need my constant attention for the next several days. He's lost a dangerous amount of blood. There could be foreign matter in the wound, which will require me to open him back up. He's not going anywhere."

"Okay, fine. I'll bring back what you need. Now, let's talk about payment. What do you want?"

She stood back from the table and twisted her shoulders to relieve the tension. Then she folded her arms and leaned against the wall.

"I saved his life. That's worth a lot, wouldn't you agree?"

Fred sighed. "C'mon, Doc. You know I appreciate what you've done. Whadya need? Food? More meds? A weapon?"

"Nope, nothing tangible. Just two things."

"One thing," countered Fred, the consummate trader.

"Two, Fred. One for the surgery and one for the aftercare."

"Fine," he said with a huff. "What?"

"First, I want you to make peace and apologize to the Cubbisons. They're good people, and you allowed their son to suffer because you asked for too much. You've got to show more compassion."

Fred scowled. "They were happy with the deal we made. At least, they said they were."

"It was too much, Fred. You've got to treat your fellow man better than that."

Fred was about to launch a tirade about how his fellow man didn't treat him very well, but he bit his tongue.

"Okay. I'll go see them. Let me know where they live."

Dr. Quinn smiled. "Thank you. Now, for the next part. You may not realize it, but this community will come to rely upon you. You've managed to corner the market on supplies that used to be available in stores. I suppose your guys cleaned them out like they cleaned out my vet truck."

Fred stood back and spread his arms wide. "I am what I am."

"Fred, what you are is an unintentional leader of this community who holds power over anybody who wants something from you. A couple of thousand years ago, someone said with great power comes great responsibility. It's time for you to recognize that you're more than a trading post. You can be the person this community needs for protection going forward. Whoever did this to your man could very well end up in Harford one day shooting innocent kids and their parents."

"That's not my deal, Doc. I didn't apply to be mayor of Harford."

Dr. Quinn allowed a slight smile. "I can't imagine the horrors of war that you and your men have been through. I have some knowledge of the way you've been mistreated since you've returned home. However, you can't spend the rest of your life punishing everyone outside your group of ex-Marines for the wrongs inflicted upon you guys. You have to turn the page on that part of your life and look forward to doing good. I know you have it in you because you would've never joined the Marines and served to protect our country otherwise."

The two stood in silence for a moment. Fred fidgeted and stared at the ceiling. Suddenly, an unexpected voice filled the room.

"She's right."

Dr. Quinn's patient had regained consciousness and was smiling at the two of them.

CHAPTER FORTY-SIX

Sunday
Yoder Place
Harford, Pennsylvania

Freeland was already aggravated by the time he led his small army of bikers to the Yoder place. By prearrangement, he'd sent Blaze to the Flying J at the Harford Road exit several miles to the north to gather up his bikers who possessed handguns or sawed-off shotguns. The rest were sent into the countryside to search for farmhouses to occupy but were ordered not to engage the locals until he gave the approval. He didn't want anything to distract from the task at hand, which was to capture, intact, this large farm and livestock operation for himself.

It was late in the afternoon by the time the group marched up the highway and turned down the Yoders' driveway. The bikers were full of nervous chatter as they cracked jokes about farm living and sister wives. It was Freeland who first noticed something was amiss.

Not that he expected a welcoming committee of women and children to rush out of the house and share hugs with his gang, but he certainly expected to see his man emerge through the front door to greet him. There was no movement whatsoever.

He was already on edge, raising his rifle to low ready as he approached the front porch. His men sensed the tension and immediately stopped talking. Freeland stopped at the location where the dead boys had been thrown on top of each other. The dried blood was visible on the grass, but the soaked soil had been raked over. He turned to seek out the two men who'd been at the Yoder house with him.

"Hey, isn't this where we piled the bodies?" He pointed at the ground with his rifle barrel.

"Um, yeah. I think so," one of the men replied, unsure how to respond. Soon, every member of the group searched the front yard for the dead kids or anything else out of the ordinary.

Now Freeland's concern grew, and he began issuing orders. "Surround the house! Two of you enter through the kitchen door at the rear. Two more of you, follow me."

As he moved quickly up the porch steps, he glanced to his right and left to confirm his men were getting into position. He shouted for the biker he'd left in charge of their hostages. There was no response. He motioned for the two men beside him to get ready. His hand signals indicated he'd open the door. He instructed one man to go right and the other to go left. He'd take the foyer toward the kitchen.

Seconds later, near simultaneously, Freeland and his men burst inside from both entries. They rushed from room to room, their weapons leading the way. The place looked exactly the way they'd left it. Next, four of the men stormed up the stairs and searched every room. There were no signs of a scuffle or anything out of place. In the master bedroom, none of them noticed the area rug from a guest room had been moved to cover the bloodstained wood floor.

The night before, John had suggested to Sam that they stop by the Yoder place on the way home. They removed the boys' bodies to the back of the property and gave them a proper burial and said a prayer for them. Then they took the dead biker's body and uncere-moniously dumped him in a ditch in the woods. After some clean-ing, the house looked like it had been abandoned. Then Sam had come up with one final touch that Freeland's men just discovered.

While Freeland wandered the upstairs hallway, dumbfounded, one of his men shouted from below, "Hey, Jack! I found a note!"

"A note? From who?"

"The traitorous son of a bitch!" was the man's response.

Jack hustled down the stairs with the other bikers following close behind. He rushed into the living room and grabbed the handwritten note out of the biker's hand. He carefully read the short letter, mumbling the words to himself. Then he handed it to Blaze.

"Is this his handwriting?" he asked, searching Blaze's face for his reaction.

Blaze scowled as he read it, shaking his head in disbelief. "I don't know, Jack. I can't honestly say that I've ever seen anything he's written."

"Can you believe this bastard?" Freeland asked angrily.

The bikers were curious.

"What's it say?"

"Yeah, what did he do?"

Jack took a deep breath to control his emotions. "He said he didn't wanna live this kind of life anymore. He said the women and children need protectin' and that he was just the guy to do it. He's takin' them to Scranton, where he figures there are FEMA camps or government-run housing to help start over."

"You can't just leave the pack!" shouted one of the bikers. Another added, "He needs to be taught a lesson. The chicks, too."

Freeland couldn't disagree. He was conflicted because he'd gath-ered his armed men with the intent to take the farm. However, he couldn't let this go because it would make him appear to be weak. Plus, his new woman had run off. That just wouldn't do.

He picked four of his men to pursue the traitor. They discussed their knowledge of the roads leading to Scranton. After assuming the man wasn't dumb enough to come by the travel plaza and use the interstate, they decided to find the first road leading south and chase him down from there. Losing four fighters before getting started wasn't in the plan, Freeland thought. However, he still had twenty-eight gunmen, plus himself and his favorite fire starter, Blaze.

With night coming upon them, Freeland resisted the urge to march up the road to do battle. Instead, like he'd learned in the military and from being on the wrong side of a predawn raid by law enforcement, it was best to get a good night's rest and hit the target in the early morning hours. This allowed him time to plot strategy with his bikers and assign them into teams.

Tomorrow was gonna be a momentous day for them all.

CHAPTER FORTY-SEVEN

Sunday
Lake Wallenpaupack
Wayne County, Pennsylvania

The Afghan community cheered as their heroic warriors returned from battle. The tractor trailer rig full of supplies was the first to arrive. It was quickly unloaded by the women and children with its contents stored throughout their compound. It was then driven several miles away and hidden at an industrial warehouse for future use.

It was late in the afternoon when Abdul and his men who had engaged Fred on the interstate made their way back. One of the pickups had run low on gasoline, so they'd had to search garages and storage sheds to siphon some out of lawn mowers. They'd killed locals and robbed their pantries in the process. Abdul and his men were now killing without compunction or remorse. After the bombing at the mall, they were at war with America and her citizens. They were all enemy combatants, regardless of sex or age.

Although the encounter with Fred and his men was heavy on his mind, Abdul wanted to celebrate with his fellow Taliban and their families. They examined the spoils of their victory, both what was taken in their pickup trucks and the supplies from the big rig. It was a haul beyond his greatest expectation. And based upon his own observations and what was relayed throughout the evening by his men, the bomb blast had created a mass casualty event that rivaled 9/11.

As they celebrated their great victory, he and his lieutenants broke off to have private conversations throughout the evening. The spotting of Jamal Khan's beloved GTO would help him exact revenge on his killers. The area around Harford where the car was spotted would also be on the way to Rochester for Vida, who was traveling on foot.

They could ill afford to waste precious gasoline and the unwanted exposure a large number of Afghans would garner if they descended upon Harford en masse. He decided to send a small number of his most trusted men to act as scouts. They would have to act surreptitiously to avoid being noticed. He recognized that would be difficult for his Afghan brothers, who were clearly not home-grown Pennsylvanians.

After the Taliban took control of Afghanistan, the government's Vice and Virtue Department, as it was called, ordered that barbershops were banned from shaving or trimming beards, as it was a violation of Shariah law. Abdul was a strict adherent to Shariah law. However, in the name of Allah, he allowed two scouts to completely shave their facial hair. They were also given what Abdul called American clothing—jeans, tee shirts promoting sports teams, and ball caps bearing merchandising branding.

From afar, they'd pass as any other resident of Northeastern Pennsylvania. Both men would do their best to look the part. However, their skills had been honed in the Afghan mountains conducting surveillance over the U.S.-led military forces in their country. If anyone could locate the GTO and the infidels who killed Khan, they could.

PART 6

Monday
"I hate Mondays."

CHAPTER FORTY-EIGHT

Monday
Cubbison's Farm
Harford, Pennsylvania

Sleepy-eyed and weary from a day of preparations, everyone at Cubbison's Farm settled in at their posts, intently focused on their surroundings. They all agreed the bikers would not wait to attack them and that it would most likely happen during darkness. It was risky for the bikers, as they did not know the terrain nor the layout of the farm. Defending your property was easier than attacking it since you were unfamiliar with the area.

Luke and Asher stood vigil at the top of the hill. They were focused on observing the bikers advancing up the road. Luke would use the hunting rifles to pick off as many men as he could while Asher would add confusion in the darkness with his own barrage of bullets from two guns, one a .22 and the other a pistol. The goal was to lend the appearance in the darkness there were at least three shooters defending the road.

John and Sam settled in along the tree line overlooking Stanley's back pasture. The men were positioned thirty feet apart, flanking the trail. They were able to communicate with each other without shouting. Flanking the trail provided them different angles of attack to deter the bikers from coming through the woods. Both men had identified a path through the trees to return to their horses without falling victim to their own improvised traps.

Closer to the farmhouse, Matthew manned the front gate alone although both Emma and Lauren roamed the property surrounding the farmhouse in a floater role. If Matthew needed a break or backup for some reason, Emma could take up a position behind a nearby barricade. In addition, whoever was guarding the front gate was responsible for giving Luke and Asher cover fire if they were forced to retreat. They also focused their attention to the east in the event the bikers managed to circle around the farm to hit the property from their blindside.

Lauren played a similar role along the creek bordering the woods up to where the trail running to Stanley's exited into the Cubbisons' fields. If John and Sam were being pursued through the trail, Lauren would provide cover fire while deploying the spiked boards full of sixteen-penny nails. Further, if the dogs began barking at the obscure trails near the trailer she and Asher were living in, she could move quickly to investigate.

Finally, the two youngest members of the group, Vida and Cat, defended the house. Vida was entrusted with Ledbetter's shotgun and was instructed to roam the front entrance to the farmhouse while monitoring any activity around the outbuildings. Cat would wander from bedroom to bedroom on the upper level of their home, gazing out the open windows and intently listening for anything out of sorts.

The eight of them had a viable plan to survive the anticipated onslaught of bikers. Their only disadvantage, they presumed, was their lack of knowledge about the enemy. They knew nothing of their numbers or their firepower. Plus, they were full of nervous anticipation, which took a toll on a body, both mentally and physically. Lack of sleep combined with the heightened state of awareness put them at risk of making a mistake. Possibly a deadly one.

Luke used the minimal amount of moonlight available to him to surveil the road through his scope. It was just after three in the morning when he caught a glimpse of a cigarette being lit.

"We've got movement," said Luke in a soft tone.

"Should I warn the others?" asked Asher.

"Hold on. Let me watch for a minute to see if they're on the move or maybe just patrolling their own grounds."

Asher tried to use the other hunting rifle's scope to view the activity, but his lack of training prevented him from focusing on the men. He decided to leave that task to Luke, who'd scoped many a deer and wild hog since he was a boy.

Luke unconsciously closed his left eye a little tighter to focus his senses on the Yoder property. As the smoker inhaled, the cherry grew bright red before fading. Seconds later, another cigarette was lit. Under the pitch-black conditions, it was easy to follow the two bouncing dots as the bikers smoked and walked up the driveway toward the street. The powerful scope enabled Luke to see the men's silhouettes in the moonlight and the glow of their cigarettes for roughly five minutes. Then, near simultaneously, both the men and their glowing smokes disappeared.

"Where'd they go?" Luke mumbled to himself. He panned his rifle back and forth, seeking out the silhouettes of the men. He concentrated on the front lawn and the driveway. Nothing.

"Did they go back inside?" asked Asher.

Frustrated, Luke lowered his rifle and responded, "Dammit! I don't know. One second they were there, and the next they were gone."

"How many?" asked Asher.

"Two, I think. I mean, I'm pretty sure. It could be nothing."

"Or they're getting organized to come at us," added Asher. "I think we should warn the others just in case."

Luke exhaled. "Yeah."

Asher began jogging down the hill toward the front gate, where Matthew greeted him. He and Emma had taken up positions behind the hay bale barriers flanking the driveway. Once Matthew confirmed it was Asher, he let Emma know, and she joined them at the gate.

He explained what Luke had observed, and Emma immediately praised the guys for letting them know. She didn't believe in taking anything for granted in this new world they were living in. Without hesitation, she ran toward the house to warn Vida, who would in turn advise Cat. Then she rushed toward the woods where Lauren was patrolling. She happened to be near the trail's exit. After explaining to Lauren what Luke had seen, Emma returned to the front gate while Lauren carefully made her way down the trail to the horses. From there, she was able to warn John and Sam in a loud enough voice to be heard yet not give away their position.

The system of disseminating information was not the best; however, it was all they had without two-way radios. They all could sense that the time to defend themselves and their property was fast approaching. In the back of everyone's mind was that gut feeling that they might not all survive, and maybe none of them would.

CHAPTER FORTY-NINE

Monday
Yoder Place
Harford, Pennsylvania

Blaze was mentally disturbed. Certainly, he was a functioning member of society in a criminal sort of way. He was able to be a part of the Warlocks motorcycle club and was capable of respecting Free-land's direction as the leader of their pack. However, for the entirety of his life since childhood, Blaze was a pyromaniac.

There were many motivations that drove people to commit arson. By far the most prevalent was revenge. This took the form of personal revenge against an enemy or societal revenge against those who didn't share the arsonist's worldview.

If the man on the street were polled, the most likely motive of an arsonist might be deemed to be insurance fraud. Some poor soul in dire straits can't pay their mortgage or car note. They look for options and then consider torching their place in exchange for a big fat settlement check. That rarely works out for the insurance fraud arsonist, and it's not even close to the second-most prevalent motive for arson, which is the psycho fire setter or pyromaniac.

Pyromaniacs come in all ages and from all economic backgrounds. The psychiatric disorder stems from being drawn to and obsessed with everything about fire. Some pyromaniacs were curious about the effects of fire on a variety of flammable objects. Others feel tense and energetic before, during and after every fire event. Arson investigators and law enforcement officers are keenly aware of this trait, which was why they often scanned the onlookers during a major fire event.

Blaze had become fascinated by fire at the age of three when he observed his older brothers set fire to a neighbor's Christmas Nativity scene. He watched in amazement as part of the display lit up almost immediately and became fully engulfed while other aspects, generally made of plastic, simply melted.

As he grew older and began to play around the neighborhood, Blaze would steal the cigarette lighters from the members of his family who smoked. He'd ride his bike into the woods and experiment with fire. He learned what burned slowly and what burned fast. He combined various objects to create exciting colors in the flame. He would steal building materials and solvents from local house building projects. All of these building supplies enhanced his ability to burn things.

However, it wasn't until Blaze turned twelve that he used fire for more than experimentation but rather, for more nefarious purposes. He'd been bullied in middle school. Once, he had his bicycle stolen only to be returned battered and inoperable. He became angry but never let on to his family who the culprits most likely were.

The two brothers and a close friend lived three streets away from Blaze. Using gasoline from his father's lawn mower can, Blaze snuck out of the house one night with accelerant and lighter in hand. He went to the home of the two brothers and found their bikes parked on the sidewalk near their porch. Then he sought out the other bully's home and found his bike in a carport. Twenty minutes later, all three boys' bikes were piled in a heap on the front stoop.

Blaze was ready to send his message. He doused the bikes with gasoline, pouring it from the gas can into a plastic cup before splashing it all over the place. Then he lit the end of a rolled-up newspaper until it was fully ablaze. He stepped back, and with the accuracy of a seasoned paperboy, he hurled the burning newspaper toward the pile of bikes.

The explosive impact of the gasoline trapped under the wooden steps leading to the front door slammed Blaze backward onto the concrete driveway. He hit the back of his head, almost knocking himself out. However, he recovered in time to crawl away from the scene and to disappear into the shrubs at the home across the street. Then he sat on his heels, mesmerized by the aftermath.

Blaze had only wanted to destroy the boys' bikes. Instead, he burned their house down. The parents and the two sons barely escaped as the two-story structure came crashing to the ground on top of the burning tires of the bikes. It took less than a day for arson investigators to determine both the cause and source of the fire.

The culprit, however, was never officially determined although adults in the neighborhood, including Blaze's parents, had their suspicions. The bullies wouldn't admit to stealing Blaze's bike and destroying it before its return. So the crime went unsolved, and a pyromaniac was emboldened.

For the next thirty years, Blaze burned things for pleasure and profit. He'd joined political organizations, honing his craft of creating Molotov cocktails to attack their opponents. He'd lost track of how many churches, campaign offices, and politician's homes he'd torched. He didn't care squat diddly about their politics. He was an equal-opportunity arsonist.

It was Blaze who set fire to Stanley's barn and outbuilding. He'd attempted to burn the house down, but his failure to see his task to completion had resulted in failure. He'd begged Freeland to allow him to send the Onvo Travel Plaza up in flames after they left.

However, Freeland had told him to wait, as they had bigger fish to fry, something Blaze could relate to, as he'd experimented on animals as well.

His role in the mission was seen as a critical one, Freeland had told him. The head of the Warlocks didn't know if the farmers were protecting themselves with patrols. Regardless, there was nothing like a good distraction to divert attention from an oncoming threat. Blaze gladly agreed to set fires and solemnly promised not to burn the farmhouse or any important buildings around it.

And he promised not to burn the cows, either.

Blaze and his team of two men took a circuitous route to reach Cubbison's Farm. It was slow going, as they had to take frequent breaks and be careful not to damage their makeshift weapons. Unlike the men who'd be carrying handguns, knives, and rifles, each of them toted a load consisting of premade Molotov cocktails, small gas cans, and extra rags.

Although they had an hour head start, they expected to be in position at the east side of the property at the same time Freeland and the others began their advance. They traversed the back side of the Ledbetter property. Blaze paused for a moment and considered burning the house down or one of the many vehicles strewn about. Then he thought better of it, as this might just serve to awaken the occupants of the Cubbison farm. Plus, he kinda liked the look of the property and thought it suited him.

After walking well past the entrance gate to Cubbison's, the three men ran across the road and located the fence line. Blaze got into position to study the terrain with a monocular. He was able to make out the cluster of buildings around the farmhouse. They were exactly as the girl Freeland had taken up with described them.

He searched for other options. There was a barn to his right, slightly down the hill from the main house. That, he decided, was expendable.

"All right, boys. Follow me." With a smile that threatened to break his face, the pyromaniac got to work.

CHAPTER FIFTY

Monday
Cubbison's Farm
Harford, Pennsylvania

"They're comin'," said Luke, his voice full of unease. It had been a little over an hour since the men smoking cigarettes had disappeared. It now appeared the rest of the bikers were up and ready to bring the fight to the Cubbisons.

Asher stood next to Luke and used the other rifle's scope to see for himself. This time, the silhouettes were illuminated by cigarettes being lit or burning.

"Geez," he whispered. "Looks like a dozen. Maybe two."

"I agree," said Luke, who'd calmed down somewhat. "I like that they're bunched together. Quick, go warn Matthew. And, Asher, hurry back. I don't want them to get too close before I begin shooting."

Asher hustled off, running down the slope toward the front gate. Luke followed him for a moment and then turned his attention back to the coming herd of bikers. He waited to see if any of them peeled off into the fields. Thus far, they stuck together.

Distance was not his friend, so he patiently waited for them to get closer. Once he began shooting, he wanted to be deadly accurate. It was the only way to reduce their numbers advantage or scare them off completely. Or it might not.

Luke took his eye off the approaching group to confirm that the person running up the hill behind him was Asher. The out-of-breath screenwriter leaned over at the waist, desperately trying to catch his breath. Luke rearranged the position of his broken leg to prevent his foot from falling asleep.

"Are you good?" he asked Asher. Asher nodded in response. He set the ammunition in place on the Cushman's seat along with two backup magazines for the Remington rifles. Luke would be able to fire sixteen shots before reloading. As one magazine was emptied and replaced with another, Asher would reload.

"Luke, I think they've had time to pass the word to everyone. It's up to you when you want to get this war started."

The men focused on the group, especially the three men who seemed to be leading the bikers up the hill at the start of the Stanley property. If Luke began firing now, to seek cover, they'd either have to turn around or run across the tall grasses into the Stanley house. Either way, he still had viable targets to pick off.

"Let's do this," he said as he took a deep inhale of oxygen and allowed a little bit to slip out. Then he held his breath. He took aim and firmly grasped the rifle. In what felt like an excruciatingly slow period of time, he squeezed the trigger. The bullet fired, Luke held his aim, and the projectile found its mark.

The man walking in the center of the three leaders was dead in a mere second, his chest exploding from the force of the bullet. He was thrown backwards into the other bikers, immediately causing confusion. The group appeared to stand in cement as the shock of the first shot caught them off guard.

Luke fired again, striking another biker, who spun around like a top before face-planting on the pavement. At this point, the men knew they were under attack. They scattered in all directions. Two charged up the hill, firing handguns wildly at Luke.

With Asher firing his rifle in the direction of the fleeing bikers, Luke didn't hesitate to eliminate the two brave, but stupid bikers. With two successive shots, he hit one in the chest and the other in the thigh. Both men fell in a heap next to each other in the middle of the road. Another shot eliminated the man with the wounded leg.

As Luke reached for his other rifle, Asher changed the magazines in the first weapon. Not unexpectedly, gunfire erupted to their right. John and Sam had engaged the enemy.

"I got one!" shouted Sam after unleashing several rounds from his rifle.

"They all hit the deck," John shouted back.

His semiautomatic rifle would serve him better as the combatant bikers drew closer. The fact they were possibly crawling through the tall grasses concerned him. Lauren had warned them of the advance and the fact as many as two dozen men had been seen moving up the road. If the bikers split their numbers in half, they would be overwhelmed if they continued to march toward the farm.

"Hold your fire for a moment," John instructed his father.

He readied his rifle and studied the field. He could identify the last location of the bikers by using the tree-lined fence behind them as reference. John took aim on the man's position and fired two rounds into the darkness. Then he studied the tall grasses for movement. Any type of disturbance that would indicate a panicked attacker.

John moved his rifle barrel slightly to the left and repeated his actions. With a couple of shots at a time, he sought to cause a mistake. On the third effort, he did.

After shooting approximately ten yards to the side of the first hit,

John fired two rounds. One of the bikers abruptly stood and fired back. John made him pay the ultimate price for his mistake by sending a bullet into the man's throat.

This startled one of the bikers hiding in the field nearby. He rose from his crouch and broke into a run. John didn't care about military rules of engagement or honor. He shot the man in the back without hesitation. In fact, he thought during those tense moments, if they all stood to declare their surrender, he wasn't sure whether he might shoot them anyway. What was his alternative? Call the sheriff and have them arrested? No, he'd assume the role of judge, jury, and hangman.

Then, all at once, multiple gunmen let loose a barrage of gunfire. Bullets flew all around John and Sam. They embedded in the trees and shredded the leaves. Some could be heard striking the ground in front of him.

John shouted to Sam, "Move!"

By prearrangement, they had code words to be used as instructions to one another. The word *move* was an indicator to slide away from their present position farther away from the trail entrance. *Turn* would be shouted if one of them felt they needed to turn around and retreat. *Go* was to be used to break cover and charge out into the open to engage the bikers. John doubted they'd use that one now that he'd learned of the number of bikers on the road. The best they could accomplish was to kill them in the fields and hope to retreat before being overrun.

John backed up a few steps into the trees and ran quickly up the hill toward the road. Sam moved past the pile of burnt cattle, whose stench was overwhelming in the stale air. However, the old country boy had smelled worse and thought it might be an excellent deterrent to the bikers heading toward his position.

Shouting the word *move* apparently emboldened the bikers into thinking the guys were retreating. They gave each other instructions that John could not discern. He readied himself behind a large, rotting tree stump.

Here they came.

John fired at the shadows of the men running across the field, letting bullets fly out of their weapons. They struck in the general area of his prior position in the woods. With the element of surprise in the form of a new position, he shot as many targets as he could. The gunfire from his right told him Sam had seen the bikers break out in a run toward them. His dad was trading blows with the enemy just as much as John was.

Then, all of a sudden, the gunfire stopped. John strained to hear their voices. They were muffled. A slight breeze picked up, causing the grasses to blow. It made it difficult to differentiate between the bikers' movements and wind-blown grass.

For several minutes, the shooting had ceased at the roadway. What were they planning? Were they regrouping? Retreating? Something else?

CHAPTER FIFTY-ONE

Monday
Cubbison's Farm
Harford, Pennsylvania

"Cat! Can you see anything?" Vida shouted up to the second story of the farmhouse.

"No! I just hear lots and lots of shooting." Cat's voice was full of fear and trepidation. Just as she completed her response, the loud barking of the dogs caught their attention.

"Which way is that coming from?" asked Vida. She spun in a complete circle. She ran toward the barn and listened. Then she raced back across the front of the lawn toward the east side of the farm. The incessant barking confused her as it carried across the fields.

"I can't tell," said Cat. "Do you think the gunshots made them upset?"

Vida thought for a moment. That was a logical conclusion. However, she thought Sam had said they were the dead man's hunting dogs. Surely, they wouldn't be startled by gunshots, especially in the distance.

"Cat! Go to the back of the house and watch for anybody coming our way. I'll go to the side where the other two dogs are tied off."

"Okay." Cat's frightened, innocent voice was barely audible as she ran toward the rear of the house down the hallway.

Vida took a deep breath and started walking toward the east side of the farm. She walked around the gardens full of lettuce, arugula, and kale that were planted to take advantage of morning sunshine. Her eyes darted back and forth, studying the fields and listening for voices. The first signs of daylight were appearing on the horizon, but there was still insufficient light to make out any intruders.

She gripped the shotgun firmly in her hand. She had not yet fired it. She'd practiced with it unloaded by repeatedly pulling the slide and squeezing the trigger. She didn't think it was particularly difficult to operate, and Sam had told her it was forgiving for those who couldn't aim that well. However, he did warn her the shotgun was powerful and to make sure its buttstock was placed firmly against her shoulder before she fired. He'd referred to the weapon's kick, or recoil, and that the pain it could inflict upon her should not be underestimated.

Truthfully, Vida didn't want to fire the weapon. She really didn't want to be involved in any of this. However, she liked the Cubbisons, especially Luke, whom she'd grown even more fond of. She felt safe there despite the threats they faced that day. Yet she couldn't help but wonder if she'd constantly be in danger at Cubbison's Farm because they had so many resources.

Vida was startled as a fire suddenly broke out in the middle of the field. The bright flames rose upward, allowing her to make out the shape of a small barn.

"Here we go again," she said to herself as she recalled the fire that had almost led to Luke's death. She couldn't decide whether to run toward the fire to see what happened or to return to her post.

"Vida! Come back!" Cat's concerned voice provided the answer.

Blaze set the fire as Freeland had requested, but it left him unsatisfied. Just as he'd done when he was a boy, he stood for a moment taking in the glorious destruction of the barn structure. He kicked at the tall grasses in the field. He broke off a short blade and threw it upward to detect the direction of the wind. It was minimal at best, blowing from west to east away from the house.

Boring, he thought to himself.

The dogs were still barking, so he sent his men to shut them up, assuming they'd stifle the incessant barking once and for all.

Now the sun was coming up soon, and he had to make a decision. The gunfire had ceased, which meant one of two things. Freeland and his fellow bikers had killed the farmers, or they had been forced to regroup. Regrouping was most likely. Blaze had warned Freeland that these farmers were probably armed and were better shooters than the Warlocks. The best approach was overpowering them with greater numbers for so long as everyone was willing to die to get the prize. *Not me*, Blaze thought to himself.

Blaze was not part of any regrouping plan. He was on his own and left to his own devices. Which meant, as far as he was concerned, that he could do whatever the hell he wanted. So he looked around for something else to burn.

He pulled out the monocular and studied the buildings again. The coming daylight was growing brighter. He needed a little misdirection to get closer to the big prize—the farmhouse.

"See that shiny tractor over there?" he asked his men, who were able to make out the shape of the tractor behind the house.

"Yeah. Is that next?" one of the men asked.

"Yup, that's next. Light it up and then meet me beside the house. If Jack doesn't get his act together, we'll take the fight right to their heart."

Blaze clutched the crate of Molotov cocktails and rushed across the field before the rising sun betrayed his position.

CHAPTER FIFTY-TWO

Monday
Cubbison's Farm
Harford, Pennsylvania

Matthew paced back and forth along the front gate. He was frustrated by the lack of visibility and his inability to engage the shooters. He'd become more comfortable with his role within the family since the power grid collapsed. He felt appreciated for his contributions rather than being ostracized for being different. Twice, he slipped back toward where his mother was positioned to ask permission to join Luke and Asher. Both times, she was firm in her response. Absolutely not. Trust the plan.

Emma left to check with Lauren to see if she needed help along the creek. Matthew assured his mother he could handle the gate alone. Just when he was about to let his guard down to relax, he spotted three figures approaching from across the road. They were walking briskly through the field, apparently hunched over to avoid detection. His eyes grew wide when he realized they were coming straight for him.

Matthew slid behind a pile of landscape timbers they'd piled near the white rail fencing. He readied his rifle and concentrated on the three shadows that zigzagged together through the high grass. When they crossed through Ledbetter's barbed-wire fencing, he warned his mother that someone was approaching.

"Please! Help!"

A woman's voice. A child crying. Another whimpering.

"Who's there?"

"Jenna. I have my kids, too. There's shooting near our house."

Matthew stood out of his crouch but kept his rifle pointed at the trio as they began to cross the road.

"Stop! Go back to the house. The shooting is at the top of the hill, and it may be right here soon."

"But we can't protect ourselves."

"We can't protect you either. You'll die here." Matthew said out loud what every member of their group had been thinking for the last day. If they had to face thirty or forty men with guns, some of whom were killers, it was a real possibility they could all die. He gulped as the realization came over him once again.

"But—" she again began to plead with Matthew, who cut her off. "Go back. Now!"

One of the children pulled at her mother's clothing. "Momma, I'm scared. What are we gonna do?"

"Sir, can't we at least hide on your property? If it's those bikers, they'll attack us. We can't fight them like you can."

Matthew was about to respond when all hell broke loose.

As the shooting stopped and the men disappeared from sight, Luke and Asher both exhaled, relieving some tension. After several minutes, during which time they listened for any activity near John and Sam, Asher broke the silence.

"Do you think that's it? Did they turn back?"

Luke furrowed his brow and shook his head with uncertainty. "I don't know. I wish the sun would start shining so we could see. Best I can tell, they bailed out into the fields. I don't think they were running away, though. Maybe they're just lying there trying to decide what to do."

Seconds later, the guys found out. Luke had just handed his rifle to Asher for a reload when multiple gunshots rang out, sending bullets firing toward them. The rounds ricocheted off the pavement while others embedded in the cars they'd pulled across the road for ballistic protection. The sudden shooting startled both of the guys, who immediately ducked for cover.

"What the hell?" asked Luke.

Asher stuck his head above a fender only to pull it down again when bullets shattered the side windows of both vehicles. Bits of glass exploded into the cars and over the roof.

Luke picked up his hunting rifle and fired over the trunk lid, unable to focus on a particular target but simply hoping to slow down the shooters.

It didn't work. A barrage of bullets tore into the car, flattening both of its right-side tires and breaking the glass on the driver' side.

"We gotta fall back," said Asher.

"No, not yet," insisted Luke, who fought the pain searing through his broken leg. He positioned himself to see the road better. It was empty. Yet the shots kept coming. "They're in the fields, using the trees and rocks for cover." Just as he and Emma had done when they'd ambushed those four men weeks ago. Would his blood be shed on top of the men he'd played a role in killing?

CHAPTER FIFTY-THREE

Monday
Cubbison's Farm
Harford, Pennsylvania

Within seconds of John hearing the gunfire at the top of the hill near Luke's position, he and Sam came under attack. Briefly he chastised himself for not maintaining some semblance of visual contact with the bikers who'd entered the field and exchanged fire with them. When they dropped to the ground, John tried following their movements; however, it was too dark. He presumed, based upon his limited success in hitting a couple of the men, they'd retreated. He was wrong.

They had moved forward, slowly moving through the field on their hands and knees in order to get closer. By the number of bullets being fired at him, John had to assume at least a dozen or more shooters were emptying their weapons at once. If they were trying to achieve some type of shock and awe approach, it was working.

Much has been written about a human's fight-or-flight response to a perceived event, attack, or threat to its survival. In animals, the reaction varies from escape, to fight when cornered, and in some cases, like the myotonic goat, or Tennessee fainting goat, they faint to play dead. In humans, the consensus is that men tend to fight while women tend to flee. It's just human nature.

John wanted to fight. He wanted to keep the killers away from his family and their home. Fighting an angry horde who were willing to expend their bullets to kill him was a fool's errand. Either way, he had to make a decision. His hesitation might get them overrun and killed. It was his father who broke him out of his trance.

"Turn! Turn!" Sam shouted from sixty feet away.

John stuck his rifle around the tree and fired several shots wildly into the field, missing any potential target. He simply wanted to buy a few seconds to get a head start into the woods. He ran through the small pathway he'd created for his escape. In the light of day, he'd disregarded roots that stuck up through the ground and low-hanging tree limbs. He assumed he'd remember their locations if and when the time came. The heat of battle erased all memory of the trip hazards filling his escape route.

John had made it thirty feet toward the horses, bullets ripping through the foliage that surrounded him, when he tripped over a tree root jutting out of the ground. He was airborne for a second, mind racing and arms waving as he tried to brace himself. In the dark woods, he misjudged the distance to the ground and landed hard on his chest and belly.

A whoosh of air seemed to fly out of his lungs and through his mouth. Stunned, he doubled over in pain, suppressing his urge to scream. John blinked his eyes repeatedly to maintain his consciousness as he willed his body to shake off the effects of the hard fall.

The bikers' voices filled the air, emboldened by their success.

"I found a trail!"

"Over here!"

The men who were fighting their way through the underbrush suddenly stopped and returned to the field as their fellow bikers discovered the trail to the farm. John set his jaw with a newfound determination. They had a clear path to the house except for the booby-traps. He doubted all the attackers would be deterred.

He gathered himself and picked up his rifle. He began moving swiftly but carefully down the path to avoid falling again. To his left he could hear the heavy feet of the bikers making their way along the trail that ran parallel to his position.

"Turn!" Sam shouted. John was certain his father was ahead of him with the horses. So he took a chance.

He stopped and began firing in the direction of the trail. Bullets flew out of his AR-15, crashing through the trees and underbrush toward the bikers. He heard the groans and screams of several of the men as they were struck.

He moved again, running toward the horses just as the bikers fired back at his previous position. When he arrived at the point where his path merged with the trail, he stopped to fire again.

"They're in the woods! Kill 'em!"

The bikers fired wildly into the dense woods, splintering tree bark and wasting precious ammo on a ghost. John had found his way through the path and joined Sam at the horses.

"You good?" Sam asked.

As John mounted his horse, he replied, "Yeah. Listen, it sounded like a war zone up on the hill. They were taking on more gunfire than we were."

"They'll hold their own. Come on, let's get to the end of the trail and start picking them off. One by one, John. It's the best we can do."

Sam took off along the trail at a fast gallop. John wasn't far behind as he heard the cursing and groans of the bikers who'd encountered their concealed traps. By the time John reached the clearing, Lauren and Sam stood waiting with their weapons pointed at the opening. The two of them worked quickly to pull the boards filled with nails into the edge of the woods. They rushed to cover the spiked boards with leaves and vines.

John had regained his self-control after the hectic retreat. "Dad, take the horses to the barn. Lauren, take cover behind the hay bales. When they come through the clearing, just shoot 'em."

"What about you, son?" asked Sam.

"I'm gonna wait for them in the woods by flanking the barbed wire. As they get tangled, I'll add to their misery."

"You could get trapped in there," warned Lauren.

"I'll be okay. Just don't shoot me when I come running out from there." He pointed toward a gap between two sizable maple trees.

John calmly disappeared into the woods like a baseball player in *Field of Dreams*. What he encountered was more like a killing field.

CHAPTER FIFTY-FOUR

Monday
Cubbison's Farm
Harford, Pennsylvania

Matthew wandered back and forth, looking from Jenna to the farmhouse and then toward the hill that Luke was defending. He didn't know what to do. The woman was not leaving. Then he heard the sound of the Cushman starting up. Luke and Asher were falling back. Gunshots still rang out near their position as well as the woods along the trail. Bullets were flying in all directions, and soon they'd be fired at him.

"Shit! Come on," Matthew ordered. He slung his rifle over his shoulder and helped the children climb through the farm gate. Jenna was escorted around the side with Matthew stepping on the lower barbed wire and pulling up on the next line above it. She slipped through but still managed to snag the seat of her jeans on a barb.

"Ouch!" she yelled as she collapsed, rolling onto the ground. "It bit me."

Matthew examined her backside and spotted a dark trickle of

blood seeping through the hole. That might be the least of her problems, he thought to himself. He brusquely pulled her upright and whispered as the Cushman approached, "Take your girls to the house. Tell them Matthew said it was okay."

"Wait, you're not Luke?"

"Twins. Now go!" He half shoved her toward her daughters, who were hugging one another.

Matthew was able to turn his attention to the road. His job was to provide cover fire for Luke and Asher in the event they retreated. As Asher drove them down the hill, gunmen had breached their sniper hide at the top and were firing upon the farm cart. Luke was trying to fire back the best he could despite having difficulty turning in the cramped cart.

Matthew unlatched the gate and opened one side to allow Asher to quickly drive through it. He stepped into the road and waved them toward the opening while taking aim on the silhouettes at the top of the hill. Just as Asher sped past, Matthew opened fire, sending several rounds in rapid succession toward the gunmen. He could see the sparks fly as the bullets ricocheted off the vehicles behind the men. There was no indication he'd hit any of the bikers, but he did manage to stop them from shooting.

"Matthew! Fall back!" shouted Asher, who stood by the gate. Luke had hobbled out of the cart and was studying the road with his scope. He was unable to see any of the bikers.

With all three men inside the gate, they found defensive positions along the driveway behind the vehicles and hay bales the family had used so often the last couple of weeks. Emma rushed toward them, weapon at the ready, to check on the well-being of her sons and Asher.

"Anybody hurt? Luke? Matthew?"

"We're fine, Mom," Luke replied.

"Good!" she said as she ran to give him a hug. She broke their embrace to hug Matthew around the neck, too. "Where are they? How many?"

"I don't know, and it's hard to tell," replied Luke. "More than ten. We got a few, but I swear there were twenty-plus when they started."

Asher approached them, focusing on the gunfire being exchanged with the bikers near the trail. "Lauren?" he asked with trepidation.

Emma understood how a single word could set forth so much emotion. She understood. "She's holding her own. I think John and Sam had to retreat, which is why the gunshots are so close."

Matthew interrupted. "Mom, Jenna and her girls are here somewhere."

"What? Why?"

"They got scared." Matthew swallowed hard before continuing. "I tried to send them home, but then the cart started up, and I wasn't sure what to do. So I sent them to the house."

"Did she have a gun?" asked Luke.

Matthew became nervous. He hadn't thought about frisking her. "Um, what? I don't know. Why should she have one?"

"Trust no one, remember?" Luke fired back.

"Luke, you're with me," said Emma as she slid behind the wheel of the farm cart.

"No, Mom. I need to be up front when they come."

"Not with one leg covered in concrete. I need you at the house, or better yet, can you get into the loft?"

"I think so."

Emma patted the bench seat. "Let's go. I'll deal with Jenna."

"Hello? Hello? Is there anybody in here?" Jenna was frightened by the darkness inside the Cubbison home. She wanted to make her presence known but didn't want to get shot by any of the occupants. "I'm Jenna, and I have my two daughters with me."

"Don't move." Vida's voice was deep and threatening. She

pointed the shotgun at Jenna and her kids as she slowly descended the stairs. One creaky step after another, she emerged onto the ground floor to find Jenna and her girls wrapped in a trembling embrace.

"Matthew said it was okay."

"Wait. Jenna?" asked Vida.

"Hey. Is that you, Vida? We thought you left for New York or someplace."

Vida lowered the shotgun; however, she didn't release the thought of having to use it. Without responding to her questions, she asked, "Why aren't you down the road?"

"I escaped when I saw more bikers approaching. I wasn't gonna wait around to be abused again."

"What about your sister? You left her behind."

Jenna felt no remorse for her decision. She stood a little taller and released the grip on her daughters. "Sometimes, you have to step away from your family, right?"

Vida relaxed and exhaled. "Yes. Come in. You need to find a safe place. The shooting is getting closer."

"I know. Luke's brother saw a golf cart or something coming down the road. That's when he let us in."

"That was Luke and another man who lives here now. I'll explain later."

Cat was standing at the top of the stairs. "Is everything all right?"

"Yes, Cat. I'm going to get them hidden and be right up."

"The gunshots are really close," Cat replied, her fear obvious by her tone of voice. "And what about the fire?"

Vida was starting to feel the weight on her shoulders of being responsible for three kids and a frightened mother.

"I'll be up in a moment," she said before turning to Jenna. "You need to do your part to protect this home. We'll hide the girls in the root cellar downstairs while you help me keep an eye out for the bikers."

"What can I do?" asked Jenna.

"The same thing I'm doing. You'll watch through all the down-stairs windows, and I'll take care of the upstairs with Cat. Call out if you see the bad guys."

"Okay."

Vida led Jenna and the girls into the cellar under the house through a door off the kitchen. A Coleman lantern illuminated the storage room full of cured meats, root vegetables, and neatly arranged shelves of heirloom seeds. The girls were apprehensive but understanding as their mother left them alone.

Jenna relaxed and assumed her post on the main floor while Vida returned upstairs. Just as she hit the landing, Cat yelled out to her.

"Here comes Lauren and Grandpa Sam. But I don't see my daddy!"

CHAPTER FIFTY-FIVE

Monday
Cubbison's Farm
Harford, Pennsylvania

"We gotta go, John!" shouted Lauren. The sun was peeking over the horizon, and their advantage over their attackers would be disappearing. Once the men who were unfamiliar with the farm could see the lay of the land, the pendulum would shift mostly in their favor. Especially, she thought, since they could see how outnumbered the Cubbisons were.

"Go!" was John's response as he fired a couple more rounds toward the bikers who were bogged down in the woods. He began to back out of the thicket until he heard a man groan in agony to his right. If they were past him near the opening Lauren would be vulnerable as she retreated toward the house.

He raced out into the open and let go of a couple of rounds toward the man writhing on the ground with a nailed board sticking out of his foot. Another one had been embedded in his calf when he fell. Both of John's shots struck the biker in the back.

"Come on!" shouted Lauren. This garnered the attention of the bikers emerging from the trail. They shot at her and missed. She ran toward the picnic tables where the party had been held the night the lights went out. She used the trees and furniture as cover in order to make her way closer to the house.

In front of the market, Asher and Matthew were being pushed back toward the porch. The bikers had come up the slight rise from the Ledbetter farm to surprise the guys, who were just inside the gate. They fell back, alternating between laying down cover fire and retreating to the next protective barrier. However, the sheer number of gunmen approaching the market, who were also using the barriers as protection, forced Matthew and Asher to sprint for cover.

Emma, who'd returned to defend her beloved business, opened the front door for the guys and fired through the windows to hold off the approaching bikers. It became a standoff as the bikers fired their handguns and two of the AK-47s into the barnboard-clad building. The bullets ripped through the walls and shattered dozens of the glass jars of food.

"I'm gonna be out of ammo soon," warned Asher.

"I've got some, but it's the wrong caliber," said Matthew.

More bullets tore through the windows, shattering the upper glass and ripping apart the frame.

Suddenly, the sound of gunfire that appeared to be directly behind them caught all of them off guard.

"We're gonna get trapped!" shouted Emma. "We've got to try to reach the house."

Matthew warned, "Mom, if they're behind us, we'll never get across the lawn."

She thought for a moment. She rushed to the back door and looked outside. The gunfire was louder and closer. Emma risked her safety and eased along the side of the market building to get a better look at the barn. She managed a smile and nodded.

Seconds later, she ran back inside to get the guys. "Let's go. We've got backup."

It had been a struggle for Luke to make his way to the hayloft. It took all of the effort his muscular upper body could muster to drag himself and his cast-covered broken leg up the wooden ladder. Once there, he pulled himself across the hay-covered floor until he reached his perch at the hay door built within the barn's gable end. Now that there was daylight, he could pick off the bikers as they approached. There was only one problem. He was down to six bullets.

He watched Lauren make her way through the venue setting still somewhat set up for the event they'd hosted on that fateful Friday night. She wasn't being pursued, a good sign. However, she wasn't accompanied by his father.

Sam had secured the horses and gone inside the house for ammunition. He'd promised to bring Luke a box of bullets when he returned. But for now, Luke focused on the whereabouts of his father.

"Luke! Cover us!"

His mother shouted at him from near the market building although he couldn't see her. He readied his rifle and turned his body in that direction.

"I've got you," he shouted in response as he pulled the scope tight to his eye in search of targets. Seemingly out of nowhere, Matthew and Asher raced across the front yard with his mother sandwiched in between. They both fired toward the east side of the market building as bullets flew past them and struck the ground around them.

"Show yourselves," Luke hissed as he pointed the rifle at the corner of the building. "Come on, cowards. Stick your head out where I can see it."

One of the bikers, a particularly bearded one, obliged. Luke had made up his mind after he fired the first shots that morning that fear was simply a result of the thoughts he'd conjured up. He knew the day would be dangerous. However, he refused to be afraid. He focused on protecting his family, and this shot was just one of many he'd fired that day.

He gently squeezed the trigger, and the bullet crashed through the man's cheekbone, tearing open his face. He fell hard into the dirt, where his body shook for several seconds before he died.

Luke became distracted as Lauren suddenly raced across the clearing, too. He swung his rifle to the right to cover her. The loss of focus almost got him killed.

One of the bikers with a rifle stood out into the open and fired several shots toward him. Two struck the top of the hay door's frame, sending splinters and pieces of wood onto his head. The other ripped through his cast just above his knee. It burned his skin as it passed through but didn't cause damage.

Luke quickly turned and fired two shots at the man as he ducked for cover at the side of the market building. He glanced toward the front porch, where Lauren was scrambling into the house.

He quickly gathered his thoughts and took inventory of his family's whereabouts. Everyone appeared to be inside the house. His father, however, was missing. Luke did not have a clear line of sight to where the trail led onto the farm.

The gunfire had stopped except for the men shooting from the side of the market building toward the house. Luke could hear the bullets embedding into the walls or breaking out glass. He wanted to fire in their direction, but he was down to just a few bullets, which he needed to protect his father and himself. It was apparent the rest of the family was pinned down inside, possibly preventing Grandpa Sam from bringing him more ammunition.

Luke tried to keep himself hidden from the shooters while watching for his father to emerge across the field. Then a bloodcurdling scream came from near the house. It was the cry of a little girl.

CHAPTER FIFTY-SIX

Monday
Harford House Motel
Harford, Pennsylvania

Fred Stewart woke unusually early that day. He was troubled by the armed men of Middle Eastern descent who had chased them up and down the interstate. He understood that the Pontiac GTO was a valuable commodity in a world with few operating vehicles left. What puzzled him was the fact they had already been burdened with truck beds full of looted property. The men had risked losing all of it just to acquire his car.

He'd also tossed and turned thinking of the lecture he'd received from Dr. Quinn after she'd saved one of his guys. Thus far, Fred and the ex-Marines who joined him had avoided the types of gun battles they had been trained to fight. Their lives in Harford, while limited, were at least safe. Some of his men suffered from post-traumatic stress disorder, as did he. PTSD could be debilitating to many former military combatants, so he was glad they didn't have to fight the kinds of gun battles like yesterday's.

Today, he had several things on his agenda. As promised, he would try to seek out some of the town leaders and reach an accord. Also, he wanted to confirm the two exits had been abandoned by the bikers. But first, he'd call on the Cubbison family, whom he'd turned away in their time of need. He might have been bitter because people had turned their backs on him in the past. However, this family didn't deserve it.

Just as the sun peeked over the horizon, he gathered up a couple of the earliest risers in his crew to take a ride out to the farm. He wasn't sure where it was, exactly. He just knew it was several miles past the travel plaza. He instructed his men to bring their battle rifles, sidearms, and extra ammunition. After yesterday's ambush, he realized the world was far more dangerous outside the friendly confines of Harford.

As they drove to the interstate exit, he and his men speculated about the gunmen from the day prior. Fred was deep in thought, staring out the window as the driver, who'd been in the backseat the day before, relayed what he'd observed to the other two passengers.

"I'm telling ya, it could've been the streets of Kandahar or even Fallujah. ISIS, Al-Qaeda, Taliban. I mean, take your pick. They'd pack themselves into some old beater pickup, guns resting on their thighs, looking all badass. It was the same deal yesterday except they were loaded down with boxes of military-issue MREs, and they weren't wearing towels around their heads."

"I seriously doubt we've been invaded by ISIS or Al-Qaeda," said one of the men from the backseat.

"You're positive they were Middle Eastern?" added the other. "Hell, we're all sportin' beards and long hair nowadays. Ain't no Sports Clips open now."

The driver slowed as they passed the two fuel stations flanking the road. Fred looked in both directions for any signs of life. They look deserted, so he pointed forward up the hill. The driver sped up and spoke.

"Man, I've been shootin' at those people for a dozen years. I know what I saw."

"There are Afghan settlements all over Eastern PA," muttered Fred.

"He's right," said one of the men in the backseat. "They got here right after we pulled out. The only difference was that they got cell phones, reloadable debit cards, and complimentary medical care courtesy of the American taxpayer."

"Ridiculous, right?" said the other passenger.

They drove along in silence for a mile or more, admiring the beautiful countryside, when Fred suddenly leaned forward. He shielded his eyes from the blinding sun. As he fumbled for his sunglasses in his vest pocket, he instructed the driver to slow down. Then he startled them all.

"Stop! Do you see that?"

The driver jammed on the brakes, throwing his fellow passengers forward. He covered his eyes and squinted to block the bright sunlight.

One of the men in the back had leaned between the bucket seats. "I see them. Look like bodies to me."

"Weapons hot, gentlemen," said Fred as he piled out of the passenger seat. The two men in the rear followed him and immediately took up positions on each side of the road.

"What about me, sir?" asked the driver.

"Stay close. We'll go on foot, but do not leave the car. It could be a setup."

Fred walked down the middle of the deserted country road with his men flanking his left and right. They held their weapons at low ready, reminiscent of when they'd patrolled the streets of Kandahar.

They slowly approached the bodies. Each had been killed with a single gunshot to the chest. Fred knelt down and examined their wounds. He didn't bother checking for a pulse. Their bugged-out eyes told the story.

"Center mass. Like a sniper would hit 'em," he said as he rose from his crouch.

"I see more up ahead," said one of the men.

Fred led the way as they walked briskly up the slight incline toward the front of the Stanley place. They found another body and then another. Then they heard the gunfire.

"Let's roll!" Fred shouted as he waved the car forward. He believed in running toward the fire.

CHAPTER FIFTY-SEVEN

Monday
Cubbison's Farm
Harford, Pennsylvania

Blaze had grown impatient as he waited for Freeland and the rest of the Warlocks to take out these farmers. Now it was daylight, and he found himself exposed, tucked against the side of the farmhouse to avoid being discovered. He was able to listen as the frightened residents ran back to the safety of their old farmhouse. *Old* being the operative word, Blaze thought to himself. *Old*, as in perfect kindling for an epic fire.

As the sun grew brighter and Freeland was unable to seal the deal by finishing off the farmers, Blaze decided to burn them out. He didn't care about farm living or settling down with a few cows. He liked the freedom of the road. He'd find an old bike or figure out how to fix his. Something would come along that would allow him to go out on his own.

He reached down for one of the Molotov cocktails. He could see the two bikers he'd been working with off in the distance hiding behind a hay bale. He knew those two would never join the firefight, which was probably why Freeland had assigned them to be pack mules for Blaze. Hell, he'd told them to kill the dogs that might've given them away. Instead, they'd cut them loose. Luckily for them, the dogs had run off chasing a rabbit or something.

Blaze held the wine bottle full of gasoline to his side and reached for his lighter. He let the flame heat up the tee shirt remnant he'd stuffed through the neck to be used as a wick. He held it high over his head, watching the cotton burn, waiting for it to get dangerously close to the accelerant. This was when that feeling of exhilaration reached a climax for Blaze.

Then, without warning, one of the doors to the storm cellar flew open to his left. Two little girls emerged from below, wiping their eyes, which were blinded by the morning sunlight. One stumbled toward him while the other one stood in place until she saw the fire-bomb in his hand. She screamed and fell backwards into the cellar. The other blindly ran toward Blaze. He deftly grabbed her by the arm so she couldn't get away.

"Where ya goin', missy? Don't ya wanna watch?"

Jenna's daughter screamed and shouted, "Let me go!"

Blaze wrenched her arm, twisting it so hard she fell at his feet.

He looked down and snarled, "Stay put!"

That was when he heard it. The unmistakable metallic sound of someone racking a shell into a shotgun. His eyes searched the lower windows to find the shooter.

"Let her go!"

It was Vida. She was looking down at Blaze from an upstairs window with the shotgun pointed directly at his chest. She never fired a shot.

Jenna's daughter continued to try to wrestle free, pulling hard on Blaze's grip. His attention diverted by the girl's formidable effort, Blaze looked down and twisted as she tugged. He planted his left foot in a small hole and rolled his ankle, causing him to lose his balance.

And precious seconds. Blaze had tried to enjoy the torching of the Cubbison home a little too much. Instead, the Molotov cocktail burned his hand, causing him to drop it on his chest. Within seconds, the child fire starter turned full-blown pyromaniac was engulfed in flames, spinning like a top, emitting bloodcurdling screams like a deranged demon.

Jenna had reached the side windows and shouted for her daughter to get back in the basement. As her daughter complied, Jenna raced to the stairs to join her kids and to secure the open basement door. Bullets ripped through the kitchen windows, tearing up the ceiling over her head.

Men came pouring out of the woods and raced across the fields toward the barn. Luke never did spot his father, and a feeling of dread started to come over him. Only a near miss by one of the gunmen brought him back into the present. Luke was judicious about the shots he took. He reminded himself to save one, just in case.

Two gunmen came running into the open, shooting their pistols at the house like a couple of banditos in an old western. Luke efficiently took them out. The man leading the way was first. The second, after stumbling over his dead friend, looked up at the hayloft just as Luke shot him between the eyes. He should have been pleased with his effort. Then the stark reality hit him.

One bullet left.

CHAPTER FIFTY-EIGHT

Monday
Cubbison's Farm
Harford, Pennsylvania

Fred's driver raced through the open gate, weaving in and out of the obstacles lining both sides of the driveway. Drawing on their training, they immersed themselves back into war-torn Afghanistan, rushing to help out their fellow Marines who were pinned down. The car skidded to a stop, leaving it nose to nose with the Cubbisons' old pickup truck. Seconds later, Fred and his men were outside the car, ready to engage the enemy.

It didn't take long for Fred to recognize the outfits worn by the bikers. One of them was running away as they approached, the club's insignia, a blazing Phoenix between the words *Warlocks forever*, making a perfect target for his Marines.

Fred muttered as he took the shot, placing the bullet in the center of the man's back and into the heart of the Phoenix. "You're dead. No kidding."

The Warlocks motto had been—*to find us, you must be good; to catch us, you must be fast; to beat us, you must be kidding.* Clearly, they'd never met any ex-Marines who'd been itching for a fight.

Fred and his men were fearless, a trait that would soon be learned by the remaining bikers who'd been firing at will toward the Cubbison house. They weren't aiming for the people inside. They were simply making Swiss cheese of the front façade and breaking glass in the process. Their efforts were undisciplined and a waste of ammunition, a lesson they learned the hard way.

The bikers were no match for Fred and his men. They split into two teams, one flanking the right side of Cubbison's Market and the other two heading through the store itself, where they could see the back door thrown open.

While his other team dispatched the bikers huddled outside the building, he and his driver hunted down the men running toward the barn from the woods. In a low crouch, they studied the unexpected battlefield through their gunsights. They never hesitated to seek out a shooter and fire upon him. One man, fearful of getting shot, ran directly into the corner of the barn, smashing his face hard into the wood. His mouth filled with blood as he bit his tongue, and a few of his front teeth fell out.

It was Jack Freeland, and his clumsy attempt to evade the gunfire saved his life. Bullets stitched the front of the barn directly in front of his path. Had he continued, he'd be dead. Instead, he stayed low, frantically crawling across the ground with a firm grip on his handgun.

Relieved that he was still alive, he quickly regained his footing and rushed into the barn, only to find himself staring at the barrel of a rifle. It was John.

"You son of a bitch!" growled John as he pushed his gun forward as if he wanted to stick Freeland with it.

"Go ahead, Farmer John," said Freeland defiantly. "You can't shoot me point-blank. It's different than killing a man runnin' through the woods. We're face-to-face. Look in my eyes. You can't do it."

Freeland leaned forward as if to stick his jaw out to allow another boxer to get a free punch. John took the opportunity. He snarled and angrily pulled the trigger on his AR-15 multiple times. Only, the gun didn't fire. He was out of ammunition.

The look of fear on John's face emboldened Freeland. He cackled, a heinous, blood-spewing laugh coming from an evil man. He began to raise his weapon to shoot John when Luke dropped the barrel of his rifle over the edge of the hayloft.

He drew a bead on Freeland's head, fired and missed. It was his last shot.

This caused Freeland to laugh even louder. "I've got plenty of bullets for you two morons and your family." He was swinging the pistol from John to Luke and back to John again. John tensed his body, ready to lunge at Freeland, when a voice came out of the darkness.

"So do I."

It sounded like a cannon. A powerful handgun released a bullet that entered Freeland's right ear and came out the left. For a brief moment, the dead biker's body stood upright in a state of suspended animation before falling to the side into a pile of horse manure.

Grandpa Sam emerged from the shadows to reveal himself to John and Luke. The Cubbison men were about to breathe a sigh of relief when a voice boomed from outside the barn doors. "Nobody move!"

As red dots flashed across their chests, Sam and John raised their hands high. In the loft, Luke shifted his weight uneasily, immediately drawing a red laser dot of his own.

"Are you John?" one of the men asked.

"Yes."

An excruciating few seconds passed. Then Fred stepped into the barn and shouldered his weapon and spoke.

"I owe you an apology."

CHAPTER FIFTY-NINE

Monday
Cubbison's Farm
Harford, Pennsylvania

After Fred's men confirmed the perimeter was secure and all the biker combatants were dead except for a handful seen running for their lives into the woods or down the road, the group gathered together in front of the market. The Cubbisons' home had been shredded by the bullets. The siding was full of holes and reduced to splintered wood. None of the windows on the front of the home were left unbroken. Family heirlooms that had been on display in the living areas were shattered or damaged beyond repair.

However, their bodies were mostly intact. Emma had been struck by a bullet in her upper arm. It was bandaged up with one of John's tee shirts. She didn't seem to mind the pain. Vida had been near an upper window when it was shot out. A shard of glass stuck in her cheekbone, narrowly missing her eye. Matthew took a bullet that grazed the back of his thigh as he was running toward Blaze after he'd grabbed Jenna's daughter. If he hadn't been shot and knocked down, he would've been engulfed in flames like the pyromaniac. Jenna's daughter who'd fallen down the stairs had a sprained wrist, but she seemed to wear it like a badge of honor. All of them would have to find a way to deal with the carnage and the effect it had on their mental state.

The group gathered in front of the market, talking about the gun battle and what had brought it on. Fred said he had been unaware of what Freeland and the bikers had planned. Inwardly, he felt responsible because he'd knowingly armed the men whose stated intention was to move out into the farmland. However, all of that dealmaking had happened before the heart-to-heart talk with Dr. Quinn. Somehow, he thought, fate had brought them all together.

"Love your truck, Sam," said Fred as they walked around admiring the Cubbison rolling billboard. "Does it run?"

"Oh, yeah. To New York City and back, as a matter of fact."

As the two men looked at their respective vehicles, Sam gave a quick synopsis of what they'd faced on that journey. Fred was starting to get a clear picture of the bedlam occurring in the heavily populated areas. It made him appreciate their small corner of the world even more.

"Well, I love your GTO," said Fred. "I've always wanted one. I just hate the way I came about getting it. How long have you owned it?"

The conversation drew Vida's attention, who was trying to appear aloof. She'd vowed to never admit what she knew about the car her father loved. She was standing by Luke's side as he talked with one of the ex-Marines about his ability to take out the bikers in the dark from such a long distance. She focused to shut out Luke's conversation and listen to the one between Fred and Sam.

"Yeah, helluva car. I only drove it once. It's not ours."

"What?"

Sam explained. He pointed to his fellow travelers as he spoke. "Asher, Lauren, and my granddaughter, Cat, had escaped from New York. Once we turned off the interstate, we thought we were out of danger. We found an abandoned motor home on an access road to a military base. Or maybe it was an arsenal. I don't remember, exactly."

"Picatinny?" asked Fred.

"Yeah, that's it. Picatinny. Well, anyway, we were sleeping, and then Lauren heard men talking. She thought it was maybe Arabic or something like that. They definitely had foreign accents. They ended up attacking the place."

Fred interrupted Sam by raising his hand. He turned to his men. "Hey, guys. Let me get you over here for a minute. We need to hear this." He gestured for Sam to proceed.

"Like I was saying. We woke up when the gunfire started. I mean, it was like a war out there. We got spooked and decided we needed to get away from there. I mean, if they'd stopped at the motor home, we'd probably all be dead. Heck, as it was, they shot Lauren in the back as we ran away. Thank God the bullet hit her in her back-pack and just knocked her to the ground."

"What does this have to do with the car?" asked Fred.

"That's what I was about to tell you," Sam replied. "This car was leading the pack of, um, three vehicles, I think. A couple of old pickups but not as old as ours. Anyway, it was full of guys with guns."

John stepped into the conversation. "My son Matthew and I had taken our truck to the city to find Sam and Cat. It was just sheer luck that we pulled off on that side road, too. We heard the gunshots, and this car was headed straight for us. I pulled my pistol, as did Matthew, to begin firing at the car. One of us shot out the tires while Matthew, I think, shot and killed the driver."

Vida suddenly felt faint. She began shaking uncontrollably, and her knees buckled.

Luke immediately became concerned. "Vida! Are you okay?"

She didn't respond at first, so Emma jumped in to help. She knelt down and looked up at the young woman's face. Then she stood and motioned to Lauren.

"It's been a trying day for all of us. Let's get her inside."

"I'll help," said Luke, who tried to hobble to her aid.

"Me too," said Cat, who'd grown fond of Vida since she moved into their home.

Vida didn't say a word and fought back her emotions. Her father was dead. The man she'd run away from. The man who beat her mother and allowed her to be raped by his brother. The man who surely deserved to die. Yet he was her father, and now she'd learned his killer, Luke's brother, was just a few feet away. As the range of emotions overcame her, she struggled to keep them suppressed.

As they helped Vida inside, Sam continued but commented on Vida first.

"She's an Afghan immigrant. Honestly, we don't know much about her other than the fact her father was abusive of her and her mother. She was genuinely frightened of him, so she used the collapse as an opportunity to run away."

Fred made eye contact with each of his men. Then he asked, "Did you get a look at the men?"

"Nah, it was dark," replied Sam.

"What happened next?"

"The car crashed into the guardrail, leaving the dented nose in the front. The afternoon we returned was when we learned Luke had been trampled by the steer. That's when John and Emma came to you."

Fred sighed and studied the car. He tried to remember the details of the pickups that had chased them down. He asked them if anybody could remember the trucks they'd encountered, but they could not because it had been dark and happened so fast.

There had to be a connection. It made sense. The gunmen had some powerful rifles in their possession. If they'd recently robbed a military arsenal, the fact they were carrying automatic weapons was possible. All of a sudden, an ominous feeling came over Fred. He might have brought trouble right to their doorstep.

CHAPTER SIXTY

Monday
Harford, Pennsylvania

After morning prayer, the scout team left the Afghan settlement with all of the surveillance equipment at their disposal. They carried rifles, handguns, and ammunition in case they had to do battle. They'd explained to Abdul that it might take days for them to find the car and the men who'd killed their brother Jamal Khan. At some point after they entered the small town of Harford, they'd have to hide their car and conduct their surveillance on foot. Abdul praised them for their loyalty and assured them the community would pray for them.

They avoided the interstate to return to the Harford area because they'd received word that the American FBI and military were searching throughout the area for the perpetrators of the bombing. Abdul's ruse of deceiving any eyewitnesses to their escape up the interstate had worked.

However, they would be searching for any operating vehicles, and it wouldn't take long to determine that his scouts were of

Afghan descent. So Abdul assured them he would be patient as they searched while protecting themselves from capture.

They drove into Harford from the east, taking the country roads that led to Gibson and then due west toward the town. They'd just rounded a bend in the road when they heard gunfire. Curious, they parked the car behind an abandoned roadside vegetable stand and made their way on foot through the fields to avoid detection.

A muzzle flash grabbed their attention, so they stopped atop a knoll overlooking the area where the gun battle was raging. One of the most valuable items taken from the arsenal was a thermal hand-held monocular. Not only did it allow them to see in the dark, it also had a long range so they could make out facial features.

Once the sun rose completely, the battle drew to a sudden end when the Pontiac GTO sped onto the gravel driveway. Both of the scouts agreed that the ease with which the four gunmen eliminated the attackers of the farm reeked of American ex-military. They praised each other, and Allah, for locating the vehicle so quickly. They contemplated leaving before they were discovered, but the leader of the scout team decided to continue their observations.

That was when he saw her. Without a doubt, the girl was Vida, Jamal Khan's daughter. Standing there, mere feet from her father's car. Amongst her new friends, the Americans.

Rage built up inside him. He wanted to seize his weapons and kill the infidels one by one. Then he wanted to throw Vida in the trunk and take her back to Abdul to administer her righteous punishment.

Instead, he took a deep breath and suppressed his emotions. He and his fellow scout confirmed what they saw with one another. They made mental notes of the two vehicles, the presence of Vida and the name on the sign near the driveway—Cubbison's Farm.

They would inform Abdul. It was Abdul who would wage jihad on these infidels. When victory was theirs, they would stand over the dead and shout *Allahu Akbar!*

THANK YOU FOR READING PERFECT STORM 3!

If you enjoyed this installment in the Perfect Storm series, I'd be grateful if you'd take a moment to write a short review (just a few words are needed) and post it on Amazon. Amazon uses complicated algorithms to determine what books are recommended to readers. Sales are, of course, a factor, but so are the quantities of reviews my books get. By taking a few seconds to leave a review, you help me out and also help new readers learn about my work.

VISIT my website to subscribe to my email list to learn about upcoming titles, deals, contests, appearances, and more!

Sign up at BobbyAkart.com

PERFECT STORM 4, the final installment in this epic survival thriller series.
Available for preorder on Amazon by clicking here.

"Bobby Akart has written yet another engaging,believable and suspenseful thriller that keeps you on the edge of your seat!"

-Reader Review

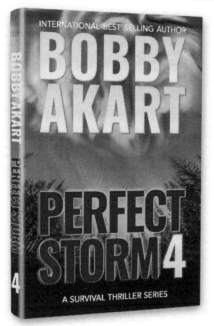

The heart-pounding conclusion.

AVAILABLE ON AMAZON

OTHER WORKS BY AMAZON CHARTS TOP 25 AUTHOR BOBBY AKART

The Perfect Storm Series
Perfect Storm 1
Perfect Storm 2
Perfect Storm 3
Perfect Storm 4

Black Gold (a standalone terrorism thriller)

Nuclear Winter
First Strike
Armageddon
Whiteout
Devil Storm
Desolation

New Madrid (a standalone, disaster thriller)

Odessa (a Gunner Fox trilogy)

Odessa Reborn
Odessa Rising
Odessa Strikes

The Virus Hunters
Virus Hunters I
Virus Hunters II
Virus Hunters III

The Geostorm Series
The Shift
The Pulse
The Collapse
The Flood
The Tempest
The Pioneers

The Asteroid Series (A Gunner Fox trilogy)
Discovery
Diversion
Destruction

The Doomsday Series
Apocalypse
Haven
Anarchy
Minutemen
Civil War

The Yellowstone Series
Hellfire
Inferno
Fallout
Survival

The Lone Star Series

Axis of Evil
Beyond Borders
Lines in the Sand
Texas Strong
Fifth Column
Suicide Six

The Pandemic Series

Beginnings
The Innocents
Level 6
Quietus

The Blackout Series

36 Hours
Zero Hour
Turning Point
Shiloh Ranch
Hornet's Nest
Devil's Homecoming

The Boston Brahmin Series

The Loyal Nine
Cyber Attack
Martial Law
False Flag
The Mechanics
Choose Freedom
Patriot's Farewell (standalone novel)
Black Friday (standalone novel)
Seeds of Liberty (Companion Guide)

The Prepping for Tomorrow Series

Cyber Warfare
EMP: Electromagnetic Pulse
Economic Collapse

Made in the USA
Middletown, DE
29 November 2023

43991356R00189